THE
LIGHT
HOUSE
GIRLS

BOOKS BY B.R. SPANGLER

DETECTIVE CASEY WHITE SERIES

Where Lost Girls Go

The Innocent Girls

Saltwater Graves

The Crying House

The Memory Bones

THE
LIGHT
HOUSE
GIRLS

B.R. SPANGLER

Bookouture

Published by Bookouture in 2022

An imprint of Storyfire Ltd.
Carmelite House
50 Victoria Embankment
London EC4Y 0DZ

www.bookouture.com

ISBN: 978-1-80314-359-0
eBook ISBN: 978-1-80314-358-3

This book is dedicated to my family.
With much love, thank you for your support and patience.

ONE

She could see the sun. Or was it the moon? The white fire balanced above the water, staying low in the sky. Shawna only saw glimpses though. He had covered her eyes with a scratchy cloth that had slipped a little. The boat lifted with a swell, testing her balance. The air was like salt, like the ocean. Or was it the bay where she'd gone crabbing with the neighbors? When he stopped paddling, she felt them drift silently. Calm waters lapped softly against the hull, interrupted with the rattle of chains. An anchor? Isn't that what he'd use to keep the boat still? When his touch came, calloused hands urging her to stand, Shawna reared away from him. The pressure to cry came again. But she held it in by biting her lip. He'd taken her. Stolen her. But what did he want with her?

"Just listen and do what I tell you," he said, cigarettes on his breath mixing with the sourness of sweat. "I'm not going to hurt you, okay?"

She nodded with a whimper, the thought of screaming circling her mind again. But her first scream had been met with a hand covering her mouth. It had been enough force to make her bleed. She could still feel a pulse in her upper lip. If Shawna had any chance to escape, she'd need to stay alert.

The tip of the boat bumped something, the bow thumping quietly as he secured it and mumbled softly to himself. She could just make out that it was a lighthouse he'd brought her to. But it wasn't one of the big ones, not one of the tall ones. She'd been to this one on a class trip. The Roanoke, her third-grade teacher had called it. It was the one on the water, but how many lighthouses were there? Had they visited them all?

The shroud slipped further over her little face. Shawna dared to lower it. But he noticed and gave her a resigned look. Shawna sat still, speaking with a hush, "It kinda fell."

"I suppose we won't be needing that," he answered, gently taking it and shoving it into his pockets. He fixed a look at her. A hard look. Though she was only eight, she knew when to fear what was in a person's eyes, when to be afraid. But this man? There was something about him that told her not to be scared. He put on a smile, forced it and told her, "We'll be there soon."

Though his face was warm, she had to remember he had taken her. She hoped Laura was okay. What fun they'd had just an hour before. It was the first carnival she'd ever been to, and they'd waited weeks to go. She tried to recall the smell of the hotdogs with the doughy rolls and the taste of the cotton candy. And the rides. Had she ever floated? It was like jumping up and down on the bed, only a hundred times better. Now she was here, when she should be at home. "Where are we going?"

He didn't answer as the massive light atop the wooden building blinded her. Turning away, Shawna tried focusing on the water's surface, an idea of swimming coming to mind. It was black like ink though. The big light was high enough to keep them hidden. He pulled on her arms, the coarse rope around her wrists itching her skin. Could she swim with her hands tied? With his finger between the knots, an almost apologetic look on his face, he told her, "I didn't want to use the ropes." Shaking his head, he added, "But it was the safest thing to do."

He turned away, chains jangling against the wood hull, the narrow boat rocking beneath his shifting weight. There were lights along the pier leading from the lighthouse to the shoreline. Their long reflections in the water rippled and shined like the soft glow of amber streetlights. She searched for a soul. A person or two. Maybe a couple taking a midnight stroll. Wasn't that what grown-ups did? Was it past midnight? Was it already morning? Shawna squinted to see how far from the shore they were. She gaped fixedly at the front of the pier. Was it like the fifty yards her gym teacher had them run? Like the ocean waters, her hope swelled. If she was right, the distance was like the pool, the one she could swim from end to end.

Shawna was a good swimmer. A lifeguard had once told her so. She could hold her breath and almost swim the full length of the pool too.

He turned his back, her gaze returning to the water. How deep was it? Did it matter? This was her chance. She could dive overboard and stay beneath the surface until she reached the pier. If she couldn't make it to the shore, there were pilings and timber, the space beneath the pier was thick with them. She could hide there until somebody found her.

She timed the shallow swells, the rise and fall. The boat was drifting from the piling as he struggled to keep hold. He pinched the rope around her wrists, but his grip loosened when the bow rose again. That's when she pushed.

Shawna shoved his body with everything she had, the muscles in her arms and legs straining. The bow's fall helped to loosen his footing, and her captor toppled over in a splash. He was gone, his body swallowed whole. She could hardly breathe as blood rushed through her, the opportunity making her heart race. There was a break in the surface that came with his gagging, along with the cough of a deep voice, his drippy arm slung over the lip of the boat, fingers clutching air.

Shawna jumped, her body crashing into the cold water, her nose and mouth and ears filling. She felt the bubbles glide across her skin like bugs crawling, and then dared a look at the lighthouse. She'd use the brightness to guide her toward life, escaping death that waited in the black depths. With her bearings, she fanned her arms down in a dolphin kick, following the smaller lights along the pier. They'd lead her to the shore like the breadcrumbs that Hansel and Gretel used. Only these weren't the breadcrumbs the birds could eat. They were like the forest fireflies, and they stayed fixed as she swam toward them.

He got her. She screamed beneath the surface, emptying her lungs as his fingers tightened around her ankle. His grip was painfully strong as she kicked with her free leg, striking his head and face. Faster, she heard in her head. And don't look back. Shawna kept her eyelids open, forcing them, ignoring the watery sting while the lights bounced above her head.

She found a piling, fingers burying into the soft moss and brushing the crust of a barnacle. Her tiny lungs ached as she stayed under water. Had she gone far enough? Where was he? The terror was immense, the need to cry stifled by pressure all around. When she couldn't stay beneath any longer, she broke the surface. Her breathing came in a ragged gasp as the saltwater touched her lungs and threatened to steal the next breath. Shaking with fright and cold, she spun around and searched for her kidnapper.

"You okay?" a voice asked from above her, the suddenness of it making her jump with a scream.

"Please help me," Shawna pleaded as she narrowed on a figure standing in silhouette. From the voice and shape, it was a woman on the pier. She could see more now. See that she'd made it halfway to the shoreline. She grabbed hold of a wood slat, the surface slimy as she managed to perch an arm over it.

The thought of rescue brought tears as the woman came close to the edge and knelt. She was three feet above Shawna, but she'd lowered herself. "Please help me. There's someone chasing me."

"It's okay, take my hand," the woman said, voice straining as she strained to grab Shawna's stretched arms, her hands clasped. There was enough light shining to show the woman's face. She was pretty, and older, her hair was a mix of dark red with streaks of white in the gray light. She took Shawna's fingers in hers, the touch supple. "You must be cold?"

"I am," Shawna answered, shivering, her teeth chattering. From behind them, the woman took a yellow rain slicker that was hung from one of the pilings.

"This is for you," she said and dressed it around Shawna's shoulder. The sleeves inside were a soft cloth, the jacket's fit a surprise to Shawna. "We'll take care of you."

"We?" Shawna asked, an unexpected strength in the woman's grip coming as she swiftly lifted Shawna onto the pier. Wet footsteps clapped the wood planks in a run. Shawna's heart ached with terror. She should have kept swimming. "You—"

The woman stood to face the man, reprimanding, "You idiot!" Shawna's heart broke and sank like the anchor the man dropped into the sea. Her kidnapper came to a stop in front of them, breathless and dripping wet. He jerked the blind from his pocket and shoved it into her mouth, the touch of salt and sweat far enough back on her tongue to make her gag. Winded and with wheezing breaths, his nose bloodied, the man dropped to his knees and wiped his brow as the woman scolded, "You almost let her get away."

TWO

The drive wasn't far from my apartment, but the hour was early, with colors from the autumn sunrise climbing above the ocean. My tires hummed steadily against the asphalt of Route 12 beneath us. The sun peeking through the clouds was beautiful, but it couldn't distract me from what I was on my way to see: the body of a young girl.

I was answering the call that had come from Jericho Flynn, his being on patrol and sighting the body that had washed ashore south of Coquina Beach. A Major in the Marine Patrols, Jericho was also my roommate and the love of my life. It wasn't often that our career paths crossed. But when they did, it was almost always with the harsh circumstance of a suspicious death.

Jericho told me to drive south toward Coquina Beach, he also told me to look to the sky for Bodie Lighthouse, saying I'd know it when I saw it. While I'd been living in the Outer Banks the last couple years, I'd yet to visit all the touristy attractions, of which there was a long list, including the lighthouses. Not far after passing a group of families roaming slowly on horseback, the tip of the lighthouse came into view. Jericho was right. I did know it when I saw it. It was the tallest structure in any direction, a black-and-white spire that was set back from Route 12 by a quarter mile. Unlike the common movie version of lighthouses, the ones perched atop jutting boulders and alone surrounded by raging seas, all but one of the Outer Banks lighthouses was on a bigger body of land. Bodie Lighthouse was located on the west side of the islands, closer to the inlet, and tall enough to see its bright lantern from the ocean and from the northern edges of Roanoke Sound.

Jericho had been patrolling the eastern side of Route 12 this morning when he called in the sighting. On a routine run up and down the ocean's coast, the body was discovered in the beach surf. At the time, it was slack tide, which meant there was no tidal movement, no threat of the body being dragged to sea and disappearing into the depths. A slack tide would only last thirty minutes though, which required Jericho to secure the body when the outgoing tide came. He assured us he'd done so using the patrol boat while preserving the crime scene. He emphasized that it *was* a crime scene.

On initially hearing about the body, my thoughts were of a drowning, a dangerous riptide perhaps. But he explained the woman was fully clothed for the autumn weather, that she was possibly adolescent or in her early twenties. With a single photograph sent from his phone, I could clearly see there were ligature marks around the victim's neck, which was all we needed to show us that this could not have been an accident. The side of the road flew by my window in a blur, my mouth turning dry as I forced a numbness to set like concrete deep inside me. From there, I pushed to spread it to my heart and soul before daring to cast an eye on the victim.

"Park over there," Tracy Fields said as I pulled up, pointing toward the medical examiner's wagon sitting along the roadside. It was parked on the grassy shoulder, the beach and ocean behind a tall berm, one of the largest sand dunes I'd seen. It was the length of a football field, creating distance between the road and the shore. On the dune, mature vegetation sprouted with sea oats and seashore elder, and saltmeadow cordgrass swaying with the breeze. A pair of buntings flew down and climbed the stalks of the sea oats, bending them until they fell, and then took turns eating the seeds. In the mix of greens and browns, I saw a path.

"I guess this is the most direct beach access," I said, slowing to stop behind the medical examiner's vehicle. A patrol car was in front of it with its lights flashing silently, an officer standing in front to wave us in. The victim's body was directly opposite of the lighthouse. Could that mean something?

"It looks like Dr. Swales and her team got here first," Tracy said with a hint of disappointment. A young crime scene investigator, Tracy grew up in the Outer Banks and joined my team soon after I'd moved here.

"We'll have plenty to do," I assured her, knowing the work we had ahead of us. As I parked, I caught a glimpse of her staring at me. It wasn't the first time and had become more common in recent months. Especially since we'd both learned that she was my daughter.

I'd started my career in Philadelphia, the home of the Liberty Bell and Betsy Ross and Independence Hall where the Declaration of Independence was signed. It was also the home of my family—Ronald, my husband, and our daughter, Hannah. Seventeen years earlier, a crazed couple suffering the tragic loss of their own child, kidnapped my little girl. The woman snatched her from the front of our house, my fingers clutching Hannah's tiny leg in a desperate attempt to save her. I'd lost the fight that morning which shattered my world, and my heart broke into a million pieces. While everyone told me she was gone, I never gave up hope. I never stopped looking for our daughter.

It was many years later when an old clue from Hannah's

case brought me to the Outer Banks, the barrier islands bordering North Carolina. What was supposed to be a short visit ended up changing my life forever. Soon after meeting Jericho, the clue I followed turned into another, and then another. And while it didn't happen overnight, we'd eventually find my daughter. We found Hannah living her life as Tracy Fields. While she had no memory of our previous life in Philadelphia, I've held on to the hope that one day she might remember me. And if not, maybe that was okay. We had a life now, and that's all that mattered to me.

"What are you staring at?" I asked, daring a faint smile, finding it was easier to joke with her than be serious some of the time. On hearing the news of being adopted and her true birth identity, Tracy decided to keep her adopted name. She also decided to keep her adopted parents and to stay on my team in the role she was hired. She'd also started coming over to our house for visits and to ask questions about the past, the missing years. That's what we called them, *the missing years*. I only knew them as being a kind of Hell, a tortuous limbo. It was an existence I would not wish on anyone. And then there were the silent moments like this one, with the most innocent and maybe perplexed looks on her face that told me she was working through many unanswered questions. "Well?"

Tracy's dimples appeared briefly as she tried hiding a smile that was inevitable. "Nothing!" she said.

I caught my own reflection in the rearview mirror. The first thing I noticed was the bloodshot red snaking through the whites of my green eyes. Tracy had visited last night, and the evening had gone on longer than expected. She'd brought a bottle of wine and her partner, Nichelle. The three of us sat next to the bay, the crisp autumn air warmed by a fire while we stayed up late and chatted. Now, in the mirror, I saw new silver-gray hairs where there'd once been the light-brown color. They were the first I'd ever had, the sight of them a surprise. "Would you look at that!" I fussed. "Grays. That's the first time I've ever seen any. I'll need to fix that."

"I can take care of it for you?" Tracy's hand dropped to my shoulder, the slight touch warming me. It was a show of affection and I'd been hungry for it. I was also strangely patient about it, fearing if I'd rushed anything, it'd push her away. "I used to dye my hair all the time when I was a teenager."

"Well, you're still a teenager," I said half joking. Tracy had multiple degrees and certificates and was a young twenty years old. She was both the youngest, and at times, the oldest soul on my team. I took her up on the invitation, saying, "I'd appreciate the help."

"Good," she answered, exiting the car. She leaned into the window, the wind batting her hair to cover her baby-blue eyes. She tucked it behind her ear and suggested, "Maybe we could try a fireball red color!"

"You think?" I asked, following her as I grabbed my badge and gun and sleeved my hands with gloves. "I always wondered how I'd look as a redhead."

"Next weekend," she offered and stepped onto the dune, following the rutted path I'd seen. I followed, my shoe sinking with sand creeping inside. I glanced to the officer, the Outer Banks having strict rules about walking on dunes. She waved us on, the beach directly on the other side. Through the mix of cordgrass and sea oats, I saw the footsteps that came before us. I showed Tracy the tiniest of them. "Dr. Swales is here."

"She must be in a field trip mood today," Tracy commented, our medical examiner often going on site when her office was slow or she felt the urge to work in the field. When the crashing waves came into view, we saw a group of children playing in the sand in the distance. They were clothed for the autumn temperatures and thundering about with laughter and squeals. Beyond them, closer to the waves, we saw Dr. Swales and her team. Even from this far, she was easy to pick out, her height under five feet, her hair a curly frizz that often looked blue. Next to her was Derek, her assistant, who made up for the height deficit. A burly man with thinning blond hair, he towered over most of us and had the strength of three men. Alongside of them was Dr. Swales's newest assistant, Samantha, a girl who looked no older than Tracy, she was a medical examiner in training. She was also the doctor's niece, a mini version in the mannerisms and expressions.

"There's Jericho," I said, his patrol boat anchored in the surf as waves rolled against the hull. The tide had already turned, but I saw that he'd protected the victim, the wet sand packed behind the body remaining free of running water while the boat was there. Jericho waved to us as he spoke with Dr. Swales, the two of them like chatty old girlfriends when they got to talking, their acquaintance going back years. My calves had started to burn by the time we reached the scene. Even with the autumn air, the walk got me sweating. "What have we got?"

"Second pass," Jericho began as he walked around the victim, his hand brushing mine. He wore full gear for the ocean, the wet air and high speeds demanding it. He tucked his hands into his vest, the sea spray leaving drops of water in the tufts of graying hair sprouting from the sides of his hat. I only reached his chin in height and looked up to see myself in his mirrored sunglasses. "We were on the second pass running south to north when Tony spotted it."

Next to the patrol boat bow, Jericho's partner, Tony, stood with a rope clutched in his hand. "Ma'am," he said and tipped his hat. He nudged his chin toward the victim. "I thought it was a seal pup at first. Maybe hit by a boat. But I'd only seen them in the winter months. Never this early in the season."

"Well, it's definitely not a seal pup," I said, lowering to one knee, Dr. Swales next to me. "Doctor."

"Detective," she replied, her fingers on her chin. She

motioned toward the neck, her knuckles knobby with age, saying, "There is obvious signs of trauma around the neck."

"I see that." The victim's face was covered by her strawberry-blonde hair which was filled with sand and broken shells. On the torso, evidence of crabs, sand fleas perhaps, a purple paisley-colored fabric with holes and exposed skin. "Caucasian, age possibly adolescent, ligature marks on the side of the neck" —I lifted the girl's hair, to see the bruising continue—"and appearing on both sides. Victim's face is in the sand which appears to be a result of the surf."

"Is it possible she was placed here?" Tracy asked as she knelt close to the patrol boat, white bands of sea foam parting before reaching us. Jericho's placement of the boat had perfectly preserved the victim. "Maybe she was killed closer to the dunes, somewhere on the beach, the high tide carried her down here?"

I'd seen the results of a dead body washed ashore before. For a time they might float in the ocean like driftwood, but that changes if the tide brings them to the shore. The victim's legs and arms were folded unnaturally from rolling and tumbling violently in the surf. There was the sand throughout her hair too. Not just at the surface, but deep. When combing through it, we'd find grains near her scalp. "It's possible, but the state of the victim tells me she'd been murdered elsewhere and taken to the sea. Whoever did this, didn't account for the tides and bringing her back to land."

I motioned for help to move the victim. A heaviness in my chest made me pause as Dr. Swales joined my hands on the victim's shoulders. For so many years, this would be the moment I'd wait and think of my daughter, Hannah. Whenever there was a murder, a body of a girl around the same age, I'd wonder if it could be my daughter. Today was different. Today, I knew my daughter was alive. She was working with me.

"I can help," Tracy said, joining us, her gloved hands on the victim's hips. Tracy stopped, her focus on the sand as she said, "Look how she is partially buried."

"She is," I said, noting half of the girl's body was covered in sand, supporting the idea the victim had been dumped at sea.

"Poor girl," Swales commented, gently stroking the victim's hair. She peered up with a tired look on her face. "Cause of death might be obvious but finding the time of death is going to be a guess at best."

"Her body's core temperature will match the ocean's water temperature?" I asked, thinking of the extended period the girl might have been tossed around at sea.

"Yes, but perhaps we can get something from the eyes," Swales said with a grunt as we rolled the body. When the victim's face showed, Swales sighed and shook her head. "Oh dear, poor thing. I always hate this part."

"Fifteen, possibly sixteen years of age," I said, continuing with the run of the case, Tracy taking notes and doubling as our crime-scene photographer. She leaned over my shoulder with a blinding flash as the batteries cycled and recharged. The victim's eyes were half-lidded, her lips a dark purple, the blood having pooled at the lowest point while her face was buried in the sand. "Get that too." I moved the victim's hair, showing the bruises around the neck, which had become accentuated by the lividity.

"That's a significant amount of force," Swales said, using her phone to take a second picture. She saw that I was curious and held up her phone. "Colors can change. I'll use this for comparison when we get to autopsy."

I brushed my fingers across the victim's arms, saying, "There are no obvious signs of defensive wounds." She wore denim jeans, skintight, and a white shirt and black bra, the seawater showing the dark fabric beneath. Her feet were without shoes with one foot bare, but on her left foot, she wore a sock with paisley stripes. I suspected the surf had taken the shoes and the sock. Tracy photographed the victim's feet and then moved to the girl's arms and her left wrist where there was a bracelet. It was a simple thing, a few strands of leather which had been braided. It could have been made in art class or in the girl's bedroom. Inspecting her fingers, the victim's touch was as cold as the ocean surf she'd arrived on, I asked, "Would there be any possibility of defensive wounds showing this late, such as post-mortem bruising?"

Swales held Derek's hand, him helping her stand as a gust of sea air blew her sideways. "Sheesh," she said with alarm, stretching her legs. "Post-mortem bruising is likely. It depends on the length of time she's been in the ocean."

"Could have been an Amber alert," I said, Tracy catching on to the request.

"I'll get on it. If it's been more than twenty-four hours, we should have had a missing child alert," she answered, kneeling where Swales had been. A steady flash came from the camera as she recorded the lifeless grimace painted on the victim's face. "Hey, guys, I think there's something in her mouth?"

"In her mouth?" Samantha asked, moving to the side, and behind me.

A stomping beat in my chest came with ideas of a murderer leaving a clue. He'd left it in the one place where it had the greatest potential of remaining, where the ocean couldn't get to. "Let me see?" I asked, shifting to look at the back of the camera. Tracy zoomed in on the victim's teeth. Between them the gray daylight had struck a tan, possibly brown, object. "I see it!"

"My bag!" Swales demanded with excitement as she slowly took to her knees again. She placed the victim's head straight, her hand open and fingers dancing while waiting for an instrument. "Derek, hand me a pair of hemostat forceps. Five inches should do."

I shined my phone's light on the area around the mouth, thinking it would help. The forceps were like needle-nosed pliers only these were skinny and the length of my hand. Swales parted the victim's lips. When she applied pressure to the lower jaw, the mouth popped open, the rigor mortis snapping. "Shit!" Swales yelled, reeling back as a sand crab crawled from between the victim's teeth.

"Oh my God!" Samantha yelled, her face contorting with a gasp. "I think I'm going to be—"

"Walk away, dear," Swales said with calm returning to her voice. She shooed the crab away with a swipe of her hand, the critter plunking into the surf. Goosebumps shot up and down my arms with a flash, the sight of it ghastly, but not entirely unexpected given the circumstance. Swales waved me closer, sweat beading on her wrinkled brow. "There is something else in here. Casey, the light, please. Shine it inside if you can."

"Is that close enough?" I asked, the roof of the victim's mouth becoming clear. The upper row of her teeth was near perfectly straight and without a single cavity or stain. Swales nodded as I instructed Tracy who'd become awestruck by the treasure hunt, "Pictures."

"Right!" she replied, firing off a series without focusing the camera. Swales lowered the tip of the hemostat, metal scraping on something solid. "What is it?"

"Sounds like a shell," Tracy said, moving close enough to brush Swales's hair with the tip of the camera lens.

From over her glasses, she eyed us until we were silent and backed away a few inches. She held up the forceps like a long finger. "Patience people."

"Sorry," I told her, speaking for the team as the metal touched the object again, the scraping sound giving me the chills like fingernails running the length of a chalkboard.

"It is rather deep inside her throat—" Swales said, struggling to take hold. Tracy's flash went off, making her hold her breath immediately. The doctor ignored it as she eased her grip on the forceps. With a look of delight on her face, she yelled, "I got it!"

"Let's see!" Tracy said.

From the dark recesses of the victim's mouth, Swales retrieved a dark sandy-gray stone, the size of it two inches, maybe less. The face of it was pocked and coarse, and not at all smooth like a stone that had been tumbling in the ocean surf. "Wow, that was deep in there."

"What is it?" I asked and held out my gloved hand, Swales dropping it into my palm.

She looked at me sheepishly, saying, "I think I got a rock."

"Is it possible it came from the ocean?" I asked, hair blowing in my face as I flipped the thing over to find nothing notable on the other side. I ran my finger across the long edge where there were fine nubs. "I'm surprised it didn't fall out of her mouth."

"There was enough room for the crab to crawl inside," Swales said. Samantha shook her shoulders as the doctor reached for Derek's hand and stood to brush the sand from her knees. "Depending on how long this child was tumbling free in the ocean, it may have gotten washed inside?"

"You don't sound convinced," I said, passing the stone around to the team.

"The child's jaw was locked fairly firm." Swales said with a shrug. She held up her hand, adding, "Yet, there was enough room for a small crab to crawl inside, passing between the upper and lower row of teeth. But a stone that size?"

"It's not a stone," Derek said abruptly, his voice resonating deep as he held it against the sky. The wind blew his thinning hair to one side as he rolled the stone between his thick fingers. "Nope. This isn't a stone at all."

"Do tell," Dr. Swales said, one hand on his shoulder as she struggled to stay balanced. She gave him a soft jab. "Well, don't leave us hanging."

"Sorry." A self-conscious grin appeared. "It's called fulgurite," he answered, plump cheeks turning red.

"Lightning sand?" Tracy asked, stirring a mound of dry sand with her foot.

"You heard of it?" I asked, the name newer than new, my having never heard the word before.

"No kidding. It's a piece of sea glass?" Swales asked, reaching for the stone. "My husband collected those things."

"What is it?" I asked, focusing on Tracy for an answer.

"It's created when lightning strikes the sand. The heat of the electricity is like three times the surface of the sun, which is enough to melt the sand. The shape is formed by the path the lightning takes until it dissipates."

I began to understand what they were holding. "Wouldn't it be clear like glass? And smooth?"

"It is on the inside," Derek answered. Swales held it for me to take, Derek continuing, "But be careful, the tubes are hollow. It's the path the lightning bolt took, and it's kinda fragile."

"Which is why they're rare," Tracy said. "The iron and other impurities in the sand are what give it color."

I held it up against the sky to try and see the glass, sunlight breaking through the overhead clouds to warm the autumn air. "You mean to tell me that I'm holding what's left over after a lightning strike."

"That's it," Tracy said.

"And how would it get inside our victim's mouth?" Swales looked up at me, one brow raised higher than the other. "Yeah, I know what you're going to say."

"That my dear is for you to figure out," she answered anyway.

"Bag it," I said, handing it to Tracy, Derek's eyes following.

When I noticed, he said, "Beachcombers can spend weeks, sometimes months searching for one of those."

"It's that rare?" I asked, thinking the piece of fulgurite didn't just happen to wash into our victim's mouth.

"Yeah, kinda rare," he answered and nodded hard enough to make his cheeks shake. "That's a collectible."

"Then maybe that rules out the chance of it coming from the ocean." I turned to face the body, the tragedy of a life cut short. An ache of sadness came, along with ideas of beach-combers and collectors. "Then maybe we need to find who this fulgurite belongs to."

THREE

With shifting sands and tidal changes, Jericho recommended we move the investigation to the next stage, the morgue and identification. As the new day aged and the clouds parted for some sunlight, the warming temperatures brought late season vacations to the beach. There were tourists behind the black and yellow crime-scene tape, gawking and talking amongst themselves. Reporters had caught word of the murder, and I saw their satellite antennas sprouting from behind the shallowest points of the sand dune along Route 12.

To my surprise, the reporters behaved themselves and stood behind the crime-scene tape. Long camera lenses nosed between the tourists while they asked questions. Like the sands, the winds had shifted as well. The gusts had turned west, throwing the smell of death into the salty air, causing a few of the curious to turn their heads and decide to move on.

The beach had seen enough too, and with help from Samantha and Derek, we lifted the victim and carefully placed her inside the body bag. The blue material thick and heavy, the body bag had a zipper down the front of it, along with six black handles, though we'd only need a couple. Made for all sizes, the young victim looked tiny inside it, her body shriveled and sad. It broke my heart.

"Shove us off?" Jericho asked me as he boarded the patrol boat. Keeping things professional, I held his hand and braced his shoulder as if I was trying to help secure his balance. It was a steal, my wanting to touch him, to feel close to him if just for the moment. I wouldn't see him again until late in the evening. We were working an unkind week, the hours of our shifts not lining up. It kept us apart more than we were together. And while the circumstance was tragic, seeing him during the day was a much-needed respite. He perched his sunglasses on the brim of his hat, the daylight glinting in his blue-green eyes. He hadn't shaved in a week and the growing stubble was becoming an itchy beard for both him and me. As he pawed at his chin, he leaned over the bow and said, "I'll be home a few hours before you. I can fire up the grill. Tony gave me some fresh yellowfin he caught shore fishing."

"That's a lot better than the store-bought fish sticks I was going to heat in the microwave," I told him. He smirked, believing I was kidding. I wasn't. "Your idea sounds good."

Tony started the twin motors and I instinctively checked the ports for them, white sea foam curling around my ankle. I didn't want to see them stranded and made sure the water was flowing through the motors. They were patrolling the ocean which could take them far from the shoreline and always made me nervous. I took hold of Jericho's fingers in a quick clutch as I handed him the bow rope. The patrol boat's hull slipped easily from the sand where it had been sitting, the stern remaining in place as the bow spun around while Tony trimmed the levels on the motors. When he pushed the accelerator, the front of the boat heaved into the air, leaving behind a thin cloud. They were gone a moment later, the motors hum continuing as the sight of them grew distant.

. . .

Derek and Samantha were on their way to the morgue, Dr. Swales deciding to drive with Tracy and me. We followed her through the entry of the municipal building. Once we were in the lower level, we did as Dr. Swales insisted, changing into disposable fabric coveralls and cloth booties to go over our shoes.

"I keep a clean house," the doctor told Tracy in a faint southern accent as she handed her a box of gloves. I recalled her saying the same to me when I'd first met her. "Isn't that right, Detective?"

"Yes, it is," I answered, slipping my arms through the coveralls, the papery feel riding against my bare arms, giving me a chill. My phone buzzed with what I hoped was the victim's identification. While processing the scene, we used a digital fingerprint reader in the field and submitted the results. Though the fingerprints were shriveled and pruned from being wet, we successfully captured two. We'd only need one for an identification.

I glanced at my phone, a name and face from a student identification showing on the screen. "Her name is Laura Jackson and she's a local. Sixteen years old."

"Gosh, she's so young," Tracy said with grim sadness. "Was there a missing person's notice issued?"

I searched the listing of reports sent to my phone, expecting to find it. "There's nothing. I went back three days too."

"It could be that the victim's parents don't know she's gone missing?" Swales questioned as she lightly shoved her shoulder against a heavy resin door. Tracy followed, stopping when the refrigerated air spilled around her feet. Swales held one of the doors, asking, "Are you two coming along?"

We didn't question her and went inside. She'd make the preliminary report that I'd want to have in hand when it came time to visit the Jackson residence. The morgue was as cold as always, the air thick with a mix of refrigeration and death. Only the stench of death wasn't as strong, all the steel tables except one were empty, the Outer Banks experiencing a small reprieve. Derek and Samantha had arrived ahead of us and placed Laura's remains on the autopsy table. Like the sight of her in the large body bag, she looked small like a child on the table. "Anything here we can use to help with the time of death?"

"Better light," Swales said, flipping on the overheads and turning on the recorder. She lifted the victim's eyelid and raised her chin while studying it. "Twelve hours minimum is my estimate. Could be more."

"Are you checking for corneal cloudiness?" Tracy asked, her forehead wrinkling. Swales motioned for her to come over. Tracy stood next to her, continuing, "Since the victim's body temperature was compromised by the ocean water."

"Yes, that is correct," she answered, shining a light across the eye as though expecting a reaction. "See the cloudiness, how it's more concentrated at the center, covering the pupil?"

"I see it. But you can still tell the color of her eyes," Tracy said. "They're a light brown."

"Some more time and the color would become difficult to see," Swales went on, focusing on Tracy and enjoying the teaching moment.

"How much time?" Tracy asked impatiently. It was slight, but enough for Swales to look at me. From the doctor's expression, I suspected she wanted to comment on how much Tracy was like me. I knew it, she knew it, but it was best not to say it. "What? What did I say?"

"Nothing wrong," I answered, lifting my shoulders. "You're asking all the right questions."

"Corneal cloudiness begins around two hours after death. After that, it becomes progressively opaque. It remains measurable the first day and into the second. Beyond two days, the measure of cloudiness is difficult to see."

"Any signs of petechiae?" I asked, wondering if the cloudiness might hide it.

"Definitely," Swales answered, leaning forward as she pulled the lower eyelid down. On the inside of it, the girl's flesh was spotted bright red. "You can see it on the upper eyelid too. Pronounced petechiae in the whites of the eyes and around the face. These are significant signs of strangulation."

"We'll take a picture now, using the ring flash." I handed Tracy the camera equipment. Beneath the table was a wooden stool Swales used. She stepped down for Tracy to stand. "Tomorrow morning, we'll repeat the picture for comparison. If the cloudiness progresses, we know the death was between twelve and twenty hours. That would give us a time of death that could be as early as last night or almost thirty-five hours."

"And if there's no signs of the cloudiness progressing—" Tracy began, her voice muffled behind the camera. She focused the lens closer to the victim's eyes, and continued, "—then that would indicate more than twenty-four hours, which is Thursday, which would put her time of death during Thursday's midnight hours."

"You two make a good team," Swales commented while rubbing her fingers through the victim's hair. "I believe we've got half the beach here. I'm finding sand all the way to the scalp."

"She'd been in the ocean a while," I said and lifted the shirt where I'd found the small series of holes. Beneath it, the victim's flesh was torn and bitten, but without a single bruise or bleeding. "Crabs?"

Nodding, Swales said, "Yes, that's my guess."

"I thought there'd be a lot more?" Tracy asked, taking a picture from over my shoulder.

"Jericho found her early. That tells us she wasn't on the beach for very long."

"Tides?" Tracy asked. "Could we use the tides to determine where her body originated?"

I held up the evidence bag with the fulgurite. "There's a map that shows tidal flows over the last couple days."

"But?" Tracy asked, taking notes.

"With the undertows, we won't have anything accurate." I placed the evidence bag on the victim, laying it across her middle. "We need to find out who, or where, this came from."

"First, let's get you the preliminary autopsy report I know you need," Swales said while continuing to comb her fingers through the victim's hair. "Other than the sand, there's no injury to the head."

I ran my hands over the victim's denim jeans, wet and cold, inspecting the pockets, making certain they were empty. In the left-hand pocket, I found a few dollars folded over and showing the wet faces of Abraham Lincoln and Andrew Jackson. "Twenty-five dollars. But nothing else."

"Not exactly running away with money, if that was a thought," Tracy said, striking the moment with a camera flash. "Doesn't it seem odd there isn't a missing person's report? Even an Amber alert?"

"It does," I said, agreeing. "But as Dr. Swales mentioned, the parents may have no idea she's missing. Let's say death did take place late last night. The parents may believe she is staying at a friend's place."

With a pair of trauma shears, Swales began to cut. She struggled with the denim, wincing. "Casey, I've lost Samantha for the day." She handed me a pair of shears and motioned to the pants as she carried on with the top. "Be a dear and help with this. The material is too tough for these aching fingers."

"Of course," I said. Swales had been set to retire recently, but decided boredom wasn't for her and stayed on full time.

One day, her replacement could be Samantha. The younger version of Dr. Swales had been the doctor's right-hand the last two months. I loved working with Swales and couldn't imagine a case without her. I began at the victim's ankle, her feet as white as the sheet that would cover her when we were done.

"A straight cut works best," Swales instructed me. "We'll bag them for forensics and as evidence." She rubbed her hands, inflammation around the knuckles showing through tight gloves, muttering, "Getting too old for this."

"You always say that," I told her, trying to lighten her mood. "What would you be doing if you weren't helping us with this case?"

She paused, her shears at the middle of the victim's chest. She froze like that long enough for Tracy to look, but then shook her head, frizzy hair swaying. "I can honestly say that I have absolutely no flipping idea."

The response made me smirk as we continued to reveal the victim's body. Methodically, the three of us searched the girl's skin for any signs of trauma. "Would you mind evaluating?" I asked Swales, wanting to get one of the more difficult questions answered. Tracy stepped back, understanding. It always made me uncomfortable to ask; I suppose if the day ever came that I wasn't bothered by any of this, then that was the day I knew it was time for me to retire too.

"You're asking if there are signs of sexual assault?" Swales said, speaking loudly enough for the official recording. Tracy helped the doctor down from her stool and repositioned it by the victim's feet. The rivets in the jeans clanked the steel tray next to the autopsy table where I staged the shredded garments for us to review again. Having been in the ocean an extended time, I had doubts of finding anything beyond the dollars stuffed in the girl's pockets. Swales climbed the stool, Tracy moving her instrument tray into position, the wheels squealing. "Inner thighs and external genitalia do not show signs of bruising. Checking for hypostatic discoloration."

I found myself turning away, searching the victim's neck and face and ears for signs of trauma that we might not have been able to see on the beach. There was only the bruising around the neck. "Tracy, can you get this?" I asked, pointing out the pattern of bruising which appeared more pronounced on one side than it did on the other.

"Indications of any semen specimens is negative," Swales said as Tracy worked the camera. "I am swabbing for acid phosphatase levels. Any elevation would indicate sexual intercourse."

"Are there technicians at the lab during the weekend?" Tracy asked, concerned the swab would sit until Monday.

"We've got a possible murder investigation and the sensitivity and urgency of the timelines is understood." Swales held out her hand, stepping down from her stool. Holding the swab, she said, "They'll come in to process it. However, I suspect it will be negative. I saw no signs of any sexual assault or activity."

I let out a sigh, saying, "Glad that was one thing she didn't suffer through." Returning to the table, I held the victim's hand, having noticed her fingernails had growth and were sturdy. "Nail scraping and clipping?"

"Right on cue," Swales said, rolling the tray around the side of the table. She returned the shears, and then shook out her hands. "But I think I can take it from here."

And she was right. She could take it from here. I needed to locate where the victim's parents lived. I needed to tell them their daughter had been murdered. When the difficult questions were asked, I'd have answers to those as well. "Doctor, your preliminary assessment is strangulation?"

She gazed at the victim's naked body and studied her from head to toe, assessing what we knew. The only identifiable injuries found were around the neck, a few possible defensive wounds on her arms, and the pronounced petechiae on the eyes. Slowly nodding in agreement, she answered with a flat and haunting tone that left me colder than the morgue ever could.

"This child was murdered. She was strangled to death and dumped in the ocean like garbage."

FOUR

The hours caught up to us quickly, the autumn sun breaking through the cloudy haze to dry them up like beach towels slung over a chair. The main thoroughfare through the barrier islands was mostly clear as we traveled south again and headed toward Motts Creek. The traffic that came with summer beachgoers had been replaced with those carrying long boards, seeking the promise of tall waves to surf near Rodanthe and Avalon Piers in Kill Devil Hills. This was also one of the prime months for fishing charters, which is where we found a connection to the victim's parents. From Laura Jackson's fingerprints and her school identification, we had a home address. We were also able to get her parents' business address—a fishing charter out of Nags Head.

Tracy drove this time, the direction nearly the same as this morning. We stopped for gas and food but kept the respite short. On my phone I had a map showing the tidal movements from the previous evening, wondering if there was a possibility of determining where Laura's body had been before Jericho found her. It was an idea Tracy floated, and one I couldn't dismiss without giving the map a look. The victim's body was discovered on the shores near Bodie Lighthouse, and her parents' fishing charter was a few miles south near the Oregon Inlet Campground and Motts Creek. The lighthouse was also close to where the Jackson family lived, leading me to surmise that Laura Jackson may have been near her home when her killer abducted her. While tides are consistent, changing every six hours, the map and its charts showed the previous night's seas being calm. Whoever dumped Laura's body in the ocean, did so close to the girl's home.

We drove to a stretch of homes two miles north of Coquina Beach and the lighthouse, turning west onto single lane road and following it around a bend that took us back in the direction we had come. There was a mix of single level and multi-level homes. Some were newer, the properties looking as though they'd been rehabilitated, maybe renovated due to a past storm and the damage it brought with it. There were other homes that were older and on the smaller size. Most were cozy and well maintained, short, white picket fences with sparse lawns that had browned with the changing season. One of the smallest of the homes was the Jacksons'. It had pale siding and stained roof shingles, some chipped and sitting askew. There was a paved driveway, its asphalt cracked and rutted on the sides, and extended by gravel to carry a rusted truck and a small hunter-green sedan. As I felt a nervous flutter in my belly, Tracy glanced over to me, the look on her face telling me she felt the same. Someone was home. And we had terrible news to deliver.

The house was raised on stilts like many in the area and had a wooden deck and lattice draped from it to cover the pilings. From beneath the house, I saw movement as we pulled into the mouth of the driveway. A man appeared. He wore a straw hat with a brim large enough to shadow his neck and face. When he saw us, he ducked to clear the beams, his hand brushing across the weathered lattice while he gazed cautiously at my car. Twice he knocked on the deck boards above him, before a

woman in her forties or fifties appeared at a sliding glass door.
She was round and without a chin, her skin pink and her eyes
set back in her head, her brown hair pinned in a bun that pulled
on her forehead.

She wiped her hands vigorously and threw a kitchen towel
over her shoulder before sliding open the door. When she
stepped out, I saw the look of deep concern and worry on her
face. The sight of it told me all I needed to know. While they
may not have contacted the police yet, they'd been searching. I
could feel my mouth go dry like a river, the back of my throat
tingling with nerves as I exited the car. Clutching my badge
against my chest, I dreaded this part of the job. Already my
tongue had grown twice its size as the words I had to say stum-
bled in my mind. I'd delivered bad news before, horrible news
more than a few times. And with each, it felt worse than all the
times before it.

"You found our daughter?" the man asked, his words thick
with a brogue I'd heard only a few times since moving to the
Outer Banks. He tore his hat off, daylight gleaming from his
bald head. He glanced above him toward the sliding glass doors
and then held the hat with both hands as though begging. His
focus returned, darting from me to Tracy, his cautionary look
turning sad and garnering a pity that tugged at my heart.
"We... we were working late and didn't notice she was gone
until this morning."

The woman joined the man, presumed to be Mrs. Jackson.
Her feet bare, she braced his arm when stepping on the rocks.
She mumbled something to him, and I heard the same dialect.
Jericho had told me about it. From him, I'd learned that it was
called High Tides and was natively spoken by those growing up
in the southern parts of the islands like Ocracoke. I was
guessing that was where the couple had been from originally. I
moved to the lawn, the couple following. "Our girl! You have
her?"

"Mr. and Mrs. Jackson?" They nodded eagerly as a neighbor across the street appeared. A patrol car arrived, the lights turned off, its tires crunching pebbles lining the property as it pulled alongside and borrowed space behind my car.

"Oh God! Frank?" Mrs. Jackson said with a moan. She stared at the patrol car as the officer closed the car door and then stood to wait for my instruction. She fanned her face to fight a scream, telling him, "I thought she was in her room!"

"Could we go inside to speak privately?" I asked, extending my arm toward the steps, the neighbor standing by her mailbox.

"Yes, ma'am," he answered, with his posture slumping while he held the woman's arm. He'd read the signs, and maybe knew what I had to tell them. They climbed the steps, the woman's thick knuckles white as she clutched the railing. He looked over his shoulder at us, explaining, "Like I said, we were out on a charter and didn't get back until early this morning."

Tracy noted the comment, asking, "What time would that have been?"

When we reached their door, Mrs. Jackson collapsed onto a chair and continued to wave her hands. Her chest and face had turned blotchy and damp, a purplish color with sweat beading on her upper lip. "I'll get us some water," he said, going inside. His abrupt motions put me on edge, but a moment later he arrived with glasses and water on a tray, along with an inhaler for the woman. With his brow furrowed, he said, "Carla has asthma."

"I understand, please take a minute," I told them as we gathered chairs and sat across from one another. We were far enough from the neighbor for privacy and sitting in what was the home's den. "What time did you arrive back last night?"

"Midnight charter," Mrs. Jackson answered with a wheezing cough. She squeezed the inhaler and sucked down the vapors, her chest rising and her eyelids fluttering. She exhaled with force, blowing raspberries. "It was a charter of six, and we'd gone thirty miles to fish for nighttime blues. We'd hoped for some tunas too."

Tracy jotted down the details, choosing to use pencil and notepad today. She flipped the page, asking, "You returned at midnight?"

With a slow nod, his wife agreeing while inhaling another squeeze, he answered, "Sounds about right." He gripped the tops of his knees with the hands of a fisherman, the back of them spotted by the sunlight and wrinkled by the sea. "An hour cleaning the catch. Another two, two and a half to clean the boat—"

"—suppose we got back home about three, maybe closer to four this morning."

Mr. Jackson moved close to the edge of his seat, shaking his head slowly. "We... we slept in, been looking the last hour." He waved his hand back and forth. "I been asking neighbors up and down if they seen her."

I swallowed and held my breath, the discussion of their whereabouts and timeline delaying what I'd come here to do. "Mr. and Mrs. Jackson," I said, changing my tone enough for them to take notice. Mrs. Jackson held her breath while Mr. Jackson seemed to brace himself for a fall, brow furrowing enough to make him squint. "Your daughter was found just after sunrise this morning on the beaches across from Bodie Lighthouse."

"Found?" he asked, a look of relief flashing briefly. "She be okay then?"

I shook my head. "Sir, I'm afraid she wasn't alive when she was discovered."

The woman's face creased, her eyelids shutting tight as if it'd help her hide from the awful truth. A strong wailing sound came from deep in her chest. Mr. Jackson went to his knees, a hand on her shoulder, the two embracing. We said nothing for a moment, letting it sink in. From behind his embrace, I heard

Mrs. Jackson ask, "How? Did she drown? She doesn't swim in the ocean."

"Only swim in the pools," Mr. Jackson added.

With the woman's comment, Tracy glanced over at me, the two of us thinking the same thing. Native to the Outer Banks, the bay and the beach, a family with a fishing boat. It seemed odd that a teenager her swimming was limited to pools. "Ma'am, I'm sorry to say, but there is evidence of foul play."

With those words, Mr. Jackson was on his feet. We stood too, recognizing when the anguish becomes rage, a reaction possible. "You saying she was murdered!?" he asked, searching around his house as though the killer was present. "What happened? Was she kidnapped?"

When he began searching the windows, I asked, "Sir, do you believe someone broke in and took your daughter?" I followed him as he paced the deck and tried to open the windows. He grunted as he brushed past me. "Do you know anyone who would want to kidnap or harm your daughter?"

"Adopted," Mrs. Jackson said in a wheezing breath. She swiped at her eyes as she stared hard at her husband, his stopping in reaction to her comment.

"They are *our* daughters," he snapped gruffly with a look of scolding. "They are our family."

Mrs. Jackson sat up, adding, "Of course they are. But it could be their biological parents. They've been in contact recently." She shook her head and wiped her nose. "But they would never ever hurt them."

"And who are their biological parents?" I asked, anxious to get a name.

"Finley," she answered while flicking her fingers in the air, snapping absently while trying to remember. "It's Robert and Jane."

"Let's get started on a profile," I commented, Tracy taking notes as I texted Alice at the station. She was on duty and could begin the computer work needed to get the Finleys' contact information. "Ma'am, they've been in direct touch with you?"

"Yes. Last week," Mrs. Jackson answered with a nod. "They were asking about the girls, wanted to talk about maybe seeing them."

"Them?" I asked, unsure of what she meant, panic gripping me with the possibility of a horrible misunderstanding. "Ma'am. You said girls? You adopted two?"

"Yes, that's right," she answered and looked to Mr. Jackson, sensing confusion. "They're sisters, Shawna and Laura."

I felt my heart shoot into my throat. We had no records of there being two girls. "Could you tell us the last known where-abouts of *both* of your daughters?"

Mr. Jackson sat down, his face grim. "They went to that carnival in town. But they went with our neighbor, the Newmans."

"Then they come home afterward," she continued. "Laura, she left a note saying she was going out."

"She does that," Mr. Jackson said. "At her age, sometimes she stays the night at a friend's place. She knew we'd be home soon to take care of Shawna."

"Shawna?" I asked. There'd been a horrible misunderstanding. "She was supposed to be home?"

"Yes!" Mr. Jackson answered, raising his voice. "You would know that! You found her on the beach!"

"Oh Jesus," the woman exhaled. "Frank... Frank. It's Laura they're talking about." Her breath got louder.

"Mr. and Mrs. Jackson!" I answered, my hands raised and feeling them tremble. "Your daughter, Laura Jackson, was discovered on the beach this morning. She was unresponsive, succumbing to injuries which appear to be a result of a homicide."

"Laura is dead?" he asked, his face filled with shock. "But where's Shawna?"

FIVE

Without losing another second, I was on the phone with the station, relaying the details of the missing child and issuing an Amber alert. I could hear my pulse thrumming in my ears, the beating of it against my temples. My voice was like a distant recording, repeating the words to the officer listening who'd issue the alert, the formalities of it scripted.

"Her height?" I asked, my tone demanding, the urgency of the alert the top priority. My question went unanswered, the girl's parents locked in a confused stare. "I need a description of Shawna."

"Four feet, maybe," the woman answered, lifting her hand up and down, attempting to measure. She burst into tears and began wheezing again.

"Follow me!" her husband said, the Jacksons inviting us into their home. On the wall across from the door, he showed me pictures of the two girls, the adopted sisters. "Will these help?"

"Absolutely!" I answered, recognizing Laura immediately, the picture on the wall a recent one, perhaps a school picture taken days before the new school year began. She handed me a second picture, Mrs. Jackson's hand shaking. Laura's little sister,

Shawna Jackson. She was eight years old and in the third grade, one of her front teeth like that of an adult, but the other still a baby tooth. Like her older sister, Shawna had strawberry-blonde hair and tanned skin with freckles that bridged her nose and cheeks. Both girls' eyes were a light brown, the kind that looked almost golden when the sun touched them at the right angle. The combination of hair and eye color was distinct and helpful in the description supplied for the Amber alert.

With my hand on Mrs. Jackson's arm, steadying her as she placed the girls' picture back on the wall, I told her, "All possible agencies have been notified about Shawna's disappearance."

"Thank you," she answered, sweat running down the side of her head, the inside of the small house stuffy. She saw me look around and nervously grabbed a handful of newspapers, crumpling them with one hand. In the other, she spread her fingers to pick up and carry three plastic cups, the kitchen on the other side of a small peninsula island. "Didn't have a chance to clear."

"Please, ma'am," I said, a gust of air coming from an oscillating fan in the corner. There was a small bookcase with a collection of encyclopedias, and a television hung like a painting on the longest of the wood-paneled walls. "Don't worry about that."

"So what are you going to do next?" Mr. Jackson asked with a look of disdain, his tone scornful. He followed his wife's lead, picking up around the room, depositing the previous day in the kitchen. I sensed he was agitated, his body language rigid. It was annoyance about the misunderstanding, I'm sure. In my career, I'd never experienced a slip like this. Certainly not about a victim and their sibling. When his shoulders slumped, he returned to the couch, asking, "What happened to Laura? Who would do such a thing?"

"I'd like to ask you some questions about Laura, her whereabouts—" I began, Mrs. Jackson shaking her head.

"Tell me Laura didn't suffer," Mrs. Jackson asked abruptly, hope in her voice, desperation on her face.

I heard the words leaving my mouth. "We believe she died quickly." A white lie. A necessary part of our language when speaking to the loved ones of the deceased.

"I want to see my girl," Mrs. Jackson demanded, urging her husband to join as she went to the sliding glass doors.

"Yes, certainly. We have a patrol car to escort you to visit with our medical examiner," I explained, Tracy standing by my side. I could come back to ask the questions I needed to. As she opened the door, I asked, "With your permission, we'd like to take a look at their rooms?"

"There's just the one," Mr. Jackson answered, the sharp tone remaining. "It's a small house, only got the two bedrooms."

"Yes," his wife answered, leaving. She turned around, adding, "You'll know which one is theirs."

Though angry, the politeness wasn't lost. "Ma'am," Mr. Jackson said and slid the glass, the door shutting with a thump. He nodded once and then escorted his wife to the patrol car.

When they were gone from the deck, Tracy said, "Hope you don't mind my saying, but that was awkward."

I could only close my eyes and shake my head. In my mind I heard Mr. Jackson yelling, *You found our daughter?* "It happened," I said, finding a lack of words to describe the disconnect, the professional embarrassment I was feeling.

"Still, the way they came out of the house asking about their daughter. I would never have guessed they weren't talking about Laura."

"We should have known about them being sisters," I said, voice unsettled. "Let's get a look at the room and then talk to the neighbors."

As the parents had said, we knew which of the two bedrooms was the girls'. It was a perfect square that had been split down the middle. Laura's side had all the signs of an older

teen, including the heart-shaped poster-board cutouts on the
wall, their tacked along the edge of posters of boy bands and
rock stars. There was a desk and chair topped with schoolbooks
and an iPad, the cover with a barcode and a *Property of East
OBX High School*. Tracy went to the desk and began thumbing
through a binder.

The other side of the room was dolled in pretty, bright
colors, the kind I'd expect for an eight-year-old. Her bed was a
foldout cot, the mattress thin and without a box spring. Though
small, it was topped with enough oversized stuffed animals to
dwarf any size bed. Shawna had started tacking posters on the
wall too, only these were popular kids shows and cartoon
movies.

There was one item that stood out: a bright yellow flier for a
carnival at the Outer Banks Soundside Event Site in Nags
Head. The thick black lettering was for the Delight's Traveling
Funfair, the dates listing the last week, their stay ending tomorrow. At the center of the page was a clown wearing billowing
pants and gigantic rubber shoes. His face was painted and
beneath his chin was an oversized ruffled red collar. A ceiling
fan lifted the bottom of the paper enough to make the clown
dance, the sight of it giving me a creepy vibe. Then again,
clowns always gave me the willies—maybe I'd watched one too
many horror movies growing up.

"Tracy," I said with a wave to get her attention. From the
wall, I untacked a flier advertising the carnival in Nags Head
and held it up for her. "The parents mentioned the girls going
with the neighbors to a carnival. Must be the Delight's Traveling Funfair."

"Clowns," she commented and then cringed. "Anything but
clowns."

"Really? Me too," I said, curious. I held the flier to take a
picture with my phone. We'd use it when meeting with the
neighbors. "I'm more into watching the acrobatics myself."

"Trapeze artists," she said with a nod. "And the high-wire act."

"Definitely. They make my stomach knot when watching them up there." I returned the flier and then shoved my hands beneath the cot, metal creaking as I leaned onto the mattress. Tracy did the same as we searched the first place most kids kept their secrets, her arm shoved shoulder deep beneath Laura's mattress. Kids tend to forget that adults were their age once too. "Anything on your side?"

She held up a paper fortune teller, the origami flattened to show bubbly red and yellow hearts on one side. "I haven't seen one of these since the ninth grade." Tracy flipped it over, staring with fond reminiscence, the other side marked with blue and green hearts. She opened the fortune teller, unfolding it and bringing it back to life. Ancient memories I'd thought lost to the tragedy of growing up returned from my childhood. Tracy stuffed her fingers inside the paper folds and presented it to me, instructing, "Pick a heart. You've got red, blue, yellow and green."

"Seriously?" I asked, briefly looking at my phone, a vibration confirming the Amber alert for Shawna had been issued. Tracy urged me on, inching the fortune teller closer. "Fine, fine! I'll pick the blue heart."

"Casey picks, blue," she stated with a look of content. The fortune teller flapped as she worked it, the inside like a mouth with more colors and choices. With each iteration, she called out a letter, spelling the words, "Blue heart."

I couldn't help myself and watched with each pass, the folded panels showing a colorful number. When she stopped, I said, "I pick the number four."

"Number four. Let's see your fortune," Tracy said, eyelids rising, her dimples showing. She unfolded the fortune, only it wasn't a fortune at all, but instructions. "It says here that you are to *kiss* the one you love and then you have to—"

I covered the paper fortune, cutting her off as she laughed. "Yeah, I think I get it. Can we get back to work now?"

"Lucky Jericho," she joked, setting the origami aside, and shoving her hands back under the mattress. Turning serious, she asked, "We'll take the iPad?"

"With permission from the parents," I answered. "It's issued by East OBX High School."

"They should be able to access it?"

"That's what I'd expect," I said, my gaze returning to the origami fortune teller, a drawing on the paper where Tracy had put her fingers. I took the fortune in hand to read what was written.

Tracy, seeing it in my hands, asked, "Oh good, my turn?"

"There's something written on the inside," I told her, bending the paper edges, unfolding it.

"She probably made it from a piece of scrap paper," Tracy said, looking disappointed as I dismantled it. "When you fold all the corners, the one side gets hidden."

"I think it's a heart," I said, but wasn't surprised by the find. Young love and the first high school years. A thought occurred to me, the victim's age and my trying to recall the joys of paper trinkets and playing with them during study hall. "Tracy, the victim is a young sixteen, her birthday was last month. Doesn't that seem a little old to keep one of these?"

"I dunno," she answered with a shrug. Tracy spread the paper folds as I grabbed a picture of the heart and the initials. "We don't know how long it's been under her mattress. Could be from years ago."

"I suppose that's true," I said, searching the room, seeing that it was well kept and clean.

"It could be she made it while in middle school or when she was a freshman?"

"Maybe. She might have forgotten all about it."

Tracy eyed the inside folds, reading the initials, "It looks like an LJ and a GN?"

I studied my phone's screen, agreeing. "Something for us to track," I said and pointed to the flier and the clown as it continued a fan dance. "That's the work we need to do next."

"You mean visit the carnival?" Tracy asked, her voice lifting.

"I think we'll come back to talk to the neighbors," I answered, tapping the date on the flier and checking the time. "The carnival is in town until tomorrow, but they're not opening until later tonight. Let's visit the grounds before then."

"Do you think one of the fair's workers would remember the girls?"

I had my doubts, Tracy seeing it on my face. At a busy funfair, what were the chances of the two girls standing out? But we had to try. "It's the last place her parents said the girls would have been. It could be the last place Laura was seen alive."

SIX

From the Jacksons' home, we drove to the ten acres of land on the Roanoke Sound in Nags Head. Called the Soundside Event Site, Delight's Traveling Funfair was there for one more night. As I drove south, the sun dipped low, the days beginning to end earlier. Tracy opened her laptop and kicked off the research into the Jackson couple. I was interested in the adoption history and the birth parents that Mrs. Jackson had mentioned. She'd said they'd been in contact recently, and had given us a name and a possible lead. A part of me understood kidnapping your own child, but murder? Was this one case or two separate cases?

There was Laura's tablet too. We'd come back for it in the morning, requesting permission from the Jacksons. There was also the school Laura attended. They might have the account access in the cloud. With Laura Jackson murdered, it was vital for us to review the account, the child's email and anything else she'd saved.

"Over there," I said seeing a Ferris wheel with red and blue and green lights twinkling against a dusky sky. "I think they're already open."

"Really?" Tracy asked, voice jumping as she shoved her

laptop in her bag.

"Really," I answered, rethinking our approach. Would the carnival workers talk to us?

I turned into the Soundside Event Site location, Tracy's fingers digging into my car's dashboard as she lowered her front to see all the carnival's attractions. The parking lot was already full as I turned right into it, driving straight ahead until hitting a turnabout. It took me around in a circle, a second parking lot acting as an overflow, our arriving much later than I'd hoped.

"The place is packed," Tracy said, gawking at the crowds, her gaze drifting upwards toward a Ferris wheel and chain swing. As I backed the car into what might have been one of the last open spots, she asked, "You know, I'm actually kind of hungry."

"Is that right?" I asked, my belly stirring in agreement. I holstered my gun out of sight and draped my badge around my neck. I wore slate gray slacks and a light beige jacket with an inside pocket that was a perfect fit for my badge. It was near evening on a Saturday, the day having gotten away from us without a break. "I suppose we could grab a bite once we're done."

"Really? You don't mind?" she asked, her face lighting up as she sniffed the air. I followed her lead and could already smell the carnival—the hay on the ground and the warm scent of kettle corn and funnel cakes. She nudged her chin toward the chain swing that was closest to the entrance, the seats filled, yells and screams warbling into the late afternoon. "Wanna give that a try?"

"Before or after we eat?" I asked, half kidding. There were bells and whistles from games being played, the ageless sound of carnival workers barking to the crowd, enticing them to play if they wanted to win a prize. Tracy stood in awe, her mouth open, face brightened, her eyelids peeled back. "Have you never been to a carnival?"

Tracy put on a pout and shook her head as we worked through the crowded line. "Nothing like this."

When we reached the entrance, the fair's attendant expecting ten dollars, I flashed my badge, telling her, "We're here to see the owner."

"Jimmy?" she said, squinting one eye as she chewed, her cheeks moving fast, the gum snapping. She waved us through, telling, "Go ahead, he's in there somewhere."

Something told me we'd be here a while. The place was shoulder-to-shoulder busy. There were kids running back and forth with parents chasing, and every attraction had a line wrapped around it. The concessions had lines too, as did the games and even the row of white and lime colored port-o-potties. I didn't stop walking until we were at the center of the carnival where I could get my bearings. Furthest from us was a funhouse, two-stories high with tall, ruby-colored flags that flapped violently in the ocean's winds. There were strobe lights filling the windows, and a circled entrance with its insides striped like a barber pole. And nowhere in sight did I see the clown from the flier. We had no idea what the owner looked like, but something told me I'd recognize him when I saw him.

"Let's try the concessions and games," I said, leading us to one of the food stands. "The girls will have definitely done the cheaper activities."

"How do you know that?" Tracy asked, her gaze rising as a man on stilts walked by, his gait like a giraffe's.

"A child and a teenager," I answered. "Not much money from the parents."

There were games everywhere, this section of the carnival laid out like players around a poker table. From where we stood, I could pick any game. The one I wanted was without a single customer, the game's attendee sitting in wait, a look of boredom frozen on their face. It was the game table with tin discs and a red dot that I found. I went to it, some cash in hand.

"A dollar?" I asked the attendant. He was in his twenties and wore a dingy, white collared shirt, with a red armband above the elbows.

He had a skimmer hat on and tipped it once as he plucked the dollar from my fingers. "Ever seen this game before?" Without waiting for an answer, he held the tin discs and plopped them one at a time until the red dot was completely covered. "If I can't see red, you win a prize."

"Not sure that'll fit in the car," Tracy said looking at the stuffed bears and lions.

"Have you been working here long?" I asked him, poising the first disc an inch above the dot. I dropped it along the edge, his giving me a nod. I moved to the next two discs, covering the red dot some more and asked, "Were you working last night?"

"If we're open, we're working," he answered, taking a swig from a thermos. From the reaction on his face, I didn't think it coffee he was drinking. I dropped the fourth disc, the red dot nearly completely covered. He held up a finger, tobacco stains showing in the blue overhead light. "Just one more."

I held the disc longer than I'd held the others, centering it just right to make the move. When I dropped it in place, the red dot was gone. "Casey!" Tracy yelled, hands clasped. "How'd ya do that!?"

"Tsk tsk," the attendant said, correcting Tracy, pointing to one tiny speck of red. "Sorry miss, but that's a miss."

I shrugged and showed him my phone with a picture of Laura Jackson. "Do you recognize her?"

The attendant's politeness changed then, his expression flat. "Are you a cop?"

"I'm just someone asking," I answered.

"Nah, ain't seen her," he said with a shake as he collected the discs. "We get a lot of people through here."

His gaze shifted behind us, a voice asking, "Can I help you with something?" I turned to face a man in his fifties, his head bald, his nose plump, and from the jowls and the way the corners of his eyebrows rose, from the resemblance around the eyes and mouth, I could see he was also the clown on the flier. He was the owner. Only question, how did he know who we were? "Sheila at the booth says you was looking for me?"

I pulled my badge from beneath my jacket's hem, the attendant slinking away to sit on his stool. There was no reaction from the owner standing in front of us. I answered, "My name is Detective White."

"Jimmy Delight," he replied. "Now you gonna tell me what this is about?"

I showed him Laura's picture, watching his face, his reaction, gauging it. There was nothing. "This girl was found this morning dead. A homicide."

Jimmy crossed his arms. "Sorry to hear that." He motioned us to the center of the courtyard when a pair of boys held up a dollar to play the disc game. "What's that got to do with us?"

"Her parents said she was here last night." I flipped to an image of Shawna, adding, "She was with her sister—"

"Amber alert," Jimmy said, surprising me. When he noticed, he said, "Seen it come across the news this afternoon."

"Do you recognize either of them?" I asked but sensed where the questioning was going.

He waved his hands toward the crowds, answering, "As you can see, we're full most of the time."

"Any chance you have security cameras?" Tracy asked as she searched above, looking for any semblance of technology.

"Look, we're a small operation." Jimmy Delight's brow wrinkled while he scratched his chin. "We're made to travel. The road is our home. We don't have cameras."

"Mind if we ask around?" I asked, showing my phone's screen again.

"Can't stop you," he said. And he was right. "But would ask you let my people work."

"Of course," I answered and handed him my card. He eyed my name and number, glancing over the edge of it at us. "Please contact us if you remember anything."

"Sure thing," he said, tucking my card into a shirt pocket. He was gone then, disappearing into the dark shadows between two game trailers.

Jimmy Delight had said they were made to travel. By tomorrow night, the grounds would be empty.

"Let's ask around," Tracy said. "We can split up and meet back here?"

"You've got the pictures?" I asked as I moved to the next game trailer, the center filled with a hundred long-neck Coke bottles, game players tossing plastic rings at them.

"I got them," she answered, showing her phone as she went to another gaming trailer. She stopped to watch a game called Balloon Blast with water guns pummeling a pair of clown heads as balloons inflated above their heads. When a balloon popped, the attendant shouted, *winner winner chicken dinner*, and then handed a furry, oversized purple dinosaur to a ten-year-old girl. "See you in an hour."

"An hour," I agreed.

It was another two hours before we finally sat down to let the day rest. We covered a square picnic table with two trays full of carnival foods. Staring at the savory delights, I was sure to regret it by the time I took to my side of the bed. There were hotdogs and doughy pretzels with cups of melted cheese, we also added a plate of funnel cake and Tracy bought a candied apple, a chunk of it already missing with evidence of sugary caramel stuck on her cheek. And though the food eased the gnawing hunger in our bellies, my mind was restless with questions. In all the booths, the workers, there was not a single hit. Not even a look of recognition from anyone. It was as if the Jackson girls had never been to Delight's Traveling Funfair.

SEVEN

Black clouds sparked lightning and edged the ocean as an autumn storm crept across the horizon like a nightmare lulling its victim to sleep. It was that time of year when the Atlantic Ocean spun seasonal storms and threatened the barrier islands. Hopefully, if this one stayed its course, it would travel away northeast, and dissipate somewhere above Bermuda. If lucky, we could have sunshine by late this afternoon and enjoy pink clouds in an amazing sunset over Kitty Hawk Bay tonight.

Still, the sight of the dark clouds was something to behold, and I respected what it represented. Having called the Outer Banks my home the last couple of years, I'd learned what to expect with the late summer and autumn months. A stiff, shifting breeze meant something to those living here year-round. It was enough to gaze east and south to see what threats might be looming. After our last year, we needed a break. It was only a few months ago that a case turned on me the way a storm can sometimes turn on the islands. It turned on Jericho too, a killer threatening our lives with a raging fire. He'd burned the both of us, and when it was over, there was nothing left of Jericho's home. With everything I am, I can never let a case get that close to us again.

When the sand dunes were shallow enough for me to see over, I couldn't help but glance at the ocean while we drove to the Jacksons' home that morning. Soundless lightning continued, sparks at the fray of black and purple mass, the winds turning up the surf with giant swells and crashing waves. The beaches were bare, the gulls and sandpipers and other birds gone, having flown inland to take refuge.

Jericho and his partner were out there too, my heart heavy with nerves as they patrolled the storming waters. I'd never think anyone would go into the ocean with such turbulence riding up the coast. But I was wrong. Tracy saw them first, pointing ahead, another sand dune breaking our view to see a group of kids daring the ocean. Dressed in skintight black suits, three of them were swallowed whole by a wave, their boards spearing the air before tumbling in a white rush. Another two were rising with a bigger wave, the ocean behind them empty of boats and ships.

"That's a crazy risk," I said as we turned onto the street to the Jacksons' home. "I get the thrill, but still."

"You've never done anything crazy?" Tracy asked, a smirk on her face which quickly faded with the muted sounds of shouting. "Casey?"

"I see it," I told her. In the middle of the street, Mrs. Jackson stood toe-to-toe with another woman, a neighbor perhaps. The two were in a heated exchange, both waving their hands and pointing their fingers. Mrs. Jackson looked to have come from her bedroom, wearing pink slippers which had faded in the years, a lime-green robe and her hair pinned. The other woman was around the same age, mid forties or so, slim and attractive and already dressed for the day. She wore a gray suit with yellow-colored blouse, her face and hair were made for a day working in an office building. While today was Sunday, the real-estate signs next to her car told us she was working. She carried a briefcase in her hand, and stomped expensive heels as the two carried on, their faces cramped in scowls, eyes blazing. "I suppose that might be Mrs. Newman?"

"I suppose that is." The Jacksons had mentioned the girls going to the carnival with the neighbors. Without warning Mrs. Jackson waved her hand close to the neighbor's head to brush her hair, a tuft of golden-blonde hair rising abruptly. The neighbor took a step back, Mrs. Jackson's face turning fierce. "Better get out there."

Hitting the brakes, I stopped the car in front of the women and opened the door. When Mrs. Jackson recognized me, she began to point and yell, "This is the neighbor we told you about."

"Mrs. Newman?" I asked.

Forcing a smile, the neighbor patted her hair, touching it gently with the palm of her hand. "I'm Barbara Newman," she said, a business card perched between two fingers. I shook my head. She showed a look of apology, saying, "Force of habit."

"Mrs. Jackson, could I have a word?" I asked, wanting to defuse what I suspected was her asking questions about Laura and Shawna. It could be that Barbara Newman was the last person to see both girls. As Mrs. Jackson considered my request, her focus jumped to the Newmans' front door where a short girl about the age of Shawna appeared. Dressed for outdoor play, she carried a playset called Ponyville, a knitted bag with plastic pony figures that were wildly colorful.

"Abigail!" Mrs. Jackson greeted the girl. I knew the look on her face. It was the same that I'd worn after my daughter had been kidnapped. It said everything I felt too. The want of your daughter's return. The deep and dark jealousy of those who had their babies while I did not. Immediately, Mrs. Newman began to retreat, keeping herself in the path between her neighbor and daughter. The Newman girl stopped where she was, a pony tumbling from the bag. Mrs. Jackson approached, her step heavy enough to hear. "Abigail! Where did you and Shawna go Friday night!"

"Mom?" Abigail said with a look of fright.

"Enough!" Mrs. Newman shouted.

"Mrs. Jackson!" I said, raising my voice.

But she wouldn't hear me. She continued forward, her hands raised, pleading, "Where's my Shawna? Where did you go?"

Frank Jackson ran past me, the air briefly smelling of the fish he hunted, calling out, "Carla!"

"I just want to ask Abigail some questions," Mrs. Jackson said, trying to reason with him. I held my hand toward her, offering it as her husband gently turned her away from the Newmans' child. Her eyelids were wide, the news we'd delivered still fresh like an open wound. And seeing the Newmans' little girl was like pouring salt on it. I know, because I felt what she felt. "Abigail was with Shawna! She might know something."

"Listen to me," I said, pinching her soft fingers between mine, forcing her to look at me. "Mrs. Jackson, I need you to go inside your home now. Let me do my job."

"Shawna and Abigail," she continued but nodded at the same time, telling me she'd heard what I asked. "They're the best of friends."

"I understand," I assured her.

When we reached the street and Mrs. Newman, she swiped her hand from mine, saying, "And Laura! You let them leave the carnival? How could you?"

"Carla," Mrs. Newman answered, her face cramped with a waiting cry. She shook her head, "I am so... so sorry—"

"You should be!" Mrs. Jackson snapped. "She was only sixteen."

Mrs. Newman looked to me and Tracy. "She was our babysitter—"

"We'll speak in a few minutes," I said, interrupting as I took hold of Mrs. Jackson's arm. Her rage had eased some, but her breathing turned ragged. The skin on her chest and neck grew splotchy with a deep purple, the hair around her forehead pressing flat against her head. "Tracy?" As I moved Mrs. Jackson back to her home, I motioned to the car for Tracy to park it.

"Thank you," Mrs. Jackson said, taking to the steps slowly, climbing each with effort. "I had to ask."

"I understand," I said, having done the same when Hannah was kidnapped. My neighbors were there. They'd seen the woman in the car who'd stolen my child from the front lawn. I'd gone to every neighboring home and asked the same questions over and over, hoping to hear something different. It wasn't until my husband at the time asked, rather begged, that I stop. That's when I finally moved on to work another part of our daughter's case. My neighbors never looked at me the same though. It was as if they'd felt guilty about what happened. It was sad to lose them too, but I think I was okay with that. "I lost a child once and did the same thing."

With that revelation, Mrs. Jackson turned her head to look at me, to really see me. With sympathetic eyes, she asked, "You did?" She didn't wait for me to answer as she empathized. "I'm sorry to hear that."

"Let's get you inside," her husband said, his fingers white with the grip he held her arm. "It ain't Barbara's fault."

When we were inside, Mrs. Jackson sucked in a squeeze of her inhaler, and then argued, "Frank, for all we know, Barbara was the last one to see Shawna and Laura. Why are you defending her?"

He took off his hat, his face painted heavy by days of sunlight, but the top of his head remaining untouched. On the kitchen counter he picked up a scrap of paper, pinching it between his fingers and holding it up for us to see, ignoring his wife's question. "It's the note Laura left."

Seeing it, Tracy and I snapped on our latex gloves. "May I?" I held out my hand palm facing up. When Mr. Jackson saw Tracy produce an evidence bag, the expression on his face changed. It wasn't fright that I saw, but surprise as he realized what he held could tie back to Laura's murder.

Mrs. Jackson took a heavy breath, her chest rattling as she asked, "Do you think Laura's note means something?"

"I won't know until we get it to the lab," I answered. Mr. Jackson carefully placed the note onto my hand, moving slowly as though he were handling dangerous materials. It could have been any piece of paper. A scrap torn from a notebook, the words written in blue ink, the letters ballooning in a flowing hand. "I didn't know schools still taught cursive handwriting?"

Mrs. Jackson moved within an inch of me. She was taller, able to look over my shoulder as she stared down at Laura's handwriting. "School don't teach it anymore. I showed Laura how to do that."

"She does a lot more than that too," Mr. Jackson added with a look of pride. "Some of the most beautiful writing I ever seen."

"Calligraphy, we got her a set with pens and inks two years ago," Mrs. Jackson continued. She showed us a framed print celebrating a twentieth wedding anniversary, the lettering like something I would see in an elegant Hallmark card. "She made this for us last year."

"Quite the gift," I said, returning my focus to the note. It read: *I'm going to meet up with some friends. I'll be back in a while.* Her name was beneath the words, the first letter of her name adorned with a long swooping tail. "Does she often go out with friends later in the evening?"

The couple traded glances, but I couldn't sense if it was guilt and their possibly being less involved in Laura's life than what was expected. "She goes out," Mrs. Jackson said, unsure how much to share.

"Who was looking after Shawna?" I asked, her stare remaining on her husband.

"Shawna was alone," Mr. Jackson answered, his body rigid, waiting for disapproval from us.

"It's okay to say what you need to say," I assured them. "I'm only interested in learning where and who she might've been with."

Mr. Jackson cast his eyes to the floor, saying, "That's just it." With a frown, he looked at his wife, answering, "We don't know who her friends are."

Not all parents are involved with the day-to-day of their children, but a name, a single one would be all I'd need to move on with the investigation. "She's never had a friend over?" I asked, sounding desperate. I reframed the question quickly, "Phone calls, a name you might have heard her say?"

The couple stayed frozen save for a fresh tear running down Mrs. Jackson's face, her voice a whimper. "Sorry, but like we said, don't know any of who she hung with."

This was odd. Maybe it didn't mean anything, but what parent doesn't know a single name of a single friend of their child? "Okay. What about the tablet?" I asked, their frowns reappearing, uncertain what I was referring to. "There's a school tablet in the bedroom. We'd like to take it with us?"

"Yeah, yeah, sure," Mr. Jackson answered, a sound of relief coming with the change in my questioning. "You find her phone?"

As I completed bagging Laura's note, Tracy answered, "Unfortunately, there was no phone recovered. But if you could share the details of your service provider, we could use that information."

The couple shook their heads again, Mr. Jackson answering,

"We got the landline for the fishing charters, and use the prepaid phones for everything else."

"If you can provide us Laura's phone number and the company name?" I asked. Mrs. Jackson began to write the information down. "We'll also need to ask for your fingerprints."

They gave each other a look, but Tracy gently added, "It's so we can eliminate your own prints."

"Eliminate?" Mr. Jackson asked, shaking his head, his mouth half-puckered with a question.

"We're going to dust for fingerprints in the girls' bedroom, like on the windowsill and glass. We'll expect to find yours and your wife's." An understanding began to register, and I held up the note Laura left for them. "This included, ensure it was Laura's."

"I touched that," Mrs. Jackson said, her fingers cupping her mouth as though she'd done something wrong.

"That's why we'll want your prints," Tracy said, turning on the digital fingerprint unit, the glass plate emitting a green glow.

"You think the person who took Shawna is the one who killed our Laura?" Mrs. Jackson asked.

"That's what we're going to find out."

"And you'll find a fingerprint on that?" Mr. Jackson asked, pointing to the paper. Doubt registered on his face as much as it did in my gut. Paper was hit and miss, requiring special care and techniques, the use of gold dust and the hope that it sticks to the amino acids in a fingerprint's sweat residue. If we were lucky and the gold worked, we'd apply silver next, which would cling to the gold and give us the contrast needed for fingerprint identification.

"It's not always a guarantee, but we can," I answered, holding it up to look through the plastic bag. From the search of the girls' room, we didn't have a lot to work with, but it was something.

EIGHT

Barbara Newman invited us into her home, a two-story house with coastal stylings like cedar shingles on the roof and siding. The outside was painted bright yellow with white trim, the landscaping and upkeep making it stand out on the street. She was dressed much like her home, bright and festive, her blouse as bright as the yellow paint. She also wore a creamy white silk scarf, the back of it draped over her shoulder like a long lock of hair. Mrs. Newman's only request when we entered was for us to remove our shoes and leave them near the front door. With the weekend work, I'd dressed more casual, tan capris and brown sandals. Tracy wore jeans and sneakers, her face warming when I noticed a hole in one of her socks.

"Please," Mrs. Newman said, handing us her business card again. I took one this time, being polite, the card with her real-estate company name made into a logo which looked familiar to me. She was nervous, and moved swiftly between me and Tracy, her hair thick with spray, the smell of it reaching me as she handed another card to Tracy. On her hands, I noticed the fingernails were also painted a bright yellow with one of them broken, a Band-Aid wrapped around the tip of her middle finger. With it, she tapped the top of the card, telling us, "That is the direct number to my cell phone. I want you to call me if you have any more questions after today."

Tracy side-eyed me, her noticing the pace at which the woman was moving and speaking. It was nerves, and she was full of them. As she led us into the kitchen area, I took notice of her home—it was spotless, nearly immaculate, leading me to think she'd just put it on the market. And maybe she had. "Is your house for sale?"

She turned, spinning on a foot, a frown forming. "No. Why do you ask?"

I looked around, smiling apologetically. "You have a lovely home."

Mrs. Newman looked at a real-estate magazine on the kitchen counter and pushed the corner so that the bottom edge was parallel to the gas range. It was a behavior that explained the neatness. I'd be lucky to have a fraction of the same. When she saw that I noticed, she lifted a kettle and shook it, water sloshing, asking, "Can I make you a cup of tea? Or coffee? I'm sure I have some snack cakes?"

"Some water would be fine, ma'am," I said, purposely giving her something to do. I wanted to watch her and see how this unfolded. There were nerves that needed explaining. Some people were just naturally nervous when it came to any form of questioning by the police. But not everyone was mentioned as being last to have seen a victim of murder.

"Sure," she said, opening the refrigerator, cold air brushing around my legs. The food and the containers on the shelves were lined up perfectly straight like the magazine. "And for you?"

"Water would be fine," Tracy answered, her notepad in hand, waiting for the questions. "Thank you."

From the door of the refrigerator, she handed us two bottles of water, the label on them showing the same name and logo as her business cards. These must have been water bottles she offered potential home buyers. Perhaps placing them alongside her business cards in houses that she showed. "How is the sheriff?" she asked, surprising me. When she saw my reaction, she said, "Sorry, I mean, how is Jericho doing?"

"He's doing well," I answered with a nod, the lid of the bottle snapping with a twist. I always forget how many people remember him as being the sheriff.

For the moment, Mrs. Newman looked calm as she explained, "After I got my license, he and his wife were one of my first customers."

"Buying or selling?" I asked, genuinely curious.

"I sold him and his wife the house on Kitty Hawk Bay," she answered. Her mouth opened in a mock gasp as she shook her head. "That place was a real fixer-upper. I mean, I still can't believe they bought it."

"Is that right?" I said, wondering if Jericho would remember this woman.

"But they were insistent," she went on to say. She cracked the top of her water bottle, taking a drink, the nerves gone. Her lips turned down in a frown. "What a beautiful house they made too—"

Mrs. Newman went on to tell us more about her first sale, easing into general conversation. I glanced at the faint scars covering my hands, the new skin, my baby skin I called it. It tingled with the thought of the burns I'd endured. The house Barbara Newman sold to Jericho had been purposely set on fire while the two of us were asleep. The arsonist had been inside and disabled the alarms, leaving us to barely escape the inferno. At one point, I was certain I had taken my last breath. The worst moment came with a backdraft. It exploded through the room, Jericho covering me with his body, shielding me from the scorching flames. I shuddered at the memory. He'd wear the scars of that selfless action for the rest of his life. Emotion stirred in my belly and stung my eyes. "We... we lost the house recently to a fire."

"I heard," she said, sadness in her voice. "The news reported arson."

"That's right," I answered, gulping a mouthful of water.

"Well, I do hope the insurance company does right by Jericho. He deserves it." With her Band-Aid covered middle finger, she tapped her business card that I'd placed on the counter. "Tell him if he wants to sell the property rather than rebuild, I can do that."

"I'll let him know," I said, the logo finally registering. The flowing lines were familiar. I held it up, asking, "Ma'am, can you tell me if Laura Jackson made this for you?"

Her brow rose instantly. "You know about her work?" she asked.

"She's very talented. We saw some of it earlier," Tracy commented. She turned her bottle of water around with the custom label. "I love how you've used it."

"That's her work," Mrs. Newman answered, her voice shaky. On the refrigerator, the door was covered in pictures. Fat fruit magnets held dozens of them in place, enough to cover the refrigerator. I went to them, my eyes needing the closer distance. In the pictures I saw Laura and Shawna and another girl. Mrs. Newman stood next to me, perching an elbow in her hand, her fingers covering her mouth. "It's just terrible what happened to that child."

"This is your daughter? She and Shawna are close?" I asked, lifting a pineapple-shaped magnet. The picture was newer, the three girls bundled in sleeping bags made of flowery colors, the carpet they were on a blend of beige and brown and matching the one in the adjacent room. "This was taken in the den?"

"Right over there," she answered. The semi-permanent grin she wore faded. I tacked the picture back onto the refrigerator, the magnet thumping with a snap. "The girls are like family."

I was silent, waited for her to fill in.

"Ever since our Abigail was just a baby." We walked to the den, taking a step down into it, standing on the carpet where the girls had been.

"Abigail is how old?" Tracy asked, the top of her pencil dancing. "She is eight, same as Shawna?"

"That's right. They're a couple months apart," Mrs. Newman said, her words made hollow in the larger room and the vaulted ceiling that was two-stories high.

"She's not here right now?" I asked, realizing the house was quiet. Too quiet for this time of day. Particularly on a weekend.

Mrs. Newman sucked in her lips, hiding them as she regarded my question. Her brown eyes turned glassy as a tearful response came. I didn't hesitate and took her arm and led her to the sofa. We sat down as she answered, "Geoffrey, my husband, took her to spend the day at his mother's place. It's my mother-in-law's birthday."

"When did they leave?" Tracy asked as she sat in a love seat.

Mrs. Newman glanced at the antique mantle clock, the round face like ivory, the time showing near eleven in the morning. "It was earlier, maybe seven thirty. He wanted to beat the morning traffic to Greenville."

"The mainland," I asked, unsure of the location.

"Uh-huh," she answered with a nod which began to change to a shake. "But I couldn't go with them on account of work."

"We may need to ask your husband some questions," I said, informing her there were no boundaries to who we'd question. "Possibly your daughter too."

"I understand," she said with a shallow sob.

From my phone, I showed her the picture of the Delight's Traveling Funfair flier. "Tell us about Friday night."

A smile flashed at the image I showed, but then faded with

her lips quivering. She answered, "We stayed until the carnival was closing."

"The Jacksons said their daughters did not stay with you?"

"That's right," she answered, lower lip quivering again. "And I wish to God they had."

"What time did you last see them?"

She tapped her watch, her gaze drifting toward the ceiling. "I suppose it would have been two, maybe three hours before the carnival closed?" she answered, but with uncertainty in her voice.

"Which was?" Tracy asked. Tracy showed the tablet, adding, "For our records."

Mrs. Newman shrugged. "I don't know. It wasn't something I was paying attention to."

I checked the picture of the flier, the closing time listed. "Says here that the carnival hours are five to eleven weekdays."

"Sounds about right," Mrs. Newman said. "I guess it would have been between eight and nine sometime."

I opened the weather app, checking the times for sunrise and sunset. "It was dark?"

Her gaze lifted to the ceiling again. "Dusk, I think. Maybe? There were lights on the rides. Why?"

"I'm wondering about the distance. Their house to Sound-side Event Site is at least five miles."

She shook her head with a wave of the hand. "I drove the girls."

"You left the fair, drove them home, and then went back?" Tracy asked, Mrs. Newman's head turning. "Or did you stay home?"

She cringed at the questions, shuffling her feet as we tried to establish a timeline. Frustrated, she asked, "Please. Let me start again?"

"Sure," I told her, eyeing a bright red patch on the carpet near her bare feet. A stain? "Ma'am—"

"—okay," she began, gazing into space while narrowing her eyes. It was blood on the carpet, the stain spreading from the bottom of her foot. "We were at the carnival, and it was getting dark. I remember because Geoffrey was telling the younger girls to look at the pretty lights."

"Ma'am," I said with more urgency. Her focus returned and she lowered her hands. I pointed to her feet, her eyes following, Tracy doing the same. "I think you're bleeding."

"Oh shoot," she said with a *tsk tsk* sound and perched her right foot on her knee. On the arch, between her toes and heel, there was a fresh cut. It was new enough to have happened when we entered the den. She twisted her mouth, a slight blush rising on her neck. "I've got numbness in my feet, been like that a few years now."

"Let us help you with that," I said, going to the kitchen. From the counter, I yanked a dozen paper towels, wetting some of them with cold water. When I returned, Tracy was on her knees and wearing gloves. I loved that she did that—staying prepared for anything. From a pocket, I got a pair of my latex gloves and put them on. "We'll just clean it?"

"You don't have to do that," Mrs. Newman said, prodding the cut with her fingertips and making the bleeding worse. "I can take care of it."

"Ma'am," I said, pausing until she was looking at me. "Let us help."

Reluctantly, Mrs. Newman put her hands back in her lap, taking one of the paper towels I offered. "Some light on this, Tracy." The flashlight blazed, blinding me briefly before sharply striking the cause of injury, lighting it like the facet of a ruby. "Mrs. Newman, I hate to tell you, but there's a small chunk of glass in your foot."

"Glass?" she said, asking with alarm. She searched the carpet, tracks racing back and forth from recently being vacuumed. "Where in the world did that come from?"

"No idea. But we know where it is now." Holding it with a pinch, I eased the glass out, bloody drops following. I packed the paper towels around it, Mrs. Newman taking it like it was a souvenir. "Some more bad news, I think that's going to need a few stitches."

"Really?" she replied curiously. "Well, shoot!"

"We can take you to the hospital?" Tracy said. "There's an urgent care a mile north of here."

"That's awfully kind of you," she said. There was a look of hesitation on her face while she turned the glass end over end, unable to recognize it as being from a jar or a drinking glass. "I'll be fine on my own. Please, let's continue."

"Are you sure?" I asked. I went to the kitchen and grabbed a kitchen towel and the full roll of paper towels. "It's not a problem."

"I'm sure," she answered. "I'll need to make some calls about the house I'm showing later anyway."

I handed her the towels, the emergency abating. "You were saying that your husband noticed the carnival lights?"

"Right, yes," she answered, the knuckles of her fingers white as she kept pressure on her foot. "That's when Laura said they needed to leave."

"And you drove them home?" Tracy asked, confirming the story.

"Of course," Mrs. Newman scoffed. "I wouldn't let them walk all that way."

"Did you see them go inside their house?" I asked, my mind stuck on the piece of glass, the den appearing in perfect order.

"I dropped them off," she said, not really answering, while sounding another *tsk tsk*. She wiped her foot, saying, "Doesn't look as bad. I might be able to get away with some tissue glue."

"Ma'am, you watched them go inside?" I asked, wanting to figure out the time they got home, the Jacksons' home without technology, without any security or doorbell cameras. "A rough idea of the time that was?"

"It'd have to have been before nine I guess."

"I noticed you have a doorbell camera," I said, thinking we could review the footage from that night. "Could we review the footage from that evening?"

"I can get that for you," she said, but then tilted her head, her eyes steady. "Doubt you'll see anything though."

"Why would that be?" Tracy asked.

As she continued cleaning her foot, wrapping the towel around it, she answered. "We had to dial down the motion detector. It was too sensitive. When I dropped the girls off outside their house, I went back to the carnival."

"You believe you were too far for the camera to pick you up?" I asked, disappointed.

"Right." Mrs. Newman stood and went to the kitchen. "There are the bigger trucks like the ones for garbage, the camera will sometimes pick them up."

"There's always the possibility the recording will show the girls," I said as she opened a drawer and picked up a paper and pad. "It would still be helpful to review any recordings from that evening."

"My husband set it up, but I made up the password," she said, writing down the web address. "It's secure and any video recordings are kept for thirty days."

She handed me the paper. The idea of us possibly seeing footage of the Jackson girls pressed me to leave, to get in front of my computer as soon as possible. "This is helpful," I said holding the paper with her business card, folding the one around the other. In exchange, I handed her my card. "If you can think of anything else from that evening, you can call me directly."

"Sure," she said, tacking the card on the refrigerator with a banana-shaped magnet. "And the sheriff's property, you'll mention it to him."

"Yes, thank you," I said. As we gathered our shoes, putting them back on before leaving, I asked my final question. "What were you fighting about with Mrs. Jackson?"

"That woman," Mrs. Newman said, her voice like a growl. When we furrowed our brows, she looked embarrassed. "My apologies. I know they're hurting."

"What's your relationship with her like?" I asked, thinking there was something there.

"We were friends once, but not as much these days. I'm busy and she's busy. It's just that the girls spend time together."

"And?" I pressed, hearing there was more to their argument.

"She wanted to know why I didn't check on the girls in the house when we got back from the carnival later on," she answered, her eyes turning wet again, lips tightening as she fought back the emotion. "Maybe she's right to be mad. I was just so tired by the time I got home."

"Ma'am, this isn't your fault," I said, assuring her she'd done nothing wrong.

"Yeah, well, tell that to Carla," she said, her voice deepening as the emotion caught up with her.

"This *was* helpful," I said, emphasizing with hope it would make her feel better. "Please, if you remember anything else, let us know."

"I will," she said, closing the door with a polite wave.

We walked into a damp haze that made my skin slick and my hair wet. The door handles of the car were covered with raindrops too. When we were inside, Tracy pulled her laptop from her bag and connected a cable from her cell phone. I handed her the paper with the web address and password, the ink smeared on one of the letters. "Let's see what footage we've got from the doorbell camera."

"We'll be talking with her again," I told Tracy and focused

on the house. I saw Mrs. Newman's silhouette standing behind the door's frosted windowpanes.

"We're coming back?" Tracy asked, her fingertips brushing across the keys with a practiced motion like it was a musical instrument. She curled the corner of her mouth and raised a brow. "Not to check on her foot."

"No, not to check her foot," I answered, trading the sarcasm. Mrs. Newman's figure lurked in wait, standing still until we drove away. "She didn't tell us everything."

Tracy stopped typing and looked at me while I rolled backward out of the driveway. "You think she's hiding something?"

I shook my head. "No. I don't think that's it," I answered, turning the steering wheel until we were parallel to the house. "Maybe she doesn't know she's hiding something. But if I was one to bet money, we'll see her again soon. She has more to tell us."

NINE

Monday morning at the station was thankfully calm. I could tell by the parking lot, the spaces empty, recognizing the few cars that had already arrived. There was one car that was unfamiliar, but the rear license plate showed it was North Carolina. I kicked loose stones from crumbling asphalt as I made my way to the front of the building. To my surprise, there wasn't a single reporter in sight. Not a one. The white benches by the station doors were empty, as were the steps from the walkway.

With release of the murder and the APB issued, news coverage for the Jackson sisters had been busy online and in the television rotation. It was enough to have expected some follow-up questions this morning. I stopped on the bottom step, taking a second to see it alone and quiet.

"They'll come soon enough," I mumbled to myself. While it was tragic, a dead teenager and a kidnapped little sister was a hot story. It was all anyone was talking about.

The pressure was mounting too. The days and nights and hours were stacking up behind us since the evening Shawna had disappeared. There were statistics and charts being shown. There were expert witnesses and ex-police detectives and investigators giving statements and doing interviews. I already knew the statistics though. I'd been a cop long enough to know them like the lines on the palms of my hands. I didn't need a reminder. I could feel the worry creeping into the shadows of the case, feel it lurking, ready to rear its ugly face when we reached a time of panic. My breath was hot with a heavy sigh. The horrible, unspoken truth was that if we didn't find Shawna soon, we were never going to find her.

"Thank you again for the help the other day," I said to Alice, the station manager. She'd jumped on the text I sent her, and had found Robert Finley almost immediately, giving us a DMV record to work with. But Jane Finley remained a mystery.

"Of course," she said from the front desk, greeting me with a short wave. I returned the gesture as she flipped a page of a magazine. She looked up, asking, "I can keep searching if you need the help?"

"Thanks," I said. "I'll let you know."

The holding benches were empty. The seats where we'd handcuff those waiting to be processed. The evening before must have been unusually quiet, even for a Sunday. Football season had begun, the first pro games scheduled to have started shortly after the one o'clock hour. By the evening, the station would have gotten calls for dispatch. One or two at least. But it was quiet. Maybe quiet was good. It would give me and Tracy time to work through Laura Jackson's tablet, along with the school's cloud account.

I reached the wooden gate separating the front of the station from our cubicles and saw the top of someone's head near my desk. He was tall enough to easily stand a full arm's length above the walls separating our workspace. His hair was wavy and a golden copper, the length in the back nearly reaching his collar, and the sides tucked behind his ears. Dressed in denim pants and a light-blue collared dress shirt, his shoes and belt bore the same saddle-tan. There was a holster and gun, along with a gold shield clipped to his hip. Tracy's arms were perched on the cubicle walls, her eyes large and engaged while our visitor spoke to her, an Adam's apple bouncing beneath his clean-shaven jaw.

Without realizing it, I primped my hair, the southeast winds making a mess of it. I checked my work shoes and slacks and the beige jacket I'd put on in the pre-dawn darkness. I could only hope everything matched, knowing I could be wearing two different colored shoes. It wouldn't be the first time either. With my level of experience, I had nothing to prove to anybody. However, we had a visitor to the station and first impressions meant something to me.

When the two saw me arriving, the visiting detective shook Tracy's hand, her lashes batting in a flutter while she palmed her hair. I held back a smile, Tracy's reaction reminding me how young she was, but how it also reminded me of me.

"Detective White?" he asked with a voice that was deep and level. He offered a hand while I plunked my backpack onto my chair and dropped my handbag into a drawer that screeched when I closed it. As I stood up again, I noticed his badge had an eagle, the city name of Greenville above the state's initials for North Carolina. "I'm Detective Jeremy Watson."

"Detective Casey White," I said, shaking his hand, the touch without callouses or roughness, his days spent doing paperwork or in front of a computer perhaps.

"He's here about the Laura Jackson case," Tracy said, remaining perched above her cubicle wall.

"Is that right?" I said and hung a thumb over my shoulder. "With so much news coverage, I was rather surprised to see the front of the station empty."

"They were here earlier," she answered and stood on her toes, craning her neck to search the station's front. When she saw that it was empty, she said, "Huh. That's weird."

"That was my doing," the detective from Greenville said. "I told them I would be giving them a statement around noon."

"You talked to my reporters?" I asked, speaking as though I managed them.

He dipped his chin and raised his brow with a smile. "*Your* reporters?"

"I work them when it is needed," I answered, his smile stretching.

"Yeah, I do the same thing back home," he commented and nodded with understanding. "I'd like to review a case with you first. It could be we might both have a statement for them."

"Is this about murder or kidnapping?" I asked, thinking of both the Jackson girls.

"Murder," he answered, the smile fading. He eased a leather messenger bag from one shoulder, opening the front and offered a manilla folder, the pages few, the lump at the center telling me it contained crime-scene photographs. "If you have time this morning, I'd like to tell you about my case."

I picked up my coffee cup and eyed the bottom of it. "Walk and talk?" I asked but didn't wait for a response as I headed to the kitchenette with hopes there was a fresh pot brewed.

"Yeah, sure. I could use a cup, thanks." The Greenville detective walked with long strides as he followed, keeping up easily. When we reached the counter, he made himself a cup, surprising me with his saying, "And by the way, congratulations."

I frowned for a moment, the coffee's steam rising between us. "Excuse me?"

He glanced over his shoulder toward Tracy. When he looked at me again, he said, "About finding your daughter."

I hadn't expected his words. "Thank you," I said, blowing the heat from my coffee, concentrating on that first sip as an excuse to keep my response short.

"I can't even imagine—" the detective continued, the look

on his face changing to the one I loathed. It was a mix of disbelief and awe and sadness, and a few other things I detested, "—and then to find her here. What an amazing story."

"It is," I said, remaining polite, my focus shifting to his case folder. "How about the conference room? We were already going to meet to discuss the Jackson case."

"That'd work," he answered and swung his bag around. "I brought my computer if it's okay to use."

I nodded, eager to see what it was that had him coming to us. "This way."

Tracy was in the conference room by the time we entered. It was only a few months ago that my team occupied most of the seats around the long table. But the numbers had thinned with promotions and injury, leaving the chairs vacant until I could restaff. Tracy gestured with a shrug, quietly noticing the sparseness. "I've got the monitors—"

She stopped when Detective Watson followed me. "The detective will be joining us."

"Jeremy, please," he said, removing his laptop from his messenger bag. He saw the two monitors, unsure which to use.

Tracy got up, eager to help. "You can display on both, or just the one," she said, offering a selection of cables. She handed him a cable, adding, "I like to use both, mirror the display."

"Sure," he answered with a nod and seated the cable into the back of his laptop. "I can do that."

"So you believe you have a case that could be related—" I began to ask, but then shut my mouth when the first image flashed onto the monitor. The victim was a teenager, about the same age as Laura Jackson. Her body lay crumpled on the ground, her legs folded beneath her, her arms spread to her sides in a way that indicated she did not try to break her fall. This child had been murdered while standing. The area of her death was wooded, trees thick with summer leaves, but the ground covered by a fresh fall of new autumn colors—a soup of bright yellows and orange. The victim wore black Chuck Taylor sneakers with thick rubber soles. She had jeans, tattered holes on the knees and thighs with gray skin bulging beneath. The rips appeared to be a part of the look and not a result of the attack. Her top was a maroon T-shirt with the name Aeropostale on the front in bold lettering.

"Her name is Jeanette Klause," he said with a long breath. "Sixteen years old, she is a junior in high school."

"Another girl," I mouthed, ideas of a connection stirring. I kept my ideas to myself until we learned more. Tracy was already typing, looking up the Klause victim, searching for a connection that was more than the physical likeness I saw on the screen. Noticing the victim had all her clothes, I asked, "Was there a sexual assault involved?"

"None," the detective answered. He faced me and Tracy. "The details about your case were limited. How about your victim?"

"No sexual assault," I told him, my focus locking on the victim's face, the photograph's angle not helping. "Could you show me a picture of this victim's face?"

The detective sipped his coffee as he tapped the laptop's trackpad. "This is what brought me here."

When the image showed on the screen, I heard Tracy gasp. I might have too, the photograph was gruesome, the strangulation of this young girl horribly violent. Long brunette hair was matted against the one side of her face, a line of dried blood running down the other. The color of her eyes hidden by the gray film that comes as a part of death. It was the neck area that I concentrated on, standing to move closer to the monitor. The force of the strangulation had been enough to rip into the girl's skin, leaving an impression of the murder weapon. "I'd like to share this with our medical examiner."

"Yes, certainly," the detective answered. "Do you see a likeness to your case?"

"Tracy?" I asked without answering. She plugged in her laptop and displayed the picture of Laura Jackson, zooming in on the injury around the neck. "Two girls, same ethnicity, similar in age and build and hair styles. No sexual assault. Both strangled."

"Did your victim suffer any other injuries?" he asked, taking to stand next to me, the glow of the monitor's colors on his face. He pointed to the blood on the victim in his case.

I rubbed my forearm as if there was pain, answering, "With Laura Jackson, we found what we believe are defensive wounds." I motioned to the blood on his victim's face. "That looks like an injury on her scalp?"

He lowered his head, cringing with disgust. "A tooth," he answered.

"She was bitten?" Tracy asked with alarm.

"We believe the injury on her scalp was from the killer's front teeth," he answered, shaking his head. "But not an intentional bite."

I ran my finger down the screen. "Look at the way the blood traveled. Your victim was standing when she was attacked." I turned to face the detective from Greenville. "Did you find any drops of blood on the victim's shirt?"

His brow lifted. "Yeah, a couple drops. But it was her blood."

"You know what you have?" I asked, seeing a clue glaring at me like I was on fire.

With the rise in my voice, the Greenville detective moved within inches of the monitor, searching the lake of pixels, but not seeing what was in front of him. "What do you see?"

"I think you have the height of your victim's killer."

"How?"

It was best to show rather than explain it. I waved Tracy to the front of the room and bowed my head toward the detective when I reached for his arm. He offered it, letting me position him behind Tracy. "Okay, Tracy is around the same height as our victims," I said as I spun her around to place her back against the detective's chest. "Now, you put your hands around her neck as though you were strangling her."

The detective's hands were large, his finger wrapping around much of Tracy's neck with ease. She jumped at his touch, his saying, "Sorry, my hands are cold."

"I believe your victim was standing like this when she was attacked," I explained. "And the killer's strength was enough to keep her upright until she was dead."

"Which was also long enough for the blood to travel to her chin and drip onto her shirt," Tracy added.

"But that's not all," I said, their eyes wide as I continued. "The injury to her scalp is because she fought back. She bucked."

"Bucked?" Tracy asked.

"The tooth mark is possibly from two front teeth?" I asked.

"Right," the detective answered. "When he attacked her, the victim jumped to free herself. She bucked and struck his mouth."

As though on cue, Tracy jumped, playing out the role of the victim. The top of her head brushed the bottom of the detective's chin, his rearing back with alarm. "I'm so sorry. Did I hit you?"

He waved his hands in the air. "I'm fine. You didn't get me."

"With the victim's height known," I began, "you have an approximate height of the killer."

The detective's mouth opened, his focus locking on the victim. "We know how tall she is and we can estimate how high she jumped."

"It's the depth of the injury on her scalp that tells you the force of the jump," I said, lifting my hand like a level and bringing it up to his face. "Without the science, I'd estimate your killer to be three to four inches shorter than you."

"Five foot ten or eleven," he answered. "How did I not see that?"

I went to the monitor with our victim. "If I had to guess, it was because you were looking at the bruising around her neck."

"I was," he answered. On the screens, sitting side by side, there was a likeness in the bruising, but a distinct difference on his victim. He ran a finger over the shapes, saying, "We can't figure out what created those."

"That's why I'd like to have our medical examiner review the images," I said. Although the pattern in the bruising showed there was a difference, the victims were similar in many ways. "Were you able to establish where your victim was last seen alive?"

"She was with her friends." He pinched his lips tight as he mussed his hair. "But their statements are so inconsistent."

"Inconsistent?" I asked, turning toward him with interest. "Where were they?"

"They'd gone to a town fair," he answered, his voice breaking. "But some time during the night they'd gotten split up. None of them know who last saw Jeanette, or when."

I frowned when I heard the emotion. Sensing he wasn't telling us everything, I asked, "Detective, how do you know the victim?" Tracy's eyelids flicked wide. It was forward of me to ask, but my instincts told me he knew her.

His gaze drifted toward the floor, the moment raw while he rubbed a palm against the tip of his chin, whiskers scratching. He was uncomfortable enough to make me feel uncomfortable and for Tracy to stir. But it wasn't because of the answer he would give. It was because he was mourning. He looked at me squarely, his lips turned down, and answered, "Jeanette Klause is my sister's daughter."

"Oh crap," I heard Tracy mutter.

He swiped errantly at his eyes, continuing, "The victim is my niece."

TEN

I held my words, the detective staying quiet as he finished showing the pictures of his niece's murder. All of them were as gruesome as the first. He settled on where his niece's body was found. It was a wooded area with thick brush and a dirt trail. There was a skinny footpath that was loose with sand and rock, the surface of it showing with shallow footprints, the impressions a mirror of the tread I recognized as being from the victim's Chuck Taylor sneakers.

"This is a wooded area between the high school and the housing development where the victim lived."

"You believe she'd been murdered here?" I asked, circling an area of the ground. "I'm looking at the disruption in the dirt, it's a sign of there being a struggle."

"There were also some broken branches," he said, opening a picture of an evergreen with fresh breaks, the end of the branches bleeding sap. "We found some evidence of the tree on her clothes."

"That rules out her being killed elsewhere and dumped," I said, noticing him wince at my choice of words. I decided to think harder before speaking, recognizing the detective was trying to do right by his niece. Good intentions aside, this was a murder investigation and once exposed to the blatant truth of murder, it'd forever stain your soul. Some of us have a limit to how much for one lifetime. And some of us grow thick-skinned.

"Sorry," he said and closed his eyes, his lips moving silently. When he was ready, he continued, "You were saying."

"Let me show you something." I went back to my seat, thinking of his mention about the girls having gone to a local fair. On my laptop, I flipped through images until landing on the flier we'd found tacked onto Shawna Jackson's bedroom wall. I threw the picture onto the monitor, the paper tattered along the bottom, the clown in the middle and the name in blocky, bold lettering across the top. "Any chance that fair you mentioned was a carnival? The Delight's Traveling Funfair?"

Detective Jeremy Watson leaned onto the edge of the conference room table and cradled an elbow, his fingers tapping his chin. "Where did you get that?" he asked, turning his head toward me. "None of that information has been released to the public."

I held my breath, shock rushing through me, my assumption and question striking unexpectedly on a possible connection. "Laura Jackson, our victim, and her sister were both at the Delight's Traveling Funfair."

"There has got to be a connection," he said, his fist closed as he drummed the top of the table.

"Tracy, bring up a map of the Greenville area," I asked, ideas swirling. When the map appeared, the field where the carnival would have been was empty.

The detective took to the front of the monitor to explain what we were looking at. "That's the high school's football field," he said, moving his arm in a circle. "A lot of the kids live within walking distance."

"The victim's killer could have followed her from the school grounds," I said, tracing a path on the monitor. "Did you get any security footage?"

He held up a finger as he returned to his seat. With a click, a video appeared. "This hasn't been released." He hesitated with a short breath and cleared his throat. "It hasn't been shown to anyone, including the victim's parents—my sister and her husband."

On the video, crowds of families dressed for the early autumn evening filed in and out of the high school's football field. There were bleachers rising into the night on the left and right. Between them, a concrete path was big enough to fit a bus and was filled with visitors coming and going. Beyond the bleachers, we saw the green field, the sidelines and the entrance to Delight's Traveling Funfair with its red and white striped pillars and billowing canvas and colorful balloons. "Did we see her?" I asked, thinking she'd passed the camera.

The detective held his finger near the striped canvas and stacked balloons, a group of teenaged girls wandering around the front. He answered, "That's her." Beneath the tip of his finger, I saw a pretty girl, the shape of her face long like her uncle's and her body lean and taller than most of the other girls. "We'll see her for the next minute, but then..."

"Where does she go?" Tracy asked, face perched on her fists, her elbows on the conference room table. She blew the bangs from her forehead, adding, "And all her friends were questioned?"

"Multiple times," he answered as he pointed to the screen again, his niece coming back into the frame. She shared a laugh with a boy, broad shouldered and large build, a football jersey with the number twenty-one on it. "That guy too. I've interviewed everyone in this video who had contact with her."

As we watched, his niece turned toward the camera, her face clear enough to take a portrait image. She looked as though she saw someone she knew, giving them a wave. A second later she was gone. "Who do you think that was?" I asked, believing she'd seen one other person who the detective might not have spoken to.

He shrugged, one brow raised. "I have no idea." He tapped his laptop to rewind the video, stopping it before his niece exited the frame. "I've watched this a million times to try and see if anyone in frame could have walked in that direction and turned around to wave at her."

"Well then, I guess we'll watch it one more time," I told him, putting on an encouraging smile. "We'll put some fresh eyes on it."

"Yeah," he said, agreeing. "That'd be great."

My ideas about the carnival shifted and changed, another one taking shape. I waved my hand at the map, saying, "Let's keep that open. Tracy, do a social media search on Delight's Traveling Funfair."

"Which site?" she asked, opening TikTok and Instagram and Snapchat and a few I had never heard of.

"All of them," I said, having no idea how many were out there, let alone relevant. "But specifically, the ones girls our victims' ages use most."

"Look at that," she said as we sat in the muted rattle of keyboard keys and mouse clicks. Tracy opened posts across the websites, the search field containing a hashtag for the name *Delight's Traveling Funfair*. One at a time, she displayed posted pictures of visitors on amusement rides and playing games or eating the carnival foods. More than a few of the posts showed the flier.

"Filter on posts with the flier?" I said, asking, "Can we do that?"

"We can do anything," she answered while updating the search. A fresh collection of results arrived on the screen, Tracy stopping on a post of a girl holding a Greenville North Carolina flier. "How about this one!"

"Perfect," I said, adding the picture from Shawna's bedroom alongside it.

"They are only five days apart?" Detective Jeremy Watson said, eyes widening as he ran his fingers through his hair. "They were in Greenville first and then packed up and moved to the Outer Banks."

"What do we do next?" Tracy asked, her voice rising, its pitch matching what I felt.

Cautiously, I answered, "This might be a strong lead, but we're going to need a lot more."

"More?" the detective exclaimed, spinning around. Even in the dim light, his body silhouetted by the monitors, I could see his face turning red. "We have two murders and have established that both victims were at the same carnival—"

"But Laura Jackson was driven home," I interrupted, raising my voice to match his. "The carnival isn't the last place she was seen alive." He crossed his arms with a disagreeing grimace. The detective's family connection wasn't helping, and we needed to think carefully about what it was we had. Lowering my voice, I continued, "The timing and them going to the same carnival could be nothing more than a coincidence."

"That's a hell of a coincidence," he said, his posture remaining standoffish. When I didn't offer more, he lowered his arms, asking, "Tell me what we should do next."

"Tracy," I said standing at the front of the room, staring at the mostly empty seats as the detective filled one of them. "Let's start a new search, a broader query."

"Past dates?" she asked.

"That's a start," I answered as she wove her fingers together and then clenched them until her knuckles popped. "I want to know every town and city Delight's Traveling Funfair has pitched a tent the last five years."

"Five?" she asked, her brow rising.

"Start with a couple months to get the query working," I

suggested, shrinking the scope so the effort didn't sound as over-whelming. "Then you can optimize it, broaden the date range."

"How does knowing where they've been before now help?" the detective asked.

"That's where you come in," I answered, lifting my leg to sit on the end of the table. "For every location we identify, I want a list of unsolved murders and missing persons."

There was a collective *ahh* between them as my idea took root. Tracy was first to jump in, saying, "We'll want to match the looks and the age to the victims."

"And the dates should coincide with Delight's Traveling Funfair," the detective said.

"Get what we're doing?" I asked.

"We're getting more," Detective Watson answered.

"Correct," I said. And warned, "But we're only going to find something if it's there to be found."

Detective Watson took a deep breath, his gaze fixed on his niece's murdered body. With a look of reluctance, he said, "Which rules out any coincidences."

"Exactly," I said as questions struck like a match in the back of my mind. Were there more victims? More dead girls? And where was Delight's Traveling Funfair going next?

ELEVEN

The conference room air had become stale. It was stuffy and warm as we worked the web searches: Delight's Traveling Funfair's previous locations and unsolved murders and abductions. My face was sticky damp, the back of my neck wet. Detective Watson was sweaty too, beaded perspiration on his upper lip. Tracy appeared immune to the still heat, a feat I'd often seen with her father, my ex. With the change in seasons, the station's air conditioning had been shut off, but the days had stayed warm, some even humid like today. I opened the conference room's window, our ears filling with the sound of wind blowing and the chatter of pedestrians at the street corner of a crosswalk.

"She was found," Tracy shrilled, breaking the silence. Heads turned. Chair wheels scraped.

"Shawna?" I asked, shock rocketing into my brain. But when I saw the look on Tracy's face, I knew it was about another missing girl, and clarified, "It's the Parker girl?"

"It is," she answered.

As the morning traveled north toward noontime, we'd learned of a missing child who resembled Shawna Jackson.

"Were there any arrests?" I asked, the news promising. Shawna's case wasn't moving, and we needed a break in it. And though we had her biological parents' address, a picture of Robert Finley from the DMV, and a squad car in front of their home, our efforts to track them down had come up without a single sighting. We only needed one chink in the case's armor to break through. "Was it a kidnapping?"

"A misunderstanding is all," she answered, the disappointment in her words matching how I felt. "Sorry?"

"The Parker girl is safe," I said, the spirit of hope fading in the room. "That's the important part."

"You want some water?" Tracy asked.

"Yeah, sure," I answered facing the breeze while I considered the lead we'd discovered.

"Detective?" she continued.

"Please," he answered.

While the connection we were working might be a strong lead, I wasn't about to pump a fist in the air in celebration. Tracy and Detective Jeremy Watson were high on the idea that the murders must be connected, but I stayed reserved. Call it purposeful pessimism. We needed more. If there was a killer traveling with the Delight's Traveling Funfair, had they followed the Jackson girls to their home? And where was Shawna Jackson?

"Casey?" Tracy said, my back turned. "I think that's Mrs. Newman."

I left the open window and stood on my toes to search the front of the station. It was the hair I saw first, poofy and shoulder length that moved with Mrs. Newman. She was dressed for work, carrying a briefcase, her slacks a dark blue, her blouse light pink and a silk scarf that complemented her ensemble. She saw me through the conference room glass and stood at the station's gate. To the station manager, I waved an approval, allowing Mrs. Newman through. She walked with a limp, leaving me to wonder if the cut on her foot had actually needed the stitches like I'd thought.

"So it is," I said to Tracy while moving around the table. "We still have her home's security footage to review?"

"We do," Tracy answered, her gaze darting from empty seat to empty seat. My team was depleted and with the addition of the case brought by Detective Watson, we needed extra hands. Tracy tilted her head, asking, "What should be the priority?"

As Mrs. Newman limped past my desk toward the conference room, Detective Watson said, "My niece's case is the only thing I am working on." He held his phone, showing the screen filled with text messages. "I've sent in notice. I'm committed. Tell me what to do."

"Terrific," I said, frowning when Mrs. Newman waved for me. I'd already seen her but began to think she was here about Jericho's property, wanting to get a bite of the real estate. I hoped I was wrong. "Tracy, help the detective continue with the location queries. Cue up the videos from the Newmans' security camera."

"Got it," she answered, my small impromptu team working shoulder to shoulder and hunched over their laptops.

I tugged on my top, straightening it while pushing against the glass door. It swung closed, Mrs. Newman hurrying to reach me, the air following coming with a thick wave of hairspray. It wasn't until she was closer that I saw the tears brimming in her eyes. This wasn't about Jericho's property. Not about real estate. "Yes, Mrs. Newman? How can I help?"

"I... I think the Jacksons killed their girls," she said quickly, quietly, her hand shaking as she clutched my arm.

With her words, I froze. "Here, let me help you," I said, forcing myself to break her stare and take her to a chair. There were eyes surfacing above cubicle walls, Mrs. Newman's disruption stirring the office. Her face was flushed and wet; she sniffed back the emotion and sat. I rolled a chair across from her and asked, "Now, could you explain what you mean by this claim?"

"Well," she began, taking a tissue from my hand and wiping the end of her nose. She dipped her chin, her eyelashes thick with mascara, clutching her chest and speaking rapidly. "I just feel it. Those girls were a part of my family for so long. But I always knew something like this would happen."

When she slowed to take a breath, I held up my hands. "Ma'am, wait a second. I'll need you to back up."

Mrs. Newman dammed her eyes, black ink dotting the corner of her tissue. "There was a reason those girls were at our house so much." She shook her head with disgust. "You've seen how they live."

"Ma'am," I said, feeling offended for the Jacksons. Their house had been humble, but I'd seen far worse conditions to raise children in. "These accusations. They require evidence to substantiate."

"Substantiate?" she asked, the corner of her mouth curving. "Well I don't have—"

"Understood," I said with interruption to reframe the question. I shifted to sit closer. "How about you tell me what you're thinking."

Mrs. Newman seemed to relax then, leaning into her seat and crossing her legs. "Those poor children, they are alone most all the time."

"When they're not at your house?" I asked, seeking to clarify.

"Right," she answered. "When they're not over our house, which is all the time, mind you."

She paused to wait for me to acknowledge what she'd said, a trait I found annoying. "Understood. So was there a particular incident you're referring to?"

"Several hospital and the urgent care visits," she answered with a slow nod. "You wanted evidence? How about that!"

"Mrs. Newman. Are you telling me the Jacksons physically abused their daughters? Were violent toward them?"

"Just Laura." She maintained eye contact, continuing, "Shawna has always been fine."

There might be something in what Mrs. Newman was telling me. Either way, we had to investigate. I scooped a notepad and pencil from the nearest desk to jot down notes. "Were you ever an eyewitness to any abuse or violence?"

She uncrossed her legs and planted her feet, wincing with the injury to her foot. "Not once." But that didn't mean anything. Domestic abuse goes on behind closed doors.

"Why didn't you mention this yesterday?" I asked, underlining urgent care in my notes. I pointed the end of the pencil toward her injured foot. "We offered to take you to the urgent care that was a mile from your house. Were you distracted? You didn't think to tell us your suspicions?"

That was a hard question. I knew it would be. Mrs. Newman swallowed her lips, her mouth disappearing while she considered what was asked. "I honestly have no idea. It was like I... forgot." The tears returned, the skin around her eyes swollen and red. I had no doubt that she was mourning for Laura, and worrying about Shawna too. And mourning someone was enough to gum up anyone's memory. "How about you tell me when you first suspected abuse?"

Her lips appeared again as she chewed the side of her mouth. "It wasn't until a couple years back when the absences started."

"They weren't going to school?"

"Coming over too," she answered. "And when Laura did come over, she'd have tape on her side, or one of those soft casts on a wrist or ankle."

"Bone breaks?" I asked, pulling out my phone and texting Dr. Swales, requesting full body scan to determine previous injuries.

"Fractures. She'd tell us that she fell or bumped her bureau." Mrs. Newman grabbed her rib, acting as though she'd struck the corner of furniture. "The one time she had two rib fractures."

I was beginning to believe the child could have been punched by an adult.

"I felt awful for her." Mrs. Newman remained wide-eyed, nodding, cheeks wet. "But a lot of the time she would only have a limp or struggle with her back. She'd ask for aspirin while watching the girls. But then we wouldn't see her for another two weeks or more."

School attendance records, I wrote down, underlining it as well. "When did you first notice?"

"Gosh," she said, biting on a nail and looking somewhere over me. "Our Abigail was just a baby when Laura first started to look after her for us."

"Eight years?" I asked, guessing her daughter's age to be the same as Shawna's.

"Oh no. Laura was perfectly healthy back then," she answered, shaking her head. "We started to notice when she turned eleven or so. I think Abigail and Shawna were around four."

"Did you ever confront the Jacksons? Or think to call Child Protective Services?"

With that question, Mrs. Newman covered her face, her fingers long enough to hide everything from her chin to the top of her forehead. From behind them, she mumbled, "I should have. I know I should have. But it wasn't my place."

I could have thrown insult on injury, explaining that it was her place, that it was every adult's place to guard the young. I didn't though, the woman's cries stirring the office again. "Mrs. Newman, did you ever speak to Laura about what was happening to her?"

Her face appeared as she answered, "Of course! Every time. I asked her what was wrong, what had happened."

"Did she ever indicate that her parents were abusing her?"

"Not once. Never." She wiped her face, rubbing her cheeks, mascara blotching around the bottom of one eye. I handed her the box of tissues. "She always made excuses, saying that she'd tripped or that her body just hurt sometimes. I wanted to tell you what I remembered," she said, cleaning her face with the tissues.

"Thank you for coming in," I said as Mrs. Newman stood, her phone in hand. There was nothing else we could get from her.

She showed me the screen as though I'd know what to look at, saying, "I've got a one o'clock showing."

Full body, I texted to Swales, seeing the previous messages were read. "I've informed the medical examiner of potential abuse."

"I'm sorry I didn't mention any of this yesterday."

"It's good that you came to us," I said, assuring her. "If you remember anything else—"

"Yes, of course," she answered, leaving the way she came in.

Got it, Swales texted back to me. *We'll perform full panel.*

I double-tapped the message, dropping a thumbs-up on it. When I opened the conference room door, Tracy and the detective were in nearly the exact same position as I'd left them. "That was Mrs. Newman. What did you make out on the doorbell camera?"

Tracy peered up, her eyes cast in her laptop's blue light. She perched one finger and tapped her keyboard to play a video on the monitor. "Just this from the night the girls went to the fair. Nothing else."

The screen was entirely black, the evening hiding nearly everything beyond the front porch. A pair of headlights appeared far head of the Newmans' home, the car slowing when it reached the house, and then stopping. It sat in the road a few seconds, the speakers silent, offering us nothing other than the image. It drove off, the screen turning black again. "Any videos before this one?"

"There's a package being delivered before sunset?" Tracy said, asking if I wanted to see it. I was hoping there'd be more, but their doorbell camera was a bust. When I didn't reply, Tracy asked, "Did Mrs. Newman remember something?"

"You might say she did," I told her. "She told me the Jacksons themselves killed Laura and Shawna."

TWELVE

The tablet was next on our list, my having gotten that one important email we'd been waiting for. It was from the school district, with heartfelt comments about Laura Jackson's death and offering to provide any support they could. The email ended with a paragraph containing new credentials to the school district's cloud account they'd created for me. With the access, we could work with the tablet issued to Laura.

When I got to my desk, plunking my backpack next to the monitor, I dropped into my chair with my legs spread and arms dangling. I closed my eyes and stayed that way a while, letting the day's midday fatigue drain from my brain and muscles. If I wasn't careful, a noontime catnap would have befallen me. I was sure of it. But the curiosity was stronger than my will to forgo and I forced myself to get up and make some coffee.

"I need caffeine," I mumbled, my voice a numb slur.

"I think I'll join you," Tracy said, her hand offered for me to take.

"Double espresso," I said, grabbing hold and letting her pull me from my seat. "Maybe a quad-shot latte!"

When we got to the kitchenette, she held up a pod, the label marked *Dark Roast*. "Afraid this is all we got."

"It'll do," I said and poked my head around the corner as Tracy made the coffee. Our conference room was empty, the Greenville detective taking the work we'd given him back to his station. When Tracy handed me a cup, I asked, "What's your thoughts on Delight's Traveling Funfair? The connection to the Greenville case?"

"Strong," she said, cringing at the bitter taste. "I mean the connection. I'd think it is the top of the list for us to investigate."

"Agreed," I said, returning to my chair and placing Laura Jackson's tablet on the desk. Tracy wheeled her chair next to mine, bumping me gently to make room for her. "Next to whatever we find on Laura's tablet, Delight's Traveling Funfair is a priority."

"Understood," she answered, opening her laptop, a map appearing. She launched a chat application, the window showing a conversation in progress, three dots animated as one of the participants typed. "I'm working directly with Detective Watson from Greenville."

"Good. We'll want to go as far back as possible. We want every location Delight's Traveling Funfair has been and every unsolved murder and kidnapping." She put on a frown, a response appearing in the chat window. "What is it?"

"There's no schedule," she answered, confirming one of my earlier finds.

"Seriously?" I asked, believing if there was a killer hiding amongst the carnival's staff, the town they were arriving had an unnamed victim. We needed to warn them. "It's like they finish wherever they are and then travel blindly with no destination in mind?"

"Then, wherever they stop, they print and distribute fliers while they set everything up."

"Permits?" I said, questioning. "If they aren't scheduling

anything in advance, that means their wait time to open is dictated by the permits they pull."

"Unless they are opening without permits?"

"Could be," I answered. I searched permits for one of the locations they'd been and tapped my screen. "Look at this. I'd think they *have* to be pulling permits. There's the event permit, operating permit, the food vendor permit, any liquor licensing, safety inspections, and who knows how many more. There are way too many needed to skate by without pulling a single one."

Tracy's round eyes came with a shrug. "I get it. But between me and Detective Watson, we haven't found anything that resembles a schedule."

I clapped my hands, saying, "I know what it is!" I understood how the carnival was working. "They always know where they are going. Most likely it's where they've already been. They don't list the location until everything is in place."

"But the permits, like you said?"

"They've probably already submitted applications for them," I answered, pointing at their website on Tracy's laptop. "They won't update that until they're in place and ready to operate."

She shrugged again, shaking her head. "What advantage does that give them?"

"Well, if we're right about who killed Laura Jackson and Detective Watson's niece, Delight's Traveling Funfair might skip one town and go to the next. No tickets sold. No complaints. No bad press. Just a loss on their permit costs." The idea was thin but would explain the lack of a schedule. "It's the only thing I can think of that would make sense to help keep the police off their trail."

"I suppose," she said, sounding unconvinced. With furrowed brow, she added, "We can't reach out in advance with a warning. Like putting extra patrols in place."

"To find out which town was next, without letting the fair

know we're on to them, we'd have to search every one of them within fifty to a hundred miles, and canvas the court office records for permits pulled that fit the collection I mentioned."

With a hard stare on her laptop, Tracy replied, "I wouldn't know how to do that in the time it would need to get done."

"That's the advantage to their last-minute schedule announcements. It could also mean that whoever oversees their schedule must know there's been a murder, which drives them to put some extra distance between where they are and where they've been."

"I've been learning how to code," she said, showing me her screen. "What I can do is write a job that repeatedly scrapes Delight's website. When there's been a schedule posted, the job will text us immediately."

"That's good," I told her, eyeing the source code, some of the keywords colored a bright magenta, while others were green and gray and yellow. I followed a few lines of it but got lost with the calls to services made up of cryptic names. I braced her shoulder, nudging affectionately, a feeling of admiration and pride warming in me. "When did you learn how to do that?"

"Been at it a few nights now," she said with a shy smile. "It's like a puzzle. I get the idea of what I want, and the code is the puzzle."

"You taught yourself all that?" I asked, admiring Tracy's mind and feeling awestruck by what she could do. Tracy was gifted in so many ways. Everyone knew it. I'd come to learn how much soon after meeting her. By then she was an adult, and with the memory of that moment there came a flash of remorse to sour what I was feeling. I'd missed the years of seeing Tracy blossom into the woman she was today. Selfishly, I'd always hate that I'd missed that. But gratefully, I was happy she had her adopted parents who saw it all.

Tracy caught me staring too long and scowled, asking in a funny voice, "What? I got something on my teeth?"

"Nothing on your teeth," I answered. "Add Detective Jeremy Watson's cell number to the notifications too."

"Already done," she said, returning her laptop to the desk.

"Let's see what we see." With Laura's tablet turned on, we both fixed a look at its home page, the icons tiled across it like a chess game with some on the top and others on the bottom. There were the typical apps we'd expected to see. The ones for email, maps, photos and videos. There were also the icons the school district had installed. There was one for note-taking and another for reading textbooks and for practicing arithmetic. "Well, this is somewhat unexpected."

"What?" Tracy asked, gaze jumping around to understand my comment.

"Wouldn't you expect to find social media apps the kids use?" I asked, swiping the screen to a second and third landing page, both empty save for the swirly, colorful background. "If I didn't know any better, this tablet was wiped. It was reset."

Tracy let out a sigh and rubbed her eyes. "Wait! What if Laura had a personal account?"

"It's school property. But it is possible," I said and opened the settings options, bringing them into view. There was only the *Sign Out* button available, and on this tablet, it showed no history of a previous user. "If there was another account used, then we'd have to know the ID."

"There's gotta be another one," Tracy exclaimed, crossing her arms, defiant in her suggestion. "Kids do this all the time so they can hide their online activities."

"Maybe Laura was one of the exceptions?" I asked, a lilt in my voice. With only the apps available on her school account, I opened the email next, saying, "I've got an idea."

"Search her email?"

"Correct," I answered as a flood of unopened school emails filled the screen. I ignored the folder labeled *All Inboxes* and jumped to the one labeled *All Sent*. "You'd expect most all these to be sent for schoolwork. But what if there is one that Laura sent to another account? A personal account?"

"If she did, it'll be there," Tracy answered as I sorted the sent email and listed the oldest first. Almost immediately, we found a candidate. "Casey! What's that one say?"

On the screen, there was an email addressed to Laura. No other name adornments. Nothing to indicate a hidden email address. Only her name, *Laura*. I clicked it. "It's old. She sent it almost a year ago."

"Hmm," Tracy grunted with a tone of disappointment. "The subject line says *Test*. School test... Wait! Test account?"

"That's it. Laura was testing an account she'd set up."

"I've definitely done that too!" Tracy said, excitedly.

"Guilty," I said raising a hand, my palms feeling sweaty. "We may have found another account."

"She used her school's email account to set up the second one."

"That's my guess. And you know what?" I asked, signing out of the tablet. "We have the email address she sent the test to."

"Try using it to sign on to the tablet!" Tracy said and leaned closer our focus fixed on the small screen.

I typed in the second email address, a prompt appearing for us to enter a passcode, a six-digit number. My heart jumped. "It's here! The second account is on here!" I said and grabbed my phone, opening the notes I'd written about Laura. "We need to figure out the passcode to unlock it."

"Passcode," Tracy commented, flipping open her notebook, leafing through the pages. "I've got her birthday!"

"Read it back?" I asked, wondering how many chances we'd have. Tracy read out the birthdate, my transcribing them to a six-digit format the tablet would accept. The Enter Passcode screen shook and displayed a lock. "Uh-uh! That's not it."

"We'll have to be careful. Otherwise, I think we can disable the account."

"I know, but how many attempts do we get?" We'd never get anywhere once the tablet was locked.

"What other significant dates are there?" Tracy asked, flipping a page, lips moving, her voice a whisper as she read through her notes.

When I heard her mention adoption, I jumped abruptly as though slapped by a thought. "What was the date of their adoption?" Tracy read the year, month and the day, the tip of my finger carefully touching each number on the keypad. When I reached the last, I said, "Let's hope this is it."

The tablet's screen appeared, a home page with very different icons than what the school's IT department had placed for Laura to use. "You got it!"

"Look at this," I said, a folder on the screen named, *Parents*. I opened it, a list of documents appearing, their titles official, showing they were from municipal offices belonging to the state of North Carolina. I clicked on one, the tablet's PDF reader displaying the document, confirming the adoption the date I'd just entered. I opened the email account next, and like before, I clicked on the *All Sent* folder, wanting to see who Laura had been contacting in secret. There was one email address that appeared over and over, Robert and Jane Finley, the couple using a shared email account.

"Casey, it was Laura that found her birth parents," Tracy said, tapping the tablet, opening one of the emails. "It looks like she's been talking to them every day."

"She was," I said coldly, referring to it in the past tense. I selected the last email sent. "From the dates, Laura was talking to them right up until the night she was killed."

THIRTEEN

There were more than two dozen emails. Twice that in the number of documents. Possibly ten times the total in the count of websites Laura Jackson had visited. Her secret account showed she'd been highly active in finding her birth parents. While it was impossible for Shawna to have remembered them, clearly, from the depth of research and the paperwork she recovered, Laura had remembered everything about her parents. She'd remembered them and a lot more. Laura wanted her birth parents back in their lives. I couldn't help but wonder what must be going through Robert Finley's and Jane Finley's minds? Surely, by now, the news of their daughter's murder had reached them.

It was the middle of the day, the morning and afternoon shifts trading places as the wall clock touched the noon hour. On Tracy's desk, her computer worked the tablet, copying the bits and the bytes to assure we had a backup of the accounts.

"We can still use it," she said while she snaked another computer cable from her laptop. "It might take a while to make a backup, but that's working in the background."

"That's great. I want to learn more about what happened." I

urged Tracy to join me at my desk to see what I was reviewing. It was the Finleys' court filings I'd opened, having already copied a handful of files. "These were a surprise to find."

"How did Laura get them?" Tracy asked.

I showed the most glaring of documents from the Department of Social Services, answering, "They were available online. Public record." It was filed by Child Protective Services, an agency within the department, and was dated seven years earlier when Shawna was just a baby and Laura was seven, a week before her eighth birthday. The document had me leaning wide-eyed with interest as I read through the Finleys' termination of their residual parental rights. On my other monitor, I opened all the police records we had on the Finleys, finding a vagrancy arrest in the days before the Child Protective Services filing. We'd had Jane Finley's and Robert Finley's records, which showed a single charge for him and none for her. It was a minor charge, vagrancy, which had been dismissed. Seeing the report from Child Protective Services, I suddenly understood what was thought to be minor, had had tragic consequences.

"Take a look at this," I said, showing Tracy. "They were living on the streets."

"You mean, they were homeless? With two kids?" she asked, gaze fixed and jaw slack. "But for how long? I mean, they're working now?"

"Keep in mind, this is from seven years ago," I said, reading though the pages of legal language. "The report stated that the Finleys were homeless. And this shows an arrest for vagrancy. That's when the girls were taken away."

"What happened to the charges?" Tracy asked, her breath sweet with chocolate, a wrapper unfurled on my desk. She nudged the crumpled end, offering a piece of her candy bar.

"I think the Finleys found themselves homeless—which can happen for a million different reasons. They were on the streets. It was winter in the Outer Banks. Maybe they couldn't get into a shelter and started panhandling for food?" I asked with a lift of my shoulders. "I think the state intervened to take emergency custody of the children."

"They can do that?" Tracy asked, knowing the answer, today's circumstances explained. There was a sad look on her face. "That's horrible."

"Search Laura's emails. Maybe the Finleys mentioned something about what happened to them?"

"I'll use keywords like adoption and arrest," she said while returning to her desk. As Tracy scanned the emails, I dug into the court documents. The children had been removed abruptly, one court filing citing safety and welfare concerns. "This doesn't add up."

"What's that?" Tracy asked, voice wet as she chewed.

"There's no other arrests?" I said, questioning. "With their children removed, I'd think we would see a pattern."

"Like a pattern if there is substance abuse in the home?" Tracy questioned, returning with her laptop to show me an email about Laura and Shawna meeting with the Finleys. "How about this. I think this could be something?"

"An email confirming their meeting with their biological parents. It most definitely is. Tag it," I said while searching Robert Finley's employment history. His arrest record was easier for me to find, and only showed the one vagrancy charge. To my surprise, the charge had been dropped weeks later, Robert Finley's record clean. Only, by then, he and his wife had lost their children. Dread for the girls curled in my stomach. "What was started couldn't be undone?"

"What do you mean?" Candy wrapper ripping.

I sat back in my chair, a dark anger stirring from the deep of me. Anger for the Finleys. "I think this was an unnecessary overreach."

"Overreach?" Tracy asked, giving the document a hard stare. "Not sure I follow."

"The vagrancy charge was dropped, but their children were never returned to them."

"Wait," she said, a scowl forming, feeling the same anger. "If the charges went away, why couldn't Child Protective Services undo what they'd started?"

"I'm not sure. Maybe it was the conditions at the time. There's no pattern of arrests, no frequency of them. What's even stranger, the court papers show the same home address we sent the squad car to watch for any activity."

"Then they weren't homeless?" she asked, confused.

I stole a chunk of the chocolate, chewing voraciously as I scanned the legal jargon. "Best guess is it means the homelessness must have been temporary," I answered. "Look at his employment dates. Finley has been working since then. I'm sure Mrs. Finley has too. But the courts had already taken that first step."

"That shouldn't be right," Tracy said, tone scolding. "I mean, for the clerks and lawyers and judges, the Finleys' case, didn't they check?"

I could only share in the disbelief of it all. "That first court action was like clockwork with one gear putting another gear into motion—" Closing my eyelids, I shook my head, a reverent fear for the power the court systems exercised. "I'm sure for the clerks and lawyers who'd worked the case, the matter of the Finley children was important. It was as important a case as the dozens they'd also worked that week and was one decision of the hundreds made. But for Jane and Robert Finley, the decision was life-changing."

"Jeez," Tracy said and then clapped her hands, a smear of chocolate in the corner of her mouth. "Take a look what I found in the email history when I added *sorry* as a keyword."

Tracy maximized the email on her screen, repeatedly tapping keys to increase the font. The email began with an apology and went on from there, telling Laura the events that ended with the family being broken apart. I skimmed the words until reaching a paragraph that added the insight we were seeking, and read it aloud.

"'Laura, this was never supposed to be this way. We had a home and food on the table and jobs we loved. But more importantly, we had you and your sister and a future. We could never have planned or imagined both me and your mom getting laid off within a week of one another. And we could never have planned to fall behind on the bills or losing our home and then losing you two. We want you to know, we have fought and will continue to fight to correct this and bring you and your sister to the home you belong. We love you and Shawna with all that we are. Trust that we will be together again soon.'"

"Soon! Could be they planned to kidnap them?" Tracy asked, snapping her fingers and leaning sturdily into her chair, the seat back creaking.

"It does read like they were planning something," I said, ideas stirring fresh. "But the words... this would never hold up in court as planning a kidnapping, premeditated."

"You don't think?"

"A good defense attorney would argue the couple had discussed obtaining a lawyer and shifting the fight to the courtrooms."

"Yeah," Tracy agreed with a nod. Tracy's eyes went wide, her brow rising. She nudged the tablet, saying, "Casey! What if the Jacksons *were* abusive like Barbara Newman said? What if Laura told her birth parents about the abuse?"

Tracy opened the folder with the emails, hundreds of exchanges that dated back more than a year. I answered, "If something was said, the evidence could be as small as a sentence fragment."

"What could?"

"The evidence that would show Robert Finley was defending the lives of his children."

FOURTEEN

With my eyes glued on the pursuit, the trees and shops and other cars on Route 12 careened by in a crazed blur. I didn't know how fast we were driving, but knew the speed was too much for the northern stretch of the Outer Banks main thoroughfare. Tracy clung to the dashboard with one hand, her nails digging into the vinyl. She held a police radio receiver in the other. It was a recent installment, along with patrol lights behind my car's grill and on the backside of the visors. Brilliant flashes of red and blue beamed from my car, a siren warbling to warn the surrounding traffic.

"That's right!" she yelled with a high shrill, my knuckles white as I strained to grip the steering wheel firm. "A Ford truck, an F-150 with North Carolina plates. The truck color is a light blue, the driver believed to be Robert Finley. Caution! There is a child in the front seat who we believe is Shawna Jackson! Driver is wanted on suspicion of kidnapping."

"Read out the plate numbers!" I shouted, the blue truck's sides and hood pocked by age, the wheel wells browned with rust. My car was younger. It was faster. But try as I might, I couldn't keep up with them. The truck's appearance was misleading, Robert Finley maneuvering swiftly through the traffic as black smoke billowed whenever he gunned the motor.

"License plate is CD1-55B9," Tracy said with a shout. "That's Charlie delta one five five bravo nine!"

Every muscle tightened as dispatch read the plate numbers back to us. In my rearview mirror, I saw a flicker of patrol lights appear in the sea of cars that had eased onto the side of the road and made room for our pursuit. It was distant and shimmered in the heat above the car roofs. "They're not going to catch up," I said, suddenly feeling alone in this race. "Tell them we need patrols from the north—"

"Casey!" Tracy screamed, a minivan suddenly stopping in front of us, its brake lights blazing, piercing my eyes as I stomped the brake.

"Hold on!" Tires screeching, the acrid stench of rubber in the air, I jerked the steering wheel and cut across the yellow line with car horns blaring. I sucked in a hot breath through clenched teeth as Tracy gasped at the unexpected sight of oncoming traffic. My car rocked sideways, air buffeting the minivan, the faces of the family inside pale streaks as we passed. When we were clear, I smashed my foot against the gas pedal and swerved back onto our side of the road.

"Holy shit!" Tracy screeched.

"Where are they?" I spun the steering wheel, the front tires bouncing violently against a curb, the car's front scraping the parking lot incline behind a Super Wings clothing store. "I don't see them!"

"Wait," Tracy answered, twisting around in her seat and searching where the F-150 should have been.

We came to a stop, my yelling, "Where did they go?" and dipped my head close to the windshield. "Did we lose them?"

"No freaking way!" she answered as the patrol car following pulled into the parking lot, the officer with a questioning gaze.

In the east, black smoke appeared like a blemish against the sky. "They turned on Albacore Street!"

"They're taking the backroads," Tracy said, pointing at the sky, the smoke dissipating.

"Call it over the radio. We can use the patrols north to cut them off," I demanded, yelling over the sirens. I stomped the gas pedal, steering us out of the parking lot, tires squealing when I turned the wheel to avoid a pair of bicyclists, my car's belly striking asphalt. "He must have made a right when that minivan stopped."

"There!" Tracy shouted at a fresh cloud swirling from the truck's tailpipe as it turned left onto a street of oceanfront homes. She picked up the radio, the radio speaker squelched, "We are resuming pursuit of a Ford F-150 truck onto Light-house Drive, plates CD1-55B9!"

I swung the steering wheel left, my hip grinding against the center console, my weight shoved by gravity. The F-150 was already three blocks north, moving two to three times the speed limit. I bit my lip and lifted my foot from the gas pedal, terrified of what could happen. This was a residential street, the three-story homes standing tall and colorful on both sides. Many of the properties were rentals, the driveways and lawns busy with families checking in for a new week in the Outer Banks. "The end of Lighthouse Drive dumps out onto Shad Street," I said, and continued to turn, taking us back toward Route 12.

"What are you doing!" Tracy asked, her hands against the passenger door window.

"I can beat them at Shad Street. There's a public beach access there," I told her, speeding up as we entered onto Route 12. Seeing Shawna Jackson out in the open had been a miracle of miracles. It was a chance happening like buying a winning lottery ticket. We'd reached a break from the morning's meeting with Detective Watson and took the time for a lunch away from the station. While it was out of the way, a new pizza place north of us on Scarborough Lane was where we'd decided to go and spend the hour. We'd have one of our favorite foods to eat and discuss Barbara Newman's comments.

Just as we neared the destination, I'd seen a girl matching Shawna Jackson's description. Four feet tall and with strawberry-blonde hair, I noticed the tone of her skin like her sister's and the freckles across her nose and cheeks. The little girl held the hand of a man in his forties or early fifties. He had the same skin tone, but it was darkened by the sun and with deep wrinkles around his eyes and lips. He was dressed in dungarees and wore an oversized T-shirt, his head covered with an OBX baseball cap, the bill tattered and threadbare around the edges. They crossed the street, melding with a larger crowd, a family with extended relatives which included grandparents supported by canes and walkers. When the man and girl emerged from the small group, he saw me watching, he saw that I had my police radio in hand.

But I had to check twice, jaw slack with surprise and awe. And then take another look, maybe three or four more times. After all the searching we'd done, and a constant patrol around the Finleys' neighborhood, here was Robert Finley out in the open with Shawna Jackson. Tracy had no idea what was happening, but within moments, he'd put the girl in his truck and was spinning his tires and fleeing north while we were stuck behind the crowd crossing the street.

"Two patrol vehicles are approaching from the south on Route 12," dispatch warned, but I'd already seen them far behind us.

I jumped on the gas pedal, my speedometer climbing to seventy-five, the road clear for the immediate miles ahead of us. "We're going to catch up to them," I exclaimed, the confidence climbing. "Jericho brought me up here to watch the sun setting over Currituck Sound."

"Ya know, Casey!" Tracy yelled over the noise of the motor

wailing. "When you asked if I wanted to go out for lunch, this wasn't what I had in mind!"

"Neither did I," I said, blood whooshing in my ears, a high octane of adrenaline pumping at a fevered pace. A patrol vehicle was stopped at a pedestrian crosswalk, its lights flashing, giving us a clear path. "Just another mile."

"I haven't been this far north since a field trip to see the horses on Carova beach," Tracy said as we reached Shad Street. I pulled off the road, expecting to see the rust and dusky blue color of the F-150 approaching. But we didn't. We heard it though. Heard the low groveling of fuel being sucked into the motor before igniting into a flurry of explosions. My heart dropped when I saw the cloud of black smoke rise in front of us. "Casey, they already turned!"

"I see them," I said, the chase continuing north, my speed hampered by traffic, the sight of them slipping as Finley jumped into oncoming traffic to race around ahead. When I could, I did the same, keeping his truck in sight until we hit a turn that was nearly ninety degrees.

"Casey," Tracy said, her voice short, the seat belt cutting into my shoulder.

"I got this, there's another turn to the left coming up." When we made it through the turn, I sped up and crossed the cattle grate, Route 12 and its paved road coming to an end. Thinking Finley would have had to stop, I said, "There's nothing but beach access from here."

"Can you drive on the beach?" Tracy asked, looking around at my car, saying the obvious without actually saying what I already knew.

"Not in this thing," I answered reluctantly. We crawled onto the beach, the tires spinning loose as I tempted the fate of getting stuck. I revved the motor, daring to venture a hundred yards into the loose sand. There was ocean directly in front of us, and tire tracks laid by four-wheel drive vehicles that could travel the remaining miles of the Outer Banks coastline. I rolled down my window, the smell of ocean filling the car. In the distance I heard the low roar of Finley's truck as I told Tracy, "But I'll bet you an F-150 can drive this all the way to the border."

"Yeah," she said, exiting the passenger side. I followed, the two of us standing ankle deep, hands raised to shield the sun as we followed a trail of the F-150's black smoke. "I don't think we can make that drive."

"Mrs. Newman," I said, her comments clear in my head as a flock of pelicans flew close to the surf. "What she said to me earlier. She was wrong. Shawna Jackson is alive."

FIFTEEN

The flurry of police activities to apprehend the F-150 would continue into the evening. For now, our best move—our only move—was to do something else. If I could have, I would have jumped into one of the 4x4 patrol vehicles with the lumpy rubber tires made for driving across the deepest beach sands. From there, I'd go door to door and knock until someone answered. There were patrols who'd go in our place. Who would do the knocking. Who would ask the questions. I had no idea how many houses they'd cover, or what the population living north of Corolla was. It didn't matter, we'd get it covered. When we looked at the map and the satellite images, there were unpaved beach roads throughout the northern tip of the Outer Banks. And peppered across all of it, I saw houses that numbered in the hundreds, maybe more. Robert Finley could be hiding in any of them. And Shawna was with him.

What was Robert Finley doing in Corolla? That was the question I needed answered. We stood at the south edge of Carova beach, the tide climbing as the day grew long. Towering wood poles were to our right, their descending far into the ocean like giant stilts. Each was perched by a pelican or a seagull, sometimes two. There were thick cables strung from one to the next, the height and spacing enough to let the birds fly freely while keeping the cars off the adjacent Corolla beaches. It was also to protect one of the Outer Banks greatest attractions. Wild horses. While I couldn't see any of them from where we stood, I wondered if Shawna could.

Tracy's hair blew around her face as she brought her laptop and put it atop my car hood. A cable ran down her arm, a tether to her cell phone. "Here's Robert Finley's DMV records Alice found," she said, motioning me around to her side.

"He's a lot younger here," I said, her screen showing a driver's license photograph. While the picture was years apart from the man I saw with Shawna Jackson, it confirmed for me that it was Shawna's biological father I saw with the child.

"Just the DMV photo for Mr. Finley and where he works," Tracy answered. "I'm still working on the mother, Jane Finley."

The patrol cars that had followed us during the pursuit stopped behind my car, their tires sinking into the sand. The officer I'd seen at the Super Wings approached while he searched distant homes in Carova. "We've radioed ahead to try and get air support."

"I heard," I told him, the radio sounding a rasp. "What do you think?"

Regarding my question, he yanked the brim of his hat to shade his eyes. Kicking his toe against the sand and looking to Tracy and then to me, he frowned, saying, "Four-wheel drive, there's a lot of houses back there. They go on for miles and miles all the way up to the Virginia border."

"They're stilted too," I said, thinking Finley would park beneath one of them and wait until after dark before moving again. "Odds on searching all of them before sundown?"

He pressed the heel of his hand against his chin, continuing to shake his head. "Not likely, but we've got a patrol."

"Thank you, officer," I said, taking his hand firmly. "At least we know who Shawna Jackson is with."

"What do we know about the guy who took her?" another officer asked, her eyes hidden behind dark sunglasses. "Finley? I heard someone say on the radio."

"That was me," Tracy answered, giving the officers a wave to show her laptop. "Dispatch has his photograph. He's the girl's father."

"Father?" the officer asked. She joined us at the laptop and lowered her glasses to see over them. "Is this a custody battle?"

"Robert Finley is the girl's biological father, but has no parental custody rights," I answered, the other officer looking at his phone to show the same picture we had. "The girl's older sister was murdered at the time Shawna Jackson was believed to have been kidnapped."

"Is he a suspect for the murder?" the officer asked, trudging through the sand back to his patrol car.

"Nothing solid at this time," I answered. And was quick to add, "But not ruled out."

The patrol officer with the dark sunglasses leaned over for a closer look at the picture. "Ya know, I'm pretty sure he works at the lighthouse," she said. "I just took my kids there last week."

"You've seen him recently?" Tracy asked, voice jumping.

"Which lighthouse?" I asked, my gaze leveling with interest. Could she be talking about the Bodie Lighthouse close to where Laura Jackson's body was discovered?

She turned to face the direction we drove from, answering, "About a mile away. It's the one with the red bricks."

"The Bodie Lighthouse? Striped black and white?" I asked.

"I think he works for the National Park Service," the officer said. She snapped her fingers, adding. "Currituck Beach Lighthouse. He does the tours there."

"Recently?" I asked, wondering what else the National Park

Service managed in the Outer Banks, what else Finley had access to.

"Ya know, I've got the date right here," she answered, showing her phone, a calendar. "We were there a week from this past Friday."

"And he was working?" I asked, hoping there was a record of it.

"Well, he was our tour guide," she answered.

"Thank you for the help, officer," I said and closed Tracy's laptop. "I think we'll head over there and ask some questions."

"You'll keep your radio on?" she asked, a beach patrol driving by, large tires chewing through the sand.

"Always," I answered, jumping into my car.

"The lighthouse?" Tracy asked, buckling her seat belt. "Food first?"

"Food first," I assured her, the sound of her stomach growling. Mine stirred in response as I spun my tires until feeling them grab. "But not until we get back onto solid ground."

Corolla Village Road was heavily shadowed by thick trees that lined both sides of it, the road a mix of gravel and dirt which turned the ride bumpy. With the summer crowds thinning, there was parking close to the lighthouse. But even from where we stood, we couldn't see the top of the spire until we walked onto an open field. There were four buildings, including the one we'd come to see. Gazing up, I followed the stacked bricks until I saw the top, a black balcony surrounding glass windows where the lighthouse's lantern existed. Though it was late in the afternoon, still daylight, a passing notion had me wishing the light was on for us to see.

"It's two hundred and twenty steps to the top," a woman said, catching my attention with her white polo shirt that had a logo on it. She had a deep tan and hair down to the middle of her back. In one hand, she carried a tablet. And in the other, black-and-white pamphlets, with pictures of the lighthouse. "About a million bricks were used to build it."

"That's a lot of steps," I said, seeing that she was one of the tour guides. That's when I noticed that the few others with the same shirt and logo were not dressed in the National Park Service uniforms. "That's a lot of bricks too."

She handed me one of the pamphlets, and then gave one to Tracy. "Interested in a tour?"

Tracy opened the leaflet, her lips moving as she began reading, her eyes wide. "Definitely! I don't remember this one."

I showed my badge, its metal breaking the sunlight that slipped between the trees. "Could we speak to a manager perhaps?"

"Well, I should be able to help you with that," she said and gave a wave toward the lighthouse. A guide waiting with a line of tourists tipped his hat and began to move.

"Ma'am, you work here full time?"

"I do, I'm the lighthouse site manager," she answered, rocking on her feet. She nudged her chin toward the house behind us, adding, "And I live on the property."

"That's amazing," Tracy said.

"The last ten years," the manager replied, eyeing the property. "One of the few lighthouses on the east coast that still has on-site lighthouse keepers."

"Then you would be familiar with most of the people working here?" I asked, opening my phone to the picture of Robert Finley that had been circulated.

"I should hope so," she said in a matter-of-fact tone. "I would have been the one to hire them."

I flipped my phone around for her to see, a distant yell coming from atop the lighthouse as the latest tour finished their climb. "Do you recognize this man?"

The site manager frowned, my questions bothersome. Her

expression relaxed when she recognized the face. "That's Bob. He's a part-time tour guide."

I noticed the logo on her polo shirt, which had no reference to the National Park Service. "Currituck Lighthouse isn't managed by the park service?"

"Not this one," she said, tapping the face of the pamphlet. "It's privately owned and managed. On the back is the contact information."

"We have Robert Finley listed as working for the National Park Service," Tracy said, sharing her confusion about the employment.

"That certainly helped in my hiring him," she said, glancing at my phone's screen again. "His knowledge of the Outer Banks lighthouses is excellent." Her smile appeared again. "Almost as good as mine."

"How long has he been working part-time for you?" I asked, glancing around at the buildings. Was Robert hiding in one of them with Shawna?

"Oh let's see," she said and rocked on her feet again while gazing up at the tall spire. "I'd say the last couple years now."

"Would he have access to these buildings?" I asked with a wave, pointing to the smallest of the buildings which couldn't have been more than a single room, its windows long and skinny, the points of the roof adorned with decorative points that might have been lightning rods. "Like that one there?"

"He only works as a tour guide, so he'd have access to the lighthouse." She frowned again and tucked a lock of hair behind her ear. "What's this about? He's an excellent tour guide."

I swiped my phone to show her a picture of Shawna Jackson, saying, "This is his biological daughter." The site manager held out her hand, asking to hold my phone. She held it close to her face and studied the picture. "We believe he kidnapped her from her adopted parents."

"Kidnapped?" she asked, returning my phone. "I didn't know he had any children."

"That's where things become more complicated," I said, and then quickly asked, "Have you seen either of them?"

"He was here earlier in the week, but I didn't see a child with him," she answered and looked to the lighthouse. "Then again, I might not have noticed."

"Was he working?" I asked.

"Not that day," she answered. "Bob wasn't on schedule."

"Would there be any other reason for one of your employees to go into the lighthouse? Maybe for maintenance?" I felt like I was grasping at straws and thinking Tracy was likely to get her climb today after all.

The site manager waved for us to follow her. We walked to the lighthouse's entrance, the top of it stretching into the sky as we followed. "None of them do maintenance. We have a special team for that. But I can show you where he would have been."

"Oh gosh, we're gonna get a tour," Tracy blurted excitedly under her breath.

We reached the lighthouse, the concrete steps leading inside it worn smooth. Inside the temperature dropped ten degrees, giving me a chill. We stood in a narrow hall with floor-boards that creaked, two rooms on either side of us. "He would've worked here, perhaps?"

"On occasion," the site manager answered. "But Bob is a really good storyteller, and he loved an audience."

"Most of his time was spent working as a tour guide?"

"I'd say almost all of the time," she answered. She went to the room to the left, a gift shop, dimly lit with shelves carrying mementos, a door split in the middle with the bottom closed, a woman standing motionless in the middle. "Stacy, do you recall Bob working the gift shop recently?" She turned enough to face the other room with the same Dutch door, split in the middle, an older man behind it, a credit card machine in hand. "How about ticket sales?"

"I don't believe so," the woman answered as I searched inside, looking to the corners, looking for anything that might stand out as being out of the normal. There was nothing. Tracy took the room where the tickets were sold, giving it a cursory look and coming up empty as I had. We climbed another half dozen steps, the site manager taking us into the belly of the lighthouse, the floor changing to a concrete slab that was covered in black-and-white tiles, which had yellowed with age. There were round gates, the iron spindles coated in thick black paint. The gate circled the middle of the floor, where the spiral staircase sprouted, climbing the wall. I dared a look to the top, the height dizzying even from the bottom.

"When he was here, how was he dressed?" I asked, thinking Finley may have come from his other job. A sense of enormity edged my thoughts, the Outer Banks full of locations employing National Park Service personnel. We might have to find every location and search them.

The site manager squinted with a hard look as she tried to recall. "Come to think of it, he might have been wearing his other work clothes."

"Like these?" Tracy held her phone showing a group of National Park Service employees.

"Yeah, that one in the middle. It's the service summer uniform they wear," she answered, identifying the one with the hunter-green slacks and gray short-sleeved dress shirt with mustard-gold badge embroidered on the right side. "I didn't think much of it at the time."

Tracy went to the first of the steps, eyelids peeled back with awe as she assessed the climb. "Gosh, how many did you say there are?"

"Two hundred and twenty," the site manager answered, as we took the first one to begin the ascent.

When we reached the first landing with one of the narrow windows, I asked, "Do you recall if he'd normally arrive wearing his other uniform?"

"Some of the time he would," she answered, stopping on the first landing, the circular brick walls covered in posters about the lighthouse, an empty seat in front of it. "Sometimes we have tour guides on each landing to answer questions."

Instinctively, I went to the foldout chair and ran my fingers around the lip of it. Tracy used her phone's flashlight to shine onto the brick and metal plates that made up the landing. It was a massive stretch, but the site manager said that Finley had been here. We had to check. "I'm not seeing anything," Tracy said.

"What are you looking for?" the site manager asked, creases between the eyes, the frown deep.

Tracy answered, "Anything that shouldn't be here."

The manager's brow furrowed even more.

"It could be that Finley used the lighthouse since his home was searched and continues to be surveilled."

"Well, not sure you'll find anything. With the few hundred people who've come through since Bob was here, we've broomed the floors and cleaned the stairs," the site manager said. The look on her face matched what I was feeling, our plight to find any evidence being futile. "On average there are a hundred thousand visitors every year."

"You said a hundred thousand?" Tracy lifted a foot and stared with alarm at the metal landing beneath. "How old are these stairs?"

"They're safe," the site manager said as I eyed a crack climbing up the brick wall. "That's on the inside. Those walls are six feet thick."

"Shall we?" I asked, a reservation stirring. The climb took us to another landing where we repeated the previous search. I shined my phone's light into the cavity of the second window, my mind growing wild with ideas about stuffed notes in the old window boards. It was a place where any cleaning would miss a hidden message. "This'd be a good spot to hide something."

The site manager's eyes brightened with surprise. She came to the window and followed my light. "You think he hid something up in there?"

"I've learned to never underestimate and to inspect every possibility," I told her, and motioned to the shallow landing in front of the window. "May I?"

"Yes! Yes, of course. By all means," she answered, offering her hand. I held it, her fingers petite but strong as I climbed into the opening, the aged brick putting dust onto my fingertips. In the window cavity, a recess of the lighthouse wall, I was able to see that it was at least six feet deep as the site manager had told us. The window was buried at three feet with another three feet on the outside. And with my height, I could stand straight without having to hunch over. From the landing, the height of the window was misleading. It was taller than me, making me hoist onto my toes to search the top of the frame. I stuffed my fingers between the wood and brick, prodding and needling the dark space for anything suspicious. Layers of paint cramped the place between the wood slats and brick. But there was still enough to hide something in there. "These windows are about a hundred and forty-five years old and maintained regularly."

"Well..." I said, getting down onto my knees and continuing to run my fingers along the edges. When I struck what felt like paper, my heart jumped. "Guys? I think I've got something!"

"No way!" Tracy said with intrigue, her arm extended, fingers clutching the air with an offer to help.

I carefully tweezed the paper corner until I could fish it out, handing it to Tracy. "What's it say?" I asked as Tracy unfolded the note.

Her excitement waned and her smile turned flat. She flipped the page end over end, the front side of it as blank as the back. "There's nothing on it."

"Weathered?" the site manager asked, taking it in hand to hold close to the window. The faint curving tails of cursive writing appeared, their impressions made by pencil. It wasn't new. It wasn't from Robert Finley. "There was something once, but that was a long time ago."

"Let's keep going," I grunted and worked the other side.

I hit a jumble of cobwebs and jerked my hand when a pair of legs crawled across my fingers. Tracy asked with alarm, "What was it!?"

"A spider... I think."

"Uh-uh!" she declared, stepping away. "I can't do bugs!"

"Tracy!" I exclaimed, touching paper. "There's another note."

"I never?" the site manager began, mouth open with a subtle gasp. "I had no idea tourists were doing that."

I handed the note to Tracy and wiped my hands clean as she unfolded the note. She looked at me like we'd just struck gold. "What's it say?"

"It's addressed to Jane, his wife. 'We'll have to remain separated. Too many eyes. We can't text or call, but we are safe. Wait for my instructions.'"

"We're safe?" I said, emphasizing *we're*. "He never says I... always we."

"Can't text or call?" Tracy asked. "Why not?"

"It means there are too many eyes," I told her.

"Is it me or does he sound paranoid," the site manager commented. "I don't know him to be like that."

"It is possible. He did break the law," I told her. "He and his wife had also lost their children in a manner which was questionable."

"I didn't know about their history, but I can understand it. Especially if it involves children."

Tracy handed me the note. I flipped it around to look for any type of timestamp. I found none. There were the creases to use though, the folds still fresh. I brought the paper to my nose, the smell newer, more like the ream it came from than the lighthouse's brick and wood. "I think he was here before we saw him crossing the street this morning. If I am right, his wife is going to be here soon too."

"Maybe she was already here?" Tracy asked, leaning into the staircase railing to search high and low.

Showing the note, I answered, "We wouldn't have this if she was. I suspect this arrangement was made before Shawna was kidnapped."

The site manager pointed up, saying, "There's another window."

We climbed the steps, taking two at a time until we reached the next window. Like the previous, I searched it, the wild ideas of another note fresh in my mind. My search came up empty-handed. When we continued, we had to slow to a single step at a time, the ascent pitting a fierce burn in my calves and thighs.

"Gosh, I can't even imagine doing this every single day," Tracy said, looking over her shoulder. Sweat beaded on her upper lip, her hair sticking to the side of her face.

"You get used to it," the site manager said, her face clean of sweat while mine was coated wet, hot air in my lungs. She smiled, adding, "Saves me time so I don't have to go to the gym."

"I bet it does," I told her, huffing exhaustedly more than I cared. We were at the top, facing a metal door that led to the outside. It wasn't the actual top though, there had to be more above us. "Where's the light?"

"That would be the lantern room," the site manager answered, her focus shifting to a door above our heads. It was round like the lighthouse and locked shut. "That room is closed to the public."

"How about to Robert Finley?" I asked. "Would he have access?"

She jangled a large keyring, answering, "Not without these."

"What are you thinking, Casey?" Tracy asked while drying her forehead.

I looked to the staircase, answering, "I think we wait for Jane Finley."

SIXTEEN

We sat on the lighthouse steps, a half level above the landing with the window where the note from Robert Finley was discovered. I'd carefully refolded it and tucked it into the recess where I'd found it. I was careful to place it back in the same spot in case the Finleys had a prearranged location. I suspected she was working with her husband, that she was a part of this crime. It was enough for me to bring her in for questioning. We only needed her to show up and to retrieve her husband's note.

Tracy worked a game of solitaire on her phone, the queen of diamonds beneath her thumb as she carried it home. She was finishing another game as we waited into the latter half of the afternoon. The season had cut our hours, the daylight inside the lighthouse changing. Golden rays beamed onto the far wall as the sun fell onto the edge of Currituck Sound, a dusky sunset that'd bring late season tourists to the water's edge. The traffic in the lighthouse had thankfully slowed too, my confidence in seeing Jane Finley beginning to wane.

We had no recent pictures of her, nothing to use as a reference, otherwise we would have taken to a surveillance position outside. What we needed was to see someone in the window, to see them climb onto the sill as I had, and then work the frame with their fingers. While waiting was a part of the job, it could also be the most tedious, leaving me to wonder about the building we sat in, its age, the prospect of Robert Finley using one of the other lighthouses across the Outer Banks.

We'd inspected the other windows, the site manager offering a tour, telling us about the one hundred and sixty-two foot tower, the million-plus bricks, that there were two windows on one side of us and another three on the other. Of particular surprise were their wood frames that I'd prodded, their age seeming implausible at one hundred and forty-five years. Was Robert Finley's sighting today a result of his placing the note for his wife? What if he'd placed the note days ago and Jane Finley had never arrived? What if something happened to her?

But as my speculations betrayed hopes of seeing Jane Finley, a woman arrived at the window's landing. Most tourists passing us had come and gone in pairs, sometimes more. Most of them held the informational pamphlet we'd seen the site manager passing around. Not this woman. She was alone and focused on the window. I tapped Tracy's shoulder and pulled her attention away from her phone and a new word guessing game.

My finger crossing my lips to show silence, I pointed toward the woman studying the windowsill. She was shorter than me and slightly overweight, her skin pink and damp, she had graying burgundy hair that lay flat against her scalp. She swiped at her forehead, her complexion likely from the climb. When she turned to look around, I could see the resemblance to her daughters. Though her cheeks were rounder, it was in her eyes and nose that I saw Shawna and Laura.

I leaned over, my bottom numb from sitting, and whispered to Tracy, "Act like a tourist and wait on the lower side of the landing."

"Okay," Tracy said, opening the lighthouse pamphlet to make like she was reading it.

As she stood, I pawed her arm, adding, "Careful when you walk past her."

She gave me a nod as her shoes clinked against the metal tread. With one hand on the railing, her fingers gliding against the metal, she read from the pamphlet. When the woman noticed her, Tracy nudged the pamphlet, saying, "It's quite something, isn't it?"

"It is," the woman answered as her eyes followed Tracy.

"That's a girl," I said under my breath, getting to my feet to shake the cramps from my legs. The woman waited until Tracy was out of sight before returning to face the window. I eased down one step, careful to place my foot as quietly as a church mouse. The spiral stairs were easily agitated by motion, and in the railing, I could feel Tracy continue her descent. I couldn't chance alarming the woman and needed her to search the window's frame for me to confirm that she was Jane Finley. I eased over the center of the staircase, the steps spiraling and the height dizzying. Tracy's brown hair and fading summer-red highlights were within my line of sight. She turned around to face the window and remained outside the woman's direct view. We had the woman blocked.

This is it! I thought when the woman braced the windowsill, her fingernails turning white with pressure. My tongue felt fat and dry, the anticipation of a chase itching the soles of my feet. I held my breath to lower my foot onto the next step. Toes first. Then my heel. Cringing when the metal creaked. The woman hesitated. She briefly looked over her shoulder and then ignored the noise. With a grunt she was in the air, hoisting herself, the tips of her sandals scraping the brick, scratching the surface before she had a leg in the air, a knee slapping the sill. Her shoulders jiggled. The tops of her arms shook, and for a moment I thought she might fall. But another grunt, and she had both feet up and was kneeling in front of the glass.

When her fingers dove into the dark crack between the wood frame and brick, I was clear to announce myself. "Jane Finley!" I said, footsteps echoing, Tracy joining me. The woman turned around to see us, face scrunched with disapproval. "Ma'am?!"

"I haven't done nothing," she replied as her lower lip quivered. I couldn't tell if it was a cry she was biting, or if it was sudden adrenaline of the shock.

She backed into the glass. She was too close to the window, her bloodshot eyes darting to me and the outside. How hard would it be to burst through a window that was more than a century old? I couldn't read her intentions. I couldn't risk them either. I did the one thing that I knew would shift whatever might be on her mind. "It's to your left."

"Wha—" she began, mouth twisting on undecided words. She could deny knowing what I was referring to, or she could get what she'd come for. Her eyes locked with mine and the desperation in them needled my heart. It was a look I'd seen a million times before. I'd seen it in the mirror, particularly those dark days when I felt the raw despair of losing my only child. This was a mother who had already lost her daughters once: and had just lost another to murder. I had to keep that in mind. Feeling her pain, I mouthed that it was okay, hoping she knew she was safe and that we only wanted what was best for Shawna. She understood, answering, "Thank you."

Trusting we wouldn't drag her from the windowsill, she drove her fingers into the nook, to the left where I'd indicated. I nudged my hand, adding, "Now, close to the bottom."

"I found it," she said, yanking the paper, tearing into it with an intensity that showed she was seeking answers as much as we were. She read it aloud: "'We'll have to remain separated. Too many eyes. We can't text or call, but we are safe. Wait for my instructions.'"

"Ma'am, where would they have gone next?"

But Shawna's birth mother didn't hear my question. She turned the paper end over end, searching for more words from her estranged husband. "That's it?"

"Ma'am?" I asked, offering her a hand. Reluctantly, she took my fingers in hers and paused to assess her status. I eliminated all but one option, telling her, "We're going to the station now."

Her eyes were wet, the sunlight slipping in through the window and turning them gold briefly when she took a final look at where the note was hidden. She lowered herself, taking both of my hands, answering, "Okay."

SEVENTEEN

It was growing late in the day, the sun already casting long shadows on everything it touched. Jane Finley exited the lighthouse, following me without objection, and without an ill word spoken. We passed a small family, a little boy no more than four staring up at the top of the lighthouse, eyes large and drinking in the worldly sight. Our shoes stirred the leaves with a dry rustle and crunched against the gravel path. I peered over my shoulder to Tracy, to see Jane Finley from the corner of my eye. She walked with her head down and gaze locked on the ground. If her husband was around watching us, she didn't know it. Tracy caught on and began to look at the far-off trees and shrubs to see if we were being watched.

When we'd reached my car, a patrol officer turned Finley around for a pat-down, a search for weapons. I could have done the same before we descended from the lighthouse landing, but I was convinced she was safe and not a threat. Jane Finley put on a look of disgust as the officer's hands ran up one leg, patting her knee and thigh. She felt Finley's bottom next, and then around the hips and the groin before running her fingers down the other leg.

"It's required," I said, Finley eyeing the officer with a hard look.

"Yeah, I know all about what's required," Finley scoffed.

"She's clear," the officer said, her voice steady, ignoring Finley's comments.

I nudged my chin to the note in her hand, saying, "You can drive with me."

Finley glanced at the patrol car. "Am I under arrest?" she asked and tucked a streak of gray behind one ear.

I tightened my lips to force a silent moment. I'd only question her. We lacked any evidence to link her directly to a crime. If Jane Finley had been involved in Shawna's kidnapping, could I blame her? I felt pressed to be honest with the woman and answered, "Not at this time." My hands on my hips, I warned, "Your husband is, and if we determine you participated—"

"Yeah, I get it!" she snapped with a snide look. "I know what you want to do! You want to ask me a thousand questions and make me trip up on my answers!"

The distrust of us was strong. Persistent too. It might be that I'd never be able to break through and speak directly to her. That is, the real Jane. Not with this guarding front. "We only want what is best for Shawna."

A wave of hot color climbed her neck and then her cheeks. Her fingers closed to make fists and her lips pressed white as she clenched her jaw. With a low growl, she said, "That's what the social workers told us. Almost exactly that same thing. Only they'd said *Laura* and *Shawna*."

"Mrs. Finley, I am so sorry for your loss," I said, realizing what I'd stepped into with the comment. I put my fist against my chest, explaining, "I know you're hurting, and I know how bad that ache is—"

"Do you!" she said, raising her voice.

"I lost my daughter when she was just a toddler," I started

to say and looked to Tracy a moment, her expression blanking. "And that pain will always be with me."

"You lost your girl?" Finley asked, more gently. I was grateful Tracy didn't move or say anything. If I was going to get any help from Jane Finley, I'd have to connect with her.

"It was a kidnapping," I continued, emotion rattling my words. As an officer of the law, it was rare for me to feel so conflicted. When I'd lost my daughter years before, I'd spent much of my life trying to heal from a wound that could never heal. She'd been through the same. She was still going through it.

"That's what this was!" she said, louder again and nodding fervently, her anger rising. "The government kidnapped our children. Then they gave them away." Her eyes were bugging, and she waved her arms, "They just gave them away!"

She began crying, ignoring the tourists walking around her, returning to where she'd been when finding her husband's note. My chest felt heavy, and I dared a step closer to her. "Jane, I understand."

"Now we'll never see Laura again," she wept, the emotion zapping her strength.

"Then let me help you," I pleaded and took her arm. Tracy ran to her other side, bracing as Laura's mother let out a mournful cry that weakened her knees. The dread I'd felt earlier returned and curled its ugly tail to fill my stomach. Jane Finley was right. There had been overreach. The vagrancy charges brought against them being a minor infraction. Child Protective Services took their children and now one of them was dead. It was a system with flaws and the Finleys had a right to be angry. But did that justify the kidnapping of Laura's sister?

When we got to my car, Finley asked with a sob, "You won't try and trap me with your questions?"

"No, ma'am," I began, breathing a deep sigh. "I won't try to trap you."

The officer's check was the only contact made and I waved off the suggestion to use handcuffs. This won a couple of points with Finley and I gave her the passenger seat in my car while Tracy sat in the back. While I felt we were safe, if Finley was any risk to us, then having Tracy sitting behind me was an advantage.

"What can I tell you?" she asked, opening the conversation to questions.

I decided on being direct, and asked, "We saw your husband with Shawna. What was your involvement in her kidnapping?"

"It isn't kidnapping when it's your own," she answered as I began the drive. "I gave birth to Laura and Shawna."

"I understand your position—"

"They're my girls!" she interrupted with heat in her words.

Tracy leaned forward, saying, "There's the law, ma'am."

"They're my flesh and blood. They come from me and Robert," she said defiantly. "They's our children. Always will be!"

We had to avoid debating the letter of the law against Finley's belief. It would be a futile effort. "Could you tell us anything about the night your husband picked up Shawna?"

Jane Finley read her husband's note again, the sudden silence from her disturbing. Had I lost her? Or maybe she was only interested in a wordy debate, pitting her law vs. the law I'd sworn to uphold. I said nothing and watched her turning her husband's note around, flipping it end over end, and then holding it against the window with late daylight bleeding through the page. Was she looking for something? Did I miss it? She saw me watching and answered as if she'd read my mind, "Sorry, there's no secrets here."

When she smiled, I returned the gesture asking, "No hidden codes like you'd see in the movies?"

The humor helped. "Nah. My Robert had got a big heart but lacks the depth if you know what I mean."

"Face value?" I asked, thinking I knew what she was referring to.

"Yeah," she agreed with a light chuckle. "Definitely face value."

"Did you help Robert with Shawna?" I asked directly, returning to the questions. A part of me hoped she'd say no, hoped she had no idea what her husband had planned. But when her chin dipped and she closed her eyelids, I knew. I had my answer.

As I approached the last turn to the street before entering the station's parking lot, a call came over the radio. Static broke the silence, the squelch making us jump. The dispatcher called out details about a suspect in custody for the kidnapping of Shawna Jackson. Patrol had identified the truck and had it pulled to the side of the road less than a mile from where we were. In the rearview mirror, Tracy was texting, the shock of the dispatch news needing confirmation. There was relief and surprise, my feelings mixed in a strange blend. I was eager to see Shawna safe, but I also knew what that meant for her biological father and mother.

"They talking about my Shawna?" Jane Finley asked, her hand flying to her chest. "Take me to her! Please!"

Taking Jane Finley to her husband could help us get a quick confession from Robert. The blubbering kind. His being of face value and all. I didn't expect him to be the type to manipulate his way through the court system and seek an acquittal. Instead, he'd see his wife, turn blubbery, and confess it all in a gushing spill.

"Shawna?" Jane Finley said again in a shaky voice. Turning right instead of left could also give Jane an opportunity to see her daughter again. That is, before the courts got involved. If I turned left toward the station, Shawna would be back in the custody of her adopted parents by the time tonight's full moon was hanging over the Outer Banks.

I gunned the motor and spun the steering wheel to the right, jumping back onto Route 12, adrenaline pumping as it had when we'd first chased Robert's truck. "You're taking me to her?"

"Yes, ma'am," I answered, a question on Tracy's face as she held up her phone for me to see in the rearview mirror.

"Thank you," she mouthed and palmed her cheeks to swipe them dry.

"We'll be there in a few minutes," I said, catching another look from Tracy. She couldn't get confirmation. We only had what had come over the radio.

When we were less than a quarter mile from the scene, Jane hopped in her seat, breathing heavy and saying, "That's his truck!" Her fingers clutched the door's handle, ready to fly out of the car. "Shawna! Baby?!"

"Ma'am!" I shouted, slowing down to park behind a patrol car, the sun on the horizon, beaming into my car. It was bright enough to make me squint and to keep the police activities hidden in the autumn glare. When the passenger door jerked opened with a kick, I shouted again, "Ma'am!"

"Shawna!" Jane Finley shouted again and waved me off, hitting the asphalt in a run toward the flashing red and blue patrol lights. My heart shot into my throat, the officers taking guard, their hands cradling holstered firearms, and their bodies in a defensive posture.

"She's with me," I told them, following behind her, showing the police officers my badge. A wave of relief eased the tension when I saw that two of the patrols knew me from the station. In front of the first patrol car was the truck we'd chased through Corolla and onto Carova beaches. It was a Ford truck, an F-150, the color light blue like the sky at dusk. And it had the rust spots around the wheel wells that sealed the identity. "Robert Finley?"

"Back of the squad car," the patrol officer answered, fists still clenched, but perched on his utility belt by his thumbs. "Only, he didn't have any identification."

"Who is that?" Jane Finley asked in a raucous cry, a hand shielding her eyes as she tried to see inside the patrol car. "Where's Shawna!?"

"Officers? The little girl?" I asked and peered inside the truck, the stench of gasoline and burnt oil wafting into my face. I touched the hood of the truck, the motor was still hot, telling me the patrols had their own chase in this pursuit. The officers traded looks, exchanged glances that said there was no girl. "Shawna Jackson?"

"He was the only one in the truck—" one of them began.

"Who the hell is he?" Jane Finley argued.

"What do you mean?" I raced around the other side of the squad car, cupping my hands over my eyes. "Officer?" I asked, grabbing the locked door handle.

"I don't know this man!" Jane Finley said as the suspect in custody was removed from the squad car. "I've never seen him before in my life... Oh God! Where's my baby girl?"

Tracy joined me with her tablet, showing me the one picture we had on file for Robert Finley. This man's height and build were the same. His facial features like that of a relative. But he was at least fifteen years Finley's junior. "Sir, can you tell us why you were driving this car?"

"Fifty bucks," the man answered, his mannerism unswayed by the attention. "Some dude gave me a fifty and said drive the truck south."

"The dude?" I asked. "Did he have a child with him?"

"Yeah. There was a little girl with him." He chewed the side of his cheek, rolling his tongue and spat a black slick onto the pavement, the smell of mint and tobacco turning my stomach. "Wait. Could have been a boy? Hair was chopped short."

"He offered you money to drive?" I asked, seeing Jane Finley turn quiet, her concern resting as Tracy escorted her back to my car. Doubt pinched my insides. Doubt about what was real and what was an act.

"That's right," he answered, a lace of black spittle running down his chin. "Said he'd give me another fifty when I was done."

"Thank you," I said to the officers. Before returning to my car, I told them, "We'll want forensics to inspect the truck, search it top down and inside and out for evidence the missing girl was in there."

"Understood ma'am," the officer said.

"What about my other fifty bucks?" The man's voice followed. "Aww shit," his words trailed hollowly as I closed my car door and sat behind the wheel. I realized we'd been played. We'd underestimated Robert Finley. "Face value," I muttered.

"What's that?" Jane Finley asked, her breath ragged from the run.

"Your husband knew the only picture of him on file was over a decade old. He knew to pick someone who looked like him, and to send them south, away from where we'd spotted them."

"He did that?" she asked, seeming to be dumbfounded with surprise.

I turned to face her. "Yeah, he did that. And I think you knew he did that." Her cheeks remained wet but a shallow grin appeared. "Ma'am. Where are they?"

"I honestly have no idea," she answered, glancing at me and then Tracy, the seat creaking. "Truly, I don't."

"Uh-huh," I grunted. The air of distrust we'd faced shifted, the weight of it falling on my shoulders. Robert and Jane Finley knew what they were doing. I couldn't believe anything she told us.

Jane Finley buckled her seat belt and leaned back into the seat, a sigh escaping with relief. Her emotional outburst was seemingly cured, abated like she'd downed a bottle of some miracle elixir. She commented then, turning my blood hot with humiliation and anger. "Face value," she said with a sly grin. "Robert is the smartest person I know. My baby is safe."

Not another word was spoken, the drive to the station stiff with silence. I didn't know what to do with Jane Finley. Any further questioning would get us nothing. She knew how to manipulate her answers in a way that would cause us to waste valuable time.

She didn't openly tell us she was involved in Shawna's kidnapping, but she also didn't deny it when asked. Suspicion of kidnapping was the first charge I could file against her. Obstruction of justice was the second. The evidence was thin and a court-appointed counsel could argue against them. For now, there would be enough to keep her at the station a day while the process played out. If I was lucky, we'd have her for two days.

By the time we'd reached the station, it had begun to empty. As the wall clock passed the five o'clock hour, the station played a medley of laptop bags being packed, the swishing of autumn jackets, zippers in motion, chair wheels crawling, and a steady banter filled with *goodbyes* and *see ya tomorrow*. If not for Jane Finley, my feet would be moving to join the exodus, but as it was, my evening hours would be filled with paperwork to secure her custody. Wherever Shawna Jackson was this evening, I hoped she was safe. I only needed to look into her mother's face to know that she was.

EIGHTEEN

The morning was brisk, a cold wind whistling through the evergreen trees edging the municipal building property. A gust carrying a reminder of the coming winter had me wrap my jacket tight around my front as clouds parted over the ocean. There was a beam of sunlight crawling across the empty roads and sidewalks, but it wouldn't be enough to warm me. Sunlight struck the bushes in front of the entrance and stirred wild birds who stretched their wings and took flight when I reached the steps.

I surveyed the parking lot as I sometimes do, and found Dr. Swales's car, thinking she must have arrived well before the clouds broke in the east. That's the way she liked to work—earlier than the day, and mostly alone. But this morning, there was another car parked next to hers, the front bumper with a personalized license plate that read, *SAMMI*. It was her medical assistant, an examiner in training, and Dr. Swales's niece. *Early birds*. It must run in the family. Samantha being here this early also told me that Dr. Swales was pushing her training.

In the room outside the morgue, I found an empty locker to

hold my jacket and bag. I thought twice about wearing my jacket with its cozy fleece lining, my gaze shifting to the thick resin doors where Laura Jackson's body had been opened and searched. The morgue was a refrigerator, and I'd never understand how Dr. Swales could work in those conditions all day, sometimes into the night. I kept my jacket on, slipping a gigantic lab coat over it and rolling the sleeves back until my fingers were freed.

"Morning guys," I said, shoving the heavy doors, the frigid air hitting me like a slap. Samantha gave a wave, her usual dress changed for today though her goth look of pale makeup and black hair was the same. She wore a new length lab coat, her name embroidered in blue, a pair of purple non-latex exam gloves. On her feet, she'd traded in her usual heavy-heeled Doc Martens for a pair of Crocs the same color as her gloves. To me, she was a mini version of Dr. Swales. In her hand, she held a scalpel, her arm perched above the open cavity of a body. Their examination was for a male in his seventies, his torso round like a melon and with legs skinny like stilts. If not for the lack of wearing masks, I would have thought the two were performing surgery. "You guys have a new case?"

Dr. Swales was dressed the same as Samantha, save for the pair of Crocs, which were mint green, and a step stool beneath her feet. She tilted her head back, her eyes giant behind her thick glasses. "Aren't you a sight this time of day?"

"What?" I asked, holding my wrist up to show them my watch. "Compared to the rest of the human race, I'm convinced you guys must be cut from a different cloth... getting up before the butt-crack of dawn."

"Yeah, yeah," Swales chided. "And yes, this is a new case."

"Morning, Casey," Samantha said with a smile as she lifted onto her toes. Swales narrowed a look and tilted her head, Samantha acknowledging. "Sorry. Detective White."

"Casey is fine," I told her, but secretly liked the reverence.

Maybe in another dozen years I'll keep the formality. I ventured closer, darting a look at the man's insides, his chest parted into two, giant flaps peeled to the sides, his ribs separated by a spreader, his lungs and heart and everything else showing. From the way Swales was studying his organs, I asked, "Find anything unusual?"

"Well, as a matter of fact, we did," she answered and looked up at me. "Care to venture what it is?"

I hadn't even had a second cup of coffee yet. I dared a few more steps, exploring the sight of it all, identifying each of the organs I recognized while searching for knife wounds or injuries from bullet shrapnel, but finding none. "There's no physical injuries to see."

With the end of her pen, she tapped the heart muscle, saying, "Heart attack is the likely cause of death, but we won't know until taking a closer look at the muscle and coronary arteries."

"Not a homicide. A heart attack?" I asked. "What am I looking for?"

"You'll probably never see this again." Her brow bounced above her eyes, her smile contagious. "I haven't seen one of these either. It is very cool."

"Very cool," Samantha repeated.

"Shall we offer a hint?" Swales asked Samantha, the two playing.

"Sure," she answered and looked at me. "Think mirror."

That's when I saw where the liver was but should not have been. "No way! Are his organs flipped?"

"Bingo," Swales said. "It's called Situs Inversus. A congenital condition where his organs are reversed from their normal positions."

"Complications from it?" I asked, wondering if the heart attack was preventable.

"That's a tough one to call," she answered, eyeing the microphone above the body, taking care in what she said. "Leads on the electrocardiographic for the tracings would have needed to be reversed for accuracy. But given what I suspect was a considerable blockage, it would not have made a difference."

"That's still an interesting case," I said, searching behind them, my gaze falling to the refrigerated drawers lining the far wall. In one of them was Laura Jackson's body and the reason I was here. "Can we review the Jackson case findings?"

"Now would be a good time for a break," Swales said as she flicked off the microphone's recording and began to ease herself down from the step stool. "Sammi, be a dear and give me a hand."

With the overhead lights beaming onto Swales and her niece, I saw how small the doctor had become, saw her moving slower, her body seeming frail. She had talked about retirement the first day I met her—Jericho laughing it off, the two joking that the day would never come. Since then, she'd brought it up enough times that it had become a point of humor we'd shrug off as nonsense, that it was just a thought for a future that would never be. But seeing Samantha do more for Swales with each of my visits, I wondered if Swales understood time better than us all, that she knew it was short, that she was already seeing life from a distance even though she remained a giant in our lives.

"Let me help," I said with a feeling of high regard and with a sadness for an outcome that was unavoidable. I held her hand as Samantha propped her arm, our guiding Swales down from the step stool. A thread of color rose on her face as she fixed a look that said everything I saw. This morning she made no comments or jokes about retirement. I nudged toward the drawers instead, the cold storage where Laura Jackson's body waited for us. "Shall we?"

"We shall," she said as Samantha grabbed the step stool and put a cane in Swales's hand. It had four short legs and creamy white rubber feet, Swales lifting it to show me and saying, "I've got my new *hurry cane*, I bet I can race you there."

Samantha hurried alongside of us, her Crocs making the same kissing noises as Swales's. "We just picked it up after we noticed—"

"What Samantha is saying is that I've got a bum knee is all." Swales cocked her head, giving the drawers a hard look. "You'll see, I'll be right as rain again soon enough."

"I'm sure you will," I commented, passing a look to Samantha, an understanding. I opened the drawer's door, frigid condensation swirling with the commotion. The bottoms of Laura Jackson's feet showed through the white vapor, a manilla toe-tag hanging from one of them.

Swales stood at the end as if greeting the victim, the drawer extending with a screech while Samantha put the step stool in place. "Up we go," Samantha said as we helped Swales take her place on one side while I went to the other.

"Thank you, dear," Swales said and braced the body tray. "This one was quite the find too."

"Quite the find?" I asked, pulling the evidence sheet back, the white cover thin like bed linen. Beneath it, we revealed the autopsy results, the sight of Laura's body taking my breath. I'd never get used to seeing death, especially when it was a child who'd barely scratched the surface of their life. "How so?"

"Two significant finds, I should say," Swales answered, taking Laura's right hand in hers. "First there's this."

As she rubbed her fingers over the tips of the fingernails, I asked, "You found something beneath her nails?"

"Tissue. Our girl here may have scratched her killer."

"I'm shocked it survived the time in the ocean." But I was relieved. Under-nail tissue samples have led to breaks in so many cases.

Swales made a fist. "This child's fingers may have been closed in a fist, a defensive posture at the time of her death.

With fists frozen in the moment, she'd unknowingly preserved the tissue."

Laura had fought to her death. "You secured some DNA from it?"

She wagged a finger in the air, answering, "I have already sent it to the lab and am hopeful for usable DNA results."

"That's a huge find," I said, my gaze fixed on Laura's face.

"And the next! Some light, Samantha?" Swales asked, Samantha coming to stand next to her and shining a light around the injuries to Laura's neck. Baseball stitches closed an incision that had been made from her naval up to the top of her chest, its course branching to the place between her neck and shoulder. That was another sight tough to see, the size of each stitch, making it appear as though her young body had been opened and searched brutally. But I know it was done with care and concern and with an incessant need to find the truth. Samantha shifted the light, its shine landing on Swales's fingers to show the deep purple and black patches where strangulation had been evidenced as the cause of death. "This child suffered a broken neck."

"Broken? There was enough force?" I asked with surprise. Human bone wasn't easily broken. I'd read once that ounce for ounce, bone was stronger than steel and could withstand tremendous force, which led me to believe Laura's death came in a terribly violent act. "Would a wave have caused such a break post-mortem?"

Swales shook her head and sounded a soft grunt. "While the waters were rough with a storm forecasted, this child was alive when the fracture occurred," she answered, and used Samantha as a test, pointing out an area in the middle of the neck. "It's the victim's C7 cervical vertebrae where we found the hairline fracture."

Swales moved her hand to Laura's chest, continuing, "There was no seawater in her stomach or lungs. When she was put in the ocean, she was already dead." She moved her hand to the neck and the injuries, adding, "With the injury to C7, there was swelling in the surrounding tissue, as well as the spinal cord."

"And if she was already dead, there would be no swelling," I said, understanding Laura's broken neck must have occurred before death. "You mentioned spinal cord. Did the injury paralyze her?"

"C7 is further down the cervical region, which would have spared her loss of her arms and hands." Swales gripped the body tray to move, Samantha coming to her aid, their language unspoken but understood. Swales let out a sigh, answering, "As for the child's lower extremities, there may have been a lasting injury."

"The force to break bone," I said with disbelief. "We would have to be looking for a man of substantial size and strength?"

"Perhaps," Swales answered, and then showed a coy smile. "Or perhaps not."

As if on cue, Samantha handed me a large envelope that I recognized as containing X-ray images. I pulled one of the sheets, thick with weight between my fingers. When I held it up to the ceiling's lights, the white and gray image distorted by the bend in the film, I asked, "What am I looking for?"

"Her bones are porous," Swales answered as she frowned at the ceiling. "There's probably not enough light for you to see it. But what we found was that your victim suffered from juvenile osteoporosis."

I recognized the name, having a grandmother who'd begun to suffer from it early in her life. By the time she'd reached seventy, her shoulders were slumped terribly, and she'd broken her hip twice. "You mean that her bones were weak?"

Swales nodded to me and ran her hand down Laura's left arm, leading me to guess, "And you found an old fracture?"

"More than one," she answered, placing Laura's hand in

hers. "From the count of them, the child has had osteoporosis since before puberty."

She held another X-ray up to the ceiling light to show Laura's spine, the view from the side. In it, I could see her chest was sunken and her spine had formed a small hump. "Like an old woman," I commented.

"Hey now," Swales chirped, a smirk showing briefly. It disappeared when she agreed, "But yes. It's a terrible condition at such a young age."

I thought of the urgent care visits and the number of days missed in school, the comments made by Barbara Newman. "Abuse of a child would exacerbate the condition?"

"Absolutely," Swales answered, leaning back, abhorred by the idea. "Do you believe some of these injuries are the result of abuse?"

I shook my head, unsure, doubt rising as two leads became clear when I only wanted one. What of the earlier notion that Laura Jackson had fallen victim to the same killer as the Greenville victim? What of Barbara Newman's words? Was Laura Jackson the victim of abuse in her home? I stared at the gray images, Laura's bones in the X-ray soft and less opaque than they should have been. "There are fractures, some of them old, but how did they happen?"

"The child suffered from osteoporosis, but how these injuries occurred is impossible to assess without an eyewitness," Swales answered with understanding.

"There is no way for us to know without more evidence." I handed her the X-ray, saying with emphasis, "But if Laura Jackson was in a house of abuse, her years there were filled with torture."

NINETEEN

A gust lifted my hair with the sunlight warming my face, the winds pushing the Atlantic Ocean to meet the Oregon Inlet Channel. The sun sat at high noon to dry the wet autumn day, warming the air and chasing away the morning's winter warnings. Our afternoon would be spent south of the station at the Oregon Inlet's fishing center, home to one of the largest charter fleets on the east coast. It was also home to the offshore charter boat owned by Carla and Frank Jackson. When I closed my eyes, I saw the fractures. I saw where the porous bones had mended, Laura Jackson's X-rays showing like burned afterimages in my eyes.

We had two strong leads, and with Dr. Swales's findings, I was able to obtain a search warrant, a judge signing without hesitation and giving me the authority to search the fishing boat. Though I'd learned a lot since moving to the Outer Banks, I'd need an expert to guide me and Tracy on the specifics of where to look. Jericho's status in the Marine Patrol provided enough justification for me to suggest his help. Within the hour, the upper ranks between departments worked the logistics and reassigned his time for the afternoon. He didn't mind, his whiskered face showing a faint smile when he got the call. He knew boats. Specifically, he knew everything and every kind of fishing boat there was that had come and gone from the Outer Banks.

With Tracy behind us and the smell of fish wafting strong, we walked the boards of a long dock, all of the slips full with fishing charters, their transoms sporting names like *Fishing Frenzy*, *Miss Oregon Inlet*, and a particular favorite, *Fintastic Fun*. I couldn't help but smile at the play on some of the names, Tracy reading them off as we searched for the Jacksons' charter boat.

"Jericho, sir, how are you?" I heard behind us, the voice a throaty scratch, a weaker version than I'd remembered. We turned to face old man Peterson, a crab fisherman I'd met when I first arrived in the Outer Banks. He'd also been a witness in my first case and who Jericho worked with for a brief spell. Tall and lean, he was no longer dressed in the sea-smelling coveralls I'd remembered. And the wiry sprout of gray hairs crawling from beneath a shabby fisherman's cap was also gone. Instead, Peterson was dressed in denim and a dress shirt with brown jacket, his hair neatly combed behind his ears. And glasses. He was wearing glasses and carrying a computer tablet. If not for the voice and his toothless whistle, I would have struggled to recognize him. "And Detective Casey White! How very nice to see you again."

"Mr. Peterson," I said, Jericho answering as well. I shook the man's hand, his touch tender and soft, a far cry from the calloused skin he'd worn in the past, his career as a crab fisherman in his touch. He was a businessman today and from the looks of the name plate and title on his shirt, we had business with him. "You work here now?"

Jericho saw the same, asking, "Have you finally left the sea, old man?" The two held one another in a brief hug, having shared years in and out of one another's lives. Jericho stepped back, adding, "I have to say, you look ten years younger."

Peterson clubbed his chest in a show of vitality, answering, "I feel it too. I finally sold that clunker crabbing boat." He showed his legs and shoes, his attire meant for land. "Traded in my uniform and filly days managing the inlet's business."

"I'm happy for you," Jericho said, shaking Peterson's hands again.

Peterson tipped a hat that wasn't there, bouncing on his heels, his attention steered toward Tracy, his asking, "And who is this beautiful lass?" At once Tracy smiled, her dimples flashed with color on her cheeks. He returned her smile, adding, "What a charming smile."

He hadn't seen mine or Tracy's faces in the news, the story of our reunion reigning in all the newspaper headlines. It was a relief too. It was nice to feel normal, even if it was only for the moment. "Tracy Fields, sir," she said, smile broadening as delight gleamed from her eyes. She offered her hand, and I could see she was enjoying this.

"Ma'am, it is my pleasure to meet you," he said. I almost laughed aloud when Peterson approached Tracy as he had with me the first time we met. He lowered himself gracefully, presenting himself like an old-world gentleman to accept her hand and greet her.

When he turned back to face me, she looked at me and mouthed, "So polite."

He tapped the name plate on his shirt, and eyed the badge slung from my neck, asking, "Now, how can I help you on this fine afternoon?"

I handed him the search warrant, the printed version we were required to have in hand and present when accessing a property as part of an investigation. "Could you direct us to Carla and Frank Jacksons' charter boat?"

"The Jacksons' boat?" he said, asking. He tucked his tablet beneath one arm and opened the warrant, squinting as he moved his eyeglasses up and down. "Damn progressive lenses—"

As he spoke, reading back what was printed on the paper, I saw the Jacksons, the couple dressed in bright orange coveralls and jackets. She carried a yellow nylon rope, looping it from elbow to the crook of her palm, raveling it for stowing. Mr. Jackson held a fishing rod, putting a wrench to the reel, the metal a shiny bright chrome color. I turned back to face the parking lot, the pier empty except for the folks tending to their livelihood. But an urgency had me thinking the Jacksons were going to sea, they were readying their boat for a charter, or possibly going alone.

I nudged Jericho's arm, his lowering a pair of sunglasses from the brim of his hat. "That's them?" he asked, shifting to face them, his posture instinctively blocking passage.

"Carla and Frank," I answered, while Tracy turned to see them too. I interrupted the old crab fisherman's reading, saying, "Mr. Peterson, we've found them."

Peterson lifted his head to look, nodding in agreement. "Yes. That you have." He handed the warrant back to me. "I believe our business is done?"

"Not quite," I said, tapping his tablet. "Do you have a record of the charters?"

"Certainly," he answered, opening the cover, his finger hovering over the top of the screen as he hunted for the letters and numbers that made up his passcode. I glanced back to see the Jacksons still on the pier. A family of four approached us to wait for Peterson. Jericho had explained the popularity of the autumn fishing and whale-watching charters. When the tablet's screen shook, Peterson grunted and started again. Tracy's eyes rolled with an impatience I could feel. He got it on the second attempt, showing a calendar, and asking, "What's the date and time... actually, go ahead and enter it."

He handed me the tablet, fingers knobbed and bent. I

entered the date without a time, the calendar focusing on when Laura and Shawna Jackson had gone to the Friday evening carnival. The page showed a listing of boat names like the ones around us. "I'm looking for the Jacksons' boat, on an evening charter."

Peterson took the tablet, swiping up, saying with a whistle, "Lemme see, that'd be the *Miss Myrtle*."

A motor started, the vibrations felt in my feet as smoke rose above the fleet. But in the long line of boats, I couldn't tell if it was them or not. Frank Peterson was gone from sight, Jericho saying, "Casey, they might be gearing up to leave the inlet."

"Stop them," I said, handing Tracy the warrant and nudged Jericho's arm again. Tracy understood, the two of them leaving me behind with Peterson. "Sir, the *Miss Myrtle*? Was it here that evening?"

He shook his head, mouth turned down, "Got records here that they fueled for an evening charter."

"Were you witness to the *Miss Myrtle* not being here?" I asked, needing confirmation.

He closed the tablet's cover. "Sorry to say, I only work the day shift and evening charters don't require staff."

From over my shoulder, I saw Frank Jackson appear, standing on the rear of the *Miss Myrtle* as Tracy handed him the search warrant. Carla Jackson appeared next to her husband, the two beginning to argue with Tracy, arms waving as Jericho took to stepping in front of Tracy. I braced old man Peterson's arm, thanking him for the help. "Sir, I have to leave."

"Contact the party who made the reservation for the charter," I heard Peterson say, his voice following. "They'll confirm if they'd gone fishing on the *Miss Myrtle* that night. Probably got pictures of their catch too."

As Frank and Carla Jackson argued, they had one opportunity to clear themselves as suspects. They needed to let us on

their boat and show proof they'd gone out to sea the evening
Laura was murdered.

"Mr. and Mrs. Jackson," I said, rushing over the boards, feet
clopping against the wood, ringing hollow as the couple looked
on with distress. When I reached them, they were shaking their
faces, arguing about the warrant. "Mr. and Mrs. Jackson, with
this warrant, we must ask that you exit your boat to allow us to
execute it."

"There's a charter coming in the next hour," Mr. Jackson
said, the idea they'd be working today struck me as curious
given the circumstances. He must have seen me flinch or something, and added, "It's been scheduled the last month."

"You'll have to cancel," Jericho told them and boarded the
fishing boat, passing Mrs. Jackson whose face shook with objection. "We will be here for at least the afternoon."

"Frank, I'll make the call," Mrs. Jackson said, her voice a
plea as she went to his side. "They're trying to help."

He bowed his head to rest on her shoulder, the sight of them
tugging on a string of sympathy. I had no way to know if they
were being truthful in anything they said, which is why I'm
driven to investigate everything to the best of my ability. "Sir,
you said this afternoon's charter was already booked?"

Mr. Jackson lifted his head as I boarded the rear of their
fishing boat, the deck wet and slippery. The sun showed his face
and the dark circles beneath red-rimmed eyes, the days wearing
on him. "That's right."

Tracy went to them, her phone in hand, ready to take notes.
"We'll need you to share with my associate the contact information for the charter last Friday evening."

"Yes, we can do that," Mrs. Jackson answered without
taking a breath. She eyed my progress as I made my way to
the front and two patrol officers joined us, along with Jericho's Marine Patrol partner, Tony. By now there were
gawkers and rubberneckers, the fleet of boats with their lower

and upper decks filling with bodies to see what was going on with the Jacksons' boat. Mrs. Jackson noticed it and turned facing us, shielding her and her husband, the earlier sympathy for them returning. "What... what do we do in the meantime?"

"We'll execute this as fast as possible, and please work with Tracy as she collects the additional information," I answered, disappearing inside the wheelhouse where Jericho had gone. He stood over the console, hands gloved in blue, the instrumentation older than I would have expected to see. I only had Jericho's Marine Patrol boats to compare, and asked, "GPS data?"

"That's what I'm searching for," he answered without looking up. With his index finger he tapped a Garmin unit, pressing the gray buttons up and down over a list of dates.

"There," I said, pointing to Friday evening. He selected the date, the navigation screen showing a map of the Oregon Inlet's docks, the route they'd traveled appearing as a dark blue line but clipped at the screen's edges. "Can you zoom out?"

"Sure thing," Jericho answered, running his fingers along the side. "There's a compartment door here. Probably the SD card."

"We might have to take it with us."

Jericho let out a breath, opening a drawer, the inside filled with everything from scissors to packs of hooks, and even a bundle of rubber bands. "I don't see a spare. They'll need one."

I sensed he didn't want to leave the Jacksons without navigation, but this was an open investigation. From my backpack I opened my laptop, saying, "I only need Friday's data. I can make a copy."

"You know how to do that?" he asked, a look of surprise, one brow raised.

I gave his shoulder a soft punch, "I can work around this stuff." Jericho ran through the unit's menus, selecting Manage Data and Data Transfer to create a file export for me. "I've picked up a few things. I even have an app to view any waypoints, routes and tracks saved."

"Listen to you," he said as he retrieved the SD card. "I'm quite impressed."

"Well thank you," I said, inserting the card into the side of my laptop. I found the newly exported file and copied it to my local drive, returning the card. As Jericho finished with the boat's navigation unit, I opened the viewer to show the map and trail, the waypoints showing like breadcrumbs, the Jacksons dropping one every couple miles. When I zoomed out, we saw that the boat had driven north, reaching the shores near Bodie Lighthouse and not far from where Laura Jackson's body was discovered. "Jericho, look at this!"

"That's where we discovered the victim," he said as sounds of drawers opened and closed, the patrol officers working outside the wheelhouse, the windows open. Jericho shook his head, saying, "With the tide and currents, the victim's body could have come from a number of places. And it may just be a coincidence they were in that same area."

"I suppose that could be true," I said, tightening my lips, not wanting to give up on the idea.

"I think I know what they were doing," he said, clasping his hands, the frown gone. "The water was still warm for this time of year. It could be they were catching baitfish."

"Baitfish?" I asked, voice rising, my experience limited to having fished with a bobber and worm when I was a kid. I took Jericho by the hand and walked to the opening, poking my head out and asking, "Mrs. Jackson, Friday night's charter, what were you fishing for?"

She let out a raspy cough to clear her throat. "Mostly night-time blues, but also fished for yellowfin tunas too."

"And the bait you used?" I asked.

Without hesitation, Mr. Jackson answered, "Some poppers for a topwater bite, but we also fished for baitfish. Had luck on the light tackle and rigged what we caught, some live herrings and mackerel to help pick up a tuna bite."

Jericho went back to the wheelhouse's console where he opened the drawer and showed the bundle of rubber bands I'd seen earlier. He came back to my side, asking, "What type of sinkers did you use?" With his years in the Outer Banks and an officer in the Marine Patrol, Jericho was familiar with the variety of baitfish and game fishing rigs. If the Jacksons were lying, we'd hear it.

"Torpedo," Mr. Jackson answered with a confused look. "We use a rubber band just above the knot with the fluoro-carbon and braided line."

"Thank you," Jericho said, leading me back to the console and my laptop. "I believe they were in that area to pick up some baitfish for the fishing charter. With the warmer waters, they had a better chance in shallower waters."

"I didn't know that you knew so much about fishing," I said, scrolling to the next set of waypoints, the charter traveling due east. Half joking, I added, "You never offered to take me fishing."

"Living on an island, I've learned a few things," he answered, a squint forming. "You'd go fishing?"

I half-smiled, but then shook my head. When I saw the disappointment, I told him, "But I'd go to be with you."

"That'd work," Jericho said, his focus returning to the screen, the Jacksons' boat having gone north to pass Bodie Lighthouse and then east away from the shore. When another waypoint showed more than a couple miles from shore, Jericho said, "Casey, I think they *were* fishing like they've said. Look at the times."

Around the points furthest east, there was a trail that made ragged circles, a series of straight lines, and then another spiral. "What were they doing there?"

"That's a drift there, which was probably them fishing for

tuna," he said, using his index finger to trace a path. "But then they anchored here where they spent two hours. I'd say that was a school of blues they fished for."

"That's typical?" I asked, not knowing anything about the sport.

Jericho cocked his head while scratching his chin. He offered a shrug, answering, "Tuna finishing would be what you'd go out for. But if there isn't a tuna bite and you want to give your customers something to remember—"

"You'd change gear and bait and then fish for blues which were biting," I said, interrupting and hoping I was right.

"Exactly," he agreed.

Tracy entered the wheelhouse, Jericho's partner following. "We found something," she said, motioning for the two of us to follow. I closed and packed my laptop, a copy of the SD card's memory stored safely. "There's an anchor line missing."

"Missing?" I asked, leaving the wheelhouse, guarding my eyes from the sun. Jericho's partner, Tony, stood at the transom, holding the frayed end of an anchor line. When I saw it, I asked, "How do you know that's for the anchor?"

He tipped the edge of a five-gallon bucket, the side of it showing the brand of a paint, the color named autumn sunrise. Written in bold, black marker, the word *Anchor*. Inside the bucket there was a coil of the white double-braided nylon rope a half an inch thick. When Mr. Jackson saw us inspecting the bucket, he stood up and said, "Lost our anchor to the prop. It's gonna cost me a couple hundred dollars to replace it."

Jericho inspected the rope, the frayed end, the edges tattered, Tony saying, "Line was cut."

"To free it from the propeller," Jericho said. He went to the edge of the transom, looking over it briefly and then looked to the Jacksons. "You cleared the rest of it?"

"Course we did," Mrs. Jackson answered in a gruff tone,

Jericho's question offending her. "We wouldn't dare go out if the wheel was compromised."

"Understood," Jericho said as Mr. Jackson pointed to a bag next to the anchor bucket. Jericho picked it up to show a tangle of rope, the ends shredded. "This checks out."

We worked to inspect the boat for the next three hours, losing the daylight as fast as the Jacksons lost their patience. By the time the sun was on the lip of the horizon and cast the Oregon Inlet in a rich buttery light, we'd bagged and tagged enough hair fibers and fingerprints to keep a small lab busy for the next three days. But even if we'd found evidence of Laura having been onboard, would it be enough to tell us what happened? We needed to contact the person who'd reserved a fishing charter on the Jacksons' boat. Only their statement would be enough to give Frank and Carla Jackson an alibi and clear their names.

TWENTY

She could have stayed another three hours. The carnival rides. The loud music. The games like Bottle Stand and Bucket Ball, and the Balloons and Darts. There were the foods too. So many. Funnel cakes, fried pickles and corn dogs on a stick. Had she ever tasted such delights? The carnival had a rhythm that ran through her. It had a beat she danced to. And it had a vibe that told her to never leave. It was intoxicating.

There were her friends too. It seemed as if everyone from Cynthia Harriet's school had come tonight. Even some of her teachers joined in the fun. She knew it would be all anyone would talk about the rest of the week. What stories they'd tell. With the thought came the ache of disappointment. She'd made a promise after all. Or had she been forced to make a promise? Isn't that what they did? Force her. While everyone would stay until the carnival closed, Cynthia had to be home early.

With disappointment, she eyed the entrance with the towering red and white striped canvas pillars. Dried straw crunched beneath Cynthia's white sneakers, the crowd parting as she walked against the grain of people arriving. The cars parked in the field bordered the woods, her house less than half a mile on the other side. Flavors of hot popcorn and melted caramel whirled on a breeze when she passed the confection stand one last time. It gave her thoughts of buying a bag to bring home, but she was already late, and the line wrapped around the other side.

Screams rose into the colorful night. A chorus filled with delightful shouts came from the Tilt-a-Whirl, a favorite ride of hers. She had to stop and watch, just for a minute before leaving. A blur of faces flew around and around, the bright pink and green cars passing and buffeting air with a whoosh. She saw them then. Saw Chet and Janet cozied together in one of the seats. That should've been her sitting next to him. The sight made her stomach roll with disappointment. He was the one who'd asked if she was coming tonight.

Cynthia's phone buzzed with a reminder for her to come home. It was the twins' birthday party. They were only three and too young to bring to the carnival. Why did they need her? It wasn't like the twins would remember tonight. Annoyed, Cynthia pegged the ground with the tip of her shoe. She was only a part-time daughter in her father's new family. What did she matter to them anyway?

Cynthia closed her eyelids and felt the carnival wrap around her with a tight hug that didn't want to let go. Maybe she could come back tomorrow. They'd probably be here through the weekend. Her phone buzzed again, the vibration rising from her fingers into her arm. She dared to look at the screen, a text from her father pressing, telling her the cake was ready with candles. Maybe she could come back afterward? She didn't mind paying the admission twice.

"But they'd want me to stay home," she muttered with a frown. Cynthia pressed on, walking by the funhouse next with the ruby-colored flags flapping loud enough to be heard. The house was tall and black and white with strobe lights filling the windows. In the middle, there was a circle as big as cathedral doors, the entrance forming a round mouth, its insides striped like a barber pole. The colors were a dizzying red and yellow as it spun slowly, a pair of kids tumbled comically, the mouth tricking their balance as they entered. She felt the urge to laugh but wanted to stay mad at her father and his new wife.

That's when she saw him. He had green hair that sprouted tall in a poof and wore a face that was masked in clown-white makeup. There were gigantic rubber shoes on his feet, painted red and blue and gold. He wore pants that bellowed around a hooped waist. And jutting from beneath his chin was an over-sized ruffled red collar. Cynthia was certain the clown standing on the platform in the front of the funhouse had taken notice of her, staring with intensity as she walked by. He waved a purple hanky as children frolicked and yelled gleefully around him. When she didn't respond, he mimed a frowning face and mimicked tears running down his cheeks. The sight of him lightened her mood.

The clown's hands were gloved in white. When she stopped, he made like he was painting a smile, and then encouraged her to do the same. It was enough to break the sour mood, even if for a moment. She returned his smile, but moved along, the time growing late. If she missed the cake, they might not let her out tomorrow either. Cynthia picked up the pace as she walked across the hay that covered the parking lot. She stopped once more at the edge of the woods separating her house from the carnival. It was where the older kids liked to drink and smoke funny cigarettes. But she'd seen most of them on the rides or playing games to win stuffed animals. She'd be alone, and that was okay.

The woods came with a damp chill and put goose bumps on her arms. The carnival lights, the stars, and even the light of the moon was hidden by the trees. They smelled like a new school year, like the autumn months before the winter came. A short gust swayed the treetops and scattered leaves. One dropped onto her shoulder. She blew it a kiss and watched it fall to the ground.

Water trickled over rocks in a nearby creek, the path to her home running next to it. Even in the gray light, she followed the sound. It led to a stout bridge, the gate to her backyard on the other side. She was alone and the woods were much darker than earlier. The idea of returning to the carnival felt distant now. The crack of a branch made her jump, but she dismissed it as being a raccoon or a squirrel perhaps. There were the distant carnival screams too, and the playful yelling. But then another branch broke. And another.

"Who's there!?" she asked, spinning around and making fists. Leaves rustling, she thought that maybe it was the older kids. She could only hope.

"Leaving so soon?" a voice asked, the words ending in a childish giggle. In the muted light, she saw the carnival clown appear from behind a tree. He stepped onto the dirt path, and in the dark of the woods, his colorful outfit was like a black-and-white photograph.

Alarmed by the sight of him, Cynthia asked, "What? Did you... did you follow me here?" In her head she tried to reason with his being in the woods. She wasn't far from the parking lot, and it could be that his was one of the trailers she walked by.

"Did you like our carnival?" he asked, his hands behind his back. He stepped closer, watching his feet around a pile of stones. When he stepped into a band of moonlight, she saw the makeup was cracking dry on his face. "I, I just noticed you leaving so soon."

"Yeah. I mean of course I loved it," she said, peering over his shoulder to see if they were alone. She turned back in the direction of her home, saying, "I live right there and have to go home now."

He put on a sad face, accentuating the look. "I'm taking my break, but how about a trick before you go?" he asked. His large feet inched closer. One gloved hand appeared, pinching the air. "I promise. It'll be a very small trick."

"Can it be fast?" she asked.

"Fast, of course," he answered and continued to inch forward. "Now watch."

Cynthia would entertain his plea, but only another minute, the bridge to her yard not far from them. His other hand appeared. He flailed his fingers in the air like a magician, a half dozen playing cards appearing one at a time. "Pretty good," she complimented, her tone polite, the trick not impressive.

Hearing she was unimpressed, he appealed, "But I'm not done." With his words, each card vanished from between his fingers. They disappeared as he made wet kissing sounds, the sleight of hand making it seem like real magic. When he was finished, his eyes widened and he asked, "How was that?"

"Wow," Cynthia told the clown, clapping her hands. She searched the ground around them and noticed the tips of his enormous shoes nearly touching her sneakers. "Where'd they go?"

When she looked up, he produced a string of colorful hankies, an impossible number of them appearing from between his closed fingers. "Let's find out," he said, his jocular smile turning cold.

"Okay," she said hesitantly, standing still and not wanting to be rude as he reached behind her ear. Cynthia had seen this trick before. In a moment, he was going to flick one of the playing cards from out of the thin air. But that wasn't his trick at all. Before she knew what he was doing, before the primal urge to run overcame her, the string of colored handkerchiefs was around her neck. And in a flash, the clown had her spun around as he tightened it hard enough to cut into her skin. He wrenched his arms and hoisted her body into the air.

"This is my trick," he huffed into her hear, his voice hideous. "It's to make you disappear."

TWENTY-ONE

The text message reached my phone around six in the morning, waking me enough to stare into blackness and follow the faint outline of a shadow crawling across the bedroom ceiling. Little did I know, the text would set the course for the entire day. Jericho stirred and mumbled a sleepy comment about leftovers for dinner and scrounging whatever was in the refrigerator. He usually slept deep and was probably still dreaming. With the upcoming daylight-saving time, the clocks wouldn't roll back for another week, leaving the outside like midnight and without a shred of light. The apartment was still, the winds calm. In the distance, there was the faint crash of ocean waves breaking. I rolled over to steal another minute, flipping my pillow over to the cold side to rest my head, jerking the comforter over my bare shoulder and draping a leg across Jericho's body.

I lifted my head with the chime coming from a second text, the clock showing fifteen minutes had gone by in what felt like seconds. I must have dozed, finding Jericho had turned onto his side, my leg wrapped around him. I kissed the back of his head as I dared to exit the warmth of our blankets, the cold disappearing when I saw the words on my phone. It was a text from

Emanuel Wilson, a detective who'd worked for me until recently. He'd been promoted to lead detective and moved his family to the mainland for his new job at a station in Elizabeth City. His text read:

Casey, teen girl murdered. I could use your help.

I hadn't spoken to him in weeks and grabbed my phone, the charging cable tightening and nearly yanking it out of my hands. I texted back with concern:

Are you okay?

Three dots bounced on my screen as he typed a reply. They stopped and dropped from sight, making me think wildly that something had gone wrong in Emanuel's first solo investigation. The dots reappeared, bouncing again, the text appearing:

I saw the case you're working. I also saw the Greenville carnival case. I think this is the same.

In an instant, my concerns swung from the emotions I held for Emanuel to Laura Jackson's case. From the search yesterday aboard Frank and Carla Jackson's fishing boat, we'd only walked away with a few evidence bags—hair fibers and fingerprints, the Jacksons insisting their girls were often on the boat. I believed them. I believed any of the evidence recovered would show the same. Another victim though. A third body. I was wide awake now, my fingers moving fast as I texted him back:

Was the victim strangled?

The three dots bounced again, his texting a reply:

That's what it looks like.

Text me the location, I replied, swiping the screen to send Tracy a separate message.

Tracy, field trip, I'll be there in 20 minutes!

I wasn't familiar with the area of Elizabeth City, but thankful the daylight was on us by the time we reached the crime scene. A small housing development with buildings that were both modern and upscale, and standing two- and three-stories tall with manicured lawns and expensive cars in the driveway. I parked at the address Emanuel sent, the home of the victim. Tracy grabbed her kit while I moved my badge around to the front of my chest as we exited the car. The street was already lined with patrol vehicles, red and blue lights swirling, reflections flashing in windowpanes where neighbors were huddled together on front porches and patios. This looked to be a quiet residential street, leaving me to think domestic violence behind the crime perhaps, Emanuel getting nervous and wanting some backup. But as I took a cursory look at the neighbors and their homes, I was reminded from past cases that looks can be deceiving.

The air was brisk, the smell of autumn strong with leaves rustling with each gusty breeze. I took hold of a crime-scene kit, slinging the bag over my shoulder as Emanuel appeared from the side of the house. Tracy smiled and waved. Emanuel returned the gesture but his expression stayed dead still. His frame was as broad as he was tall, towering over the patrol officers like the trees lining the rear of the houses. He'd been a basketball star in a previous life but had retired from it at a young age and decided to go into law enforcement after the murder of a close relative. A junior detective to my senior the last couple years, Emanuel earned his place as a lead detective. And already, I could see the wear of the job, the corners of his eyes and across his forehead lined with worry, and a splash of ash-colored grays accenting his hair.

I took hold of his arm with an affectionate squeeze, saying, "I'd hug you, but not sure how your team would react."

Tracy jumped between us, saying, "Poo poo on them, I'm hugging you anyway."

That brought a smile to Emanuel's face, the sight of it warming me. His voice low and soft enough for us to hear, he said, "I really have missed you guys."

When Tracy stepped back, I asked, "You got your first big case? The victim is inside?"

He closed his eyelids slowly, opening as he spoke. "She's out back," he answered, his gaze traveling over my shoulder. I turned to see a news van rolling toward us, the reporters picking up the radio chatter. "An affluent neighborhood like this, I thought they'd be here soon enough."

"Yeah, let's get moving," I said, urging Emanuel to lead us around the house. The lawn was hard and crunchy, the night cold enough to frost the tips of the grass. We followed the foot-path from the patrols that had already gone to the crime scene and reached a yard where there was a swing set and child's playhouse. I searched the back of the house and along the fence but saw no body.

From the rear door, my gaze found the faces of a mother and a father, the nightmare in their eyes telling me they were the victim's parents. Emanuel saw me looking, saying, "That's a part of the job I'll never get used to."

"No. I wouldn't expect you to." He unlatched the side gate, letting us through, and led us to the middle of the yard and stopped at the sliding board, the swings moving with a short breeze. "Where's the victim?" I asked, confused.

"Those woods," he answered, looking up to size the trees. He motioned to the houses, saying, "There's about two acres of thick woods between the highway and this housing development. It acts as a buffer for the noise."

"I bet there are plenty of trails in those woods?" Tracy asked with a grunt. "And I bet that's where the older kids go."

"We found a lot already. Most of them extend away from a small creek that runs parallel to the road you guys parked," he answered, taking us to the rear gate. From there, I saw the first of the paths, a small wooden bridge that had been painted barn-red, with an arch in the middle, the water trickling slowly beneath it. "We believe Cynthia Harriet was coming home when she was attacked."

Walking across the bridge I caught a glimpse of the crime-scene tape, the yellow and black looking out of place against the natural colors in the woods. Next came the rapid cycling of a camera flash battery, a strobe bouncing white light off the trees. The path was covered in a mural of orange and red and green, the frost on the leaves melted to give them a shine in the sharp daylight skipping through the trees. "How old is the victim?"

"Fifteen," Emanuel said, his jaw clenching.

"That's around the same age as our victim," I told him. A sinking feeling came when I saw her, saw the top of her wavy auburn hair, a blue hair scrunchy sitting on the ground. I sucked in a breath, felt the chill touch deep in my lungs where I held it while taking in the first impressions.

Cynthia Harriet's head was turned, her neck bent as though she'd been trying to see who was behind her. Her arms were out to her side, an elbow bent, her left hand empty and fingers clutching nothing. One leg was folded beneath her, the other board-straight with a shoe missing from her left foot. She wore denim jeans and a matching denim jacket, neither of them soiled or torn. She wore expensive diamond earrings with a matching necklace, her cell phone on the ground next to her. The jewelry and her cell phone told me this was not a robbery.

"Casey?" Emanuel asked, watching me. I didn't realize it, but they were all watching me. My arms folded, I'd paced back and forth, taking care where I stepped, saying nothing as I assessed what had happened. "What are you thinking?"

"She came from over there. You'll see the leaves are rustled from the path, and there's a branch on a sapling that's broken. Someone should mark it. I can see it from here."

"You think that's where she was attacked?" someone asked.

"Not there, but it could be where the killer was standing, maybe hiding," I answered. I shifted to the other side of the body, Tracy pivoting to stay opposite of me while she began to take photographs. I raised my arms, my motion swift and fast enough to catch one of the patrol officers off guard. "She was attacked here. Held from behind and tried reaching around to fight her attacker."

"That was my assessment too," Emanuel said, opening his notepad. "I believe she was strangled right there where her body is. I think she also died while standing."

"I believe you are correct," I told him, my eyes meeting his where I saw a spark of relief. "She struggled here. The ground is trampled, the struggle lasting until he was sure Cynthia was dead. That's when the killer released her and let her body fall to the ground."

"Would the killer have moved her?" someone asked.

"The leaves," I said, the earth showing where the victim had kicked while battling for her life. "She'd kicked hard enough to lose one of her shoes."

"We found it ten yards away on the edge of the creek," Emanuel said.

I went to the other side where the light was better. The victim's skin was morbid white, a look of fright fixed forever on her tiny face. She was on the smaller side for fifteen, which could be nothing, or it could be everything if that's what the killer wanted. I made a note of it, the officers and detectives continuing to make room for us. I stopped and studied the distance from the victim's home. A hundred yards away? Maybe less. Did the victim scream? Did her parents hear something, and not knowing what it was, they dismissed it? Would that haunt them for the rest of their lives? The idea of it hurt to think about, a chill rising through me. "Were there any reports phoned in from last night?"

One of the detectives working for Emanuel stepped closer, plain clothes with dress shirt and slacks, he couldn't have been more than a few years older than Tracy. "We're still checking on that, ma'am, but the victim's parents said they didn't hear anything unusual."

"Unusual?" I said, wondering if that was their words. "Get clarification on what that meant."

"You think it's something?" Emanuel asked.

"Could be nothing, or everything, but should be covered," I answered.

"Who called it in?" Tracy asked, kneeling by the victim's head, camera in hand, taking a picture of the ligature marks on the victim's neck. I saw why Emanuel texted me. Cynthia Harriet had been strangled to death.

The young detective flipped through a notebook, answering, "The first call came in around eleven last night from the parents, reporting their child hadn't come home."

"Missing persons requires more time," I muttered, thinking the parents must have started to look themselves. My heart ached when I pieced together the events of the night. I knelt next to the body, my breathing short, imagining the nightmare of being a parent and searching for your child, only to come across their remains. "One of the parents found her? Right?"

The young detective swallowed and looked to Emanuel for

direction. Emanuel gave him a nod, the detective answering, "The victim's father."

By now there were pronounced signs of lividity, the victim's skin a blotchy black and blue where her blood had settled. On her chest and neck and in the graying remains of her eyes, there were signs of petechia, the broken blood vessels forming a rash, its emerging as she suffocated. Her eyelids were open, staring fixedly at the tops of the trees. I glanced in the same direction, seeing them swaying forty feet above, parting to let the sun peer through. Did the victim watch the cloudless sky as she died? Did she see the stars or the moon? With such horrendous violence, I hoped she saw these peaceful things in her final moments. I hated the idea that it might have been her killer she saw last. "I need to open her mouth," I said while snapping the cuff of a latex glove, the powder shimmering in a small puff.

"Yeah, certainly," Emanuel answered after a moment, his not realizing I was seeking permission. "Anything you need. Was there a detail about the mouth with the other victims?"

"With the Bodie Lighthouse victim there was," Tracy said as she placed her camera equipment down to help. "But not with the Greenville victim."

The young detective knelt next to us, the look on his face telling me he was eager to learn, "Mind my asking what it is you're looking for?"

Tracy grunted as she worked to pry the mouth, the jaw sticking firmly. After a struggle, the victim's jaw separated with a pop. "In the one victim, we discovered a piece of fulgurite."

"Lightning sand?" Emanuel asked, his voice lilting with the surprise. "In her mouth?"

Shocked that he knew what it was, I said, "Am I the only one that's never heard of the stuff?"

"It's a beach prize," the young detective said. I fixed him a look, trying not to frown. "My parents are beachcombers."

"Let's see if we find any in here," I said while holding a

flashlight over the victim's mouth. I looked up at Tracy, asking, "You've got a firm grip?"

"Yeah, I've got it," she said, shifting her thumbs onto the victim's teeth while I tugged on the girl's swollen tongue and moved it to the side. I lowered my head closer, squinting to focus until I could see clear to the back of her throat. "Anything in there?"

"Empty," I said as death reached me. It filled my nostrils with a sickening breath, the victim's lungs emptying. The smell was hours old, the girl's murder taking place some time in the evening. I sat up, leaning back on my shoes and held my breath until the odor passed. But it wasn't going to pass. It was death and death was forever. "There's no fulgurite."

"You think it's a different case?" Emanuel asked.

"Not sure, but those ligature marks are damn distinct," I said, and then stopped when I saw something. "What is that?"

I shined my flashlight on the side of the victim's neck, the light landing on a red thread woven between the locks of the victim's hair. "I see it," Tracy said, handing me tweezers and an evidence bag.

"Let's take you to the lab," I said, carefully pinching an end and pulling it free. When it was safe and sealed in the evidence bag, I handed it to Emanuel, leaving my hand in the air for him to take hold. He hoisted me up with an effortless motion. "We're going to take some close-up pictures. Would you be interested in coming to the station?"

"Definitely," he answered, brows rising to form the creases I noticed on his forehead. "Greenville case too?"

"That's the idea," I said. "Let's all get into a room and compare notes, pictures, ME reports, all of it."

"I got something else to show you," Emanuel said, waving me toward him as he took to the trail I suspected the victim had traveled. "Tracy?"

Tracy followed, snapping a picture of the broken branch as she passed the sapling. "What's out there?"

Emanuel spun around, walking backward, the crime-scene tape sliding between his fingers. "You were right about the victim coming from this path. I had the team cordon off all of it."

He turned back around, his body blocking my view. Above him, I saw the trees open to a large clearing and heard the distant sound of cars, tires riding on concrete and large truck engines barking loudly. When Emanuel stepped aside, I stepped onto dried straw and saw tire marks rutted across a field, the remains from a hundred cars that had come and gone. There were twenty or more trash barrels, all of them filled with litter, the wind carrying some of it across the field, a paper flier tumbling end over end until it was near my feet. I bent over and picked it up, the surprise making me want to yell as I read, "'Delight's Traveling Funfair'!"

"What?" Tracy said in a near shout, taking the flier from my hand.

"They were here yesterday," I said.

Emanuel waved his hand toward the field, answering, "This is the last known location Cynthia Harriet was seen alive."

I tapped my phone's screen, selecting one phone number and made the call, telling Emanuel and Tracy, "It's time to bring the Bureau in on the case."

TWENTY-TWO

I could barely sleep through the night. I'd tossed and turned so much that I thought Jericho was going to pick up his pillow and a blanket to sleep on the couch. I'd never felt so restless. As soon as I'd close my eyelids, my mind began racing, my skin got hot, and my insides broiled enough to make me kick off the bed covers. Moments later, I'd ball up like a baby to try and stay warm. I'm sure it was the anticipation of the morning meeting. With a third victim, their body discovered in proximity to Delight's Traveling Funfair, we had a solid connection. But we lacked evidence. In my head, I saw the one piece of physical evidence that might make our case—a red thread.

With a tall cup of my not-so-favorite Quick Mart coffee, I arrived at the station to find a small team from the FBI already setting up computers in and around the cubicle behind mine. At the desk sat Nichelle Wilkinson, her frilly brown hair covered with a baseball cap, gold FBI lettering embroidered above the brim. Her brown eyes went wide like saucers when she saw me, her hands waving as she jumped up and down. Like Tracy, Nichelle wasn't concerned about appearance or public displays of affection. She ran around the cubicle wall and bounced against my chest as she held and squeezed me. When she was ready, she pushed back, her smile broad, and said, "You look—" she began, a frown forming. "Well, you look tired, but I love that you called me."

"No sleep," I said, making room to put my things down. "It's great seeing you."

"What do you think?" she asked, clasping her hands in front of her while I took a step back to see all of her. She spun once to show me the outfit, the sight of her putting me in awe. Nichelle had begun her career in our IT department and was the prettiest nerd I'd ever met. It wasn't long before the reality of who she was and what she could do became clear. Nichelle was our IT department. Working multiple cases that ventured nationally, and even internationally, Nichelle's cyber skills and technical prowess were quickly noticed by the FBI. I'd learned later they were talking with her regularly, asking her for help on their own cases. She'd also been the one to help me in my search for Hannah, showing me the ways of online sleuthing. It wasn't long before she'd caught the crime-scene bug and decided to train for her certification. That's when a move to the FBI became a reality. Losing Nichelle was both heartbreaking and a profoundly proud moment. Since then, I hadn't found a single soul who could fill her shoes. Deep down, I don't think I wanted to either. She spun once more, saying, "Come on, Casey, what do you think?"

Tracy stood up from her desk, her hand on Nichelle's back. "Oh, you know how amazing you look." There was a gleam in her eyes, the two living together, a relationship blossoming. Tracy faced me saying, "Doesn't she?"

"Nichelle, the uniform suits you." I pulled my laptop from my bag, looking over the cubicle wall to see Nichelle had brought every piece of hardware she and her team could carry. My gut told me we'd need it too. I just hoped the station network connection could support the demand in bandwidth.

This was a Super Bowl team joining our case. I put my laptop down and took Nichelle's hands in mine and with a serious face, I asked her, "Nichelle, are you happy?"

Her eyes lit up like she was watching fireworks on the fourth of July. In a single breath I was both ecstatic for her and deeply saddened. But I smiled to match the delight I saw on her face. "Casey, Oh my God! I love the work."

"If you're happy, then I'm happy," I said, the front of the station sounding with footsteps, the stride long and steady. "Look who's joining us this morning."

Emanuel approached with the Greenville detective close behind him, "Nichelle!" he said with the biggest smile I'd ever seen on his face. He took her in his arms, giving her a bear hug while scanning the team she'd brought with her. "Brought the cavalry with you?"

She eased back, looking up in his face, saying, "Impressive, right!"

"Damn impressive," he answered.

"Nichelle," I said, leading Emanuel aside. "This is Detective Jeremy Watson. He's the detective from Greenville, working the case of the first victim."

"Ma'am," he said, offering a hand.

"Oh please!" Nichelle answered with a laugh. "It's just Nichelle."

"Nichelle," he said greeting her. "I'm working what we believe is the first murder—"

"It's not the first," Nichelle interrupted, her face turning serious. She looked to me, adding, "After you called, I got the okay to dig into the case. I need to show you something."

I lifted the black swill in my cup, saying, "A refresh and then to the conference room."

. . .

It hadn't been that long since Emanuel and Nichelle moved on to their new roles, but still, seeing them here, listening and speaking to them, it felt really good. I leaned back in my chair to watch the room.

In a way, they were my family. I hadn't known anyone when I came to the Outer Banks that summer day a couple years back—my venturing south and then east toward the barrier islands in search of my daughter. In a very short while, I had new brothers and sisters in my team, and had found Jericho and eventually Hannah too. I imagined us being like a large family, the station our home, the children having grown and moved on, leaving the dining room table empty and the kitchen without commotion. Yet today, like holidays and family events, the house was full again, coming alive with a hundred different conversations carrying on at the same time, the feel of it warming me inside.

I held the moment dear to my heart, but then braced the table, the work at hand a morbid task. I was sure there was a killer amongst the Delight's Traveling Funfair. We had to find them before they struck again. I chose to sit at the front of our large conference room table, the men and women that made up Nichelle's team sitting along one side while my team, both old and new and extended, sat along the other. Every seat was filled, and it took a knock of my knuckles on the tabletop to douse the conversations and get their attention.

"Love to see the enthusiasm!" I said, raising my voice over the soft chatter that continued. "For those who don't know me, I'm Detective Casey White. And we're here today to catch a killer."

With my introduction, Nichelle clicked a mouse to present what her team had discovered. "Greenville," she began, the conference room's larger monitor showing a map of the town. "Now if I zoom out."

The letters making up the name Greenville shrank, a larger

area of North Carolina showing. "Northwest, we have Elizabeth City," Emanuel said.

"South and east, we've got Outer Banks and the Soundside Event Site in Nags Head," Tracy added.

"Is this where you wow us?" I asked with climbing anticipation.

"I hope so," Nichelle answered, tapping her keys, a graphic appearing over the map. I saw it near immediately and went to the monitor, stepping to the side so Emanuel and Detective Jeremy Watson had a clear view. On the map, the newly added graphics showed a thick blue line going through each of the cities, green marker showing where Delight's Funfair had been. Another set of red markers I knew to be where the victims were discovered. What was of interest, what got me up from my chair, was where the thick blue line was coming from. It appeared from the north, beyond the map she was showing. "Seen enough?"

"I don't think I have," I answered, and pointed to the top of the monitor, Emanuel and Detective Watson joining me. "Show me what's in the north."

"Oh my," I mouthed as Nichelle zoomed out further, the journeys of Delight's Traveling Funfair stretching from the northern Rockies in the west, down to the southwest states and Texas border, and over to southeast and back north. Peppered alongside their stops were more red flags, seven total, the dates on them going back two years. I punched my hip with shock, wondering how it could be these deaths had gone this long without the killer being suspected as having traveled with Delight's Traveling Funfair. "How could this happen?"

"Could it be an anomaly in the data?" Detective Watson asked as he cupped the back of his neck. He shook his head, his expression sharing the same disbelief. He held out his hands, saying, "Let me reframe my question."

"Coincidence?" One of Nichelle's team said, asking before

he could continue. "What we're showing is a correlation of missing and murdered girls matching the ages of your victims."

Nichelle clicked on a mouse, increasing the size of the font used to show the dates. "We are only showing the cases that occurred on or close to the dates of the Delight's Traveling Funfair."

The Greenville detective pardoned himself as he went to the monitor and waved his hands in front of the map. "But could it be a coincidence?"

"Correlation doesn't imply causation," I said, understanding what he was driving at.

"Exactly," he said, Emanuel putting on a frown.

"But, guys," Emanuel began with a grunt and going to the other side of the monitor, "we have strong evidence that can't be discounted."

"Which is why I said correlation doesn't imply causation," I told them. I turned to face Nichelle and her team, adding, "But it gives us reason to strongly suggest where it is we want to look and concentrate our investigation."

"I'll give you that," Detective Watson agreed. He went to his seat, wiping his brow and opened his laptop. "I just want to make sure we're focusing on the right place."

I looked at the dates again, the places where the fair had pitched their tents and stood up games and confection stands to sell candied apples and entertain children. "With these overlapping dates and locations, it would behoove us to investigate." As I looked at the count of missing and dead girls, I asked Nichelle and her team, "There is strong evidence of a killer traveling with the fair—could be they work there or it is someone mirroring their location, traveling in their shadows. How is it nobody has come across this already?"

The FBI agent who spoke earlier cleared his throat, asking, "May I?"

I looked to Nichelle to gauge if this was who she reported

to. She tilted her head, raising a brow, my seeing enough to answer, "Yes, sir. By all means, please."

He removed his hat, his jet-black hair slicked back, a red ring on his forehead remaining. "Can you open the other overlay?"

"Previous case?" Nichelle asked, clicking on her mouse before he started to nod.

"This is a case we started eighteen months ago. We've been tracking it ever since," he answered, leaving his chair to go to the monitor. On the map, three of the previous victims disappeared, as did the thick blue line to represent the fair's travels and stops. He looked at me, motioned to around his neck saying, "What started as two victims with similar markings, jumped to three and then six. We were nowhere. Agent Wilkinson came on board and joined the investigation and started working the data while we could do nothing but wait."

"Wait for another victim?" I said, asking, my understanding what he meant was a morbid truth. "Waited until I called you guys yesterday."

"We're convinced that all the victims have the same killer," he continued.

"Including the victims based on the pictures we sent Nichelle," I said.

"Yes," Nichelle said, changing the view and standing next to her manager. On the screen, tiled side by side, and up and down, every victim in their case, the pictures showing ligature marks, having the same identifiable pattern. "I could use image arithmetic and apply morphological filters, and exercise all my coding tricks I know, but that would only tell us what we can already see."

"That it is the same murder weapon," I said. Nichelle's manager dipping his head, a murmur of agreements coming from the conference table.

"Based on the pictures you sent, we joined your cases immediately to ours," he said. "Your addressing Delight's Traveling Funfair was the break we needed."

"That's when we started plotting the locations," Nichelle added. "I got the ones for the funfair from the work Tracy had started."

"And the results are what we have here," I said, leaning forward to lock eyes with Detective Watson. Any questions about the Jacksons in connection to their daughter's murder was nearly squashed. "It's a lot of correlation, but I think I've seen enough to say we're looking at the same murder weapon. That means we're also looking at these crimes being committed by the same person. A single killer."

TWENTY-THREE

We filled the monitors with pictures taken from Delight's Traveling Funfair, Tracy and Nichelle finding posts by kids, including the flier with the clown on the front, an invitation to enjoy the fun, the food and the amusement rides. The FBI had a case before ours but had not made a connection to the funfair until we'd contacted them. I had my own thoughts on that oversight, but it was too late to fix it now.

On our second monitor, we kept the map with the overlay, the dates going back a couple of years. But there was one important element missing, and it was the question that had dogged us since the funfair had first come to our attention. Where was Delight's Traveling Funfair going next?

When one of the social media posts from recent weeks showed the clown from the fliers in full garb in a live video segment, I stopped the room.

"Play that back," I told Tracy. She rewound the snippet, playing it again. "Put it on a loop."

"Continuous playback," she said, chair wheels in motion as the room took notice. A visitor to the funfair had been filming their friends when the clown appeared behind them. He had a fountain of green hair and wore thick makeup, and giant bulbous shoes. And though he had a hoop around his waist and billowing pants, the clown did acrobatics, cartwheeling and hopping up and down for a group of children. But it was the ruffled red collar around his neck that I locked my focus. "That's the clown on the flier."

"Cynthia Harriet," Emanuel said, voice rising as he went to the screen. "Pause it!"

Tracy stopped the video, the face of the clown a blur, his body in mid somersault. "What do you see?"

"Did you know my wife picks out my clothes when we go to dinner or to family?" he asked the group. We shook our heads. He put on a smile, adding, "She thinks I have terrible color coordination. That's what she calls it, color coordination. I don't know if that's even a thing." He pointed to the collar next, answering, "I might not have color coordination, but that shade of red looks damn close to the shade of red in that thread we found on Cynthia Harriet's body."

"Yes, it does," I assured him, adding, "And tell your wife, she has excellent color coordination."

"Do we know who from the funfair is dressing up as a clown?" Nichelle's manager asked, pinching his glasses.

"Tracy, open a picture of Jimmy Delight," I instructed, having seen his face and enough pictures of the funfair's clown attraction to find a resemblance. When his face appeared, I asked, "Let's do a side-by-side with one of the fliers."

When they were shown, Nichelle squinted, the makeup and hair and other clown garb concealing the identity. "The man's bone structure is definitely the same. But we couldn't get a positive match on this."

As we studied the faces, Tracy continued playing the video, the friends in the foreground dispersing, the focus falling on the clown. Then came the magic tricks, children gathering around and sitting cross-legged on the lawn while the clown made puffy red balls appear out of thin air. There were giant playing cards like the jack of hearts and ten of diamonds, their vanishing with a snap of his fingers, an ace of spades appearing in their place. When the handkerchiefs appeared, I stood. One by one, a colorful scarf came from the clown's closed fist, each one waving like a flag caught in the wind, the corners knotted to create a rope, or a chain of them. When it was draped across the clown's chest, an idea blinked into my mind like a wish. I yelled, "Pause it!" The playback stopped, my saying, "It's like a garrote."

"Garrote?" Tracy asked, fingers sweeping across the keyboard as she looked up the term. In the dim light of the room, I could see the whites of her eyes appear. "Oh, he could have strangled them with the handkerchiefs?"

"Look at the knots stringing the handkerchiefs together," I exclaimed while Tracy removed the map from the other monitor and replaced it with the bruising around the victims' necks. I ran my finger across the bruises, asking, "Am I reaching, or do you guys see it too?"

Detective Jeremy Watson stood next to me, huffing a deep breath through his nose as he crossed his arms, a deep, pensive look filling with doubt. He was our doubting Thomas, the team member to question everything. While annoying, we needed him to validate the ideas. "The shape is there. I'll give you that," he said with a nod. "But would they be sturdy enough to do that kind of damage? Could they hold?"

"I think it's called a scarf chain," Nichelle announced to the room. "It's where the magician makes a string of colorful hand-kerchiefs appear."

"There could be a wire in play," I suggested as I ran my finger across the clown's chest. "See how the handkerchiefs aren't quite flaccid? They're stiff around the knots, like a clothesline."

"And these match the bruising," Emanuel said, taking a

printed picture with the bruising blown up. "This could be the murder weapon."

"Jimmy Delight is the owner and manager. Unconfirmed, but with some computer skills at work, I think we can confirm whether or not he's the one in the clown suit and makeup," Nichelle's manager said, his buying into the direction we were going.

"The red thread we recovered from Cynthia Harriet," Emanuel said, holding up a picture of the evidence bag. "Same shade as the ruffles on that costume. With the Delight's Funfair having been in proximity to the murder, it's enough for me to question them."

"And the magic handkerchiefs trick, the way they are chained together," I said, continuing to summarize. "We're seeing them used in the clown's magic show. What else do we think he used them for?"

Nichelle asked, "Between what you guys have and what our team worked, we can investigate the carnival?"

"We can do more than that," I told her as two of the FBI agents began typing. "With state boundaries crossed, and the help of you and your team, we'll have the approvals to search every inch of the Delight's Traveling Funfair."

The municipal building's parking lot glistened wet, rainwater beading on my windshield as the wipers settled beneath the hood of my car. I opened the door and exited, covering my head, the motor clicking and clanking while it cooled. The day had grown late and I stopped by the municipal building offices before heading home. There was paperwork to file, a part of a long and arduous process involving a residential address change. Jericho's home was recently lost to a fire and estimates of a full rebuild would be a year or more. He was on patrol this afternoon and I'd offered to drop the paperwork off for him.

Only, I never made it inside the building. A pair of faded green Crocs catching my eye, their toes pointing up with one foot in a lean like a bent flower stem.

My heart grew heavy and dropped to the pit of my stomach. There was only one person in all the Outer Banks that I knew who wore those shoes. I raced around a parked car, my hand covering my mouth to stifle a gasp. It was Dr. Swales. Terri's body was sprawled across the wet pavement, hidden between two cars, her bluish hair soaked and spread across the blacktop like spilled ink. Above her head, her Walkman headset, one of the spongey orange earbuds broken. Her skin was gray and pale, her lips almost white and her eyelids shut closed with rainwater puddled on them. On her chin there was a gash, deep enough to need stitches, the open wound bleeding, streaks the color of crimson in the late daylight running down her neck.

"Terri?" I yelled, touching her cheek and listening for a breath. The feel of her skin was shockingly cold like a corpse. "Terri, can you hear me?!"

Movement. A quick breath. A gesture as she reached for my hand, her purse strap woven between her fingers. "Casey?" she answered, her voice a dry rasp.

"Terri, I'm here," I said, the rain dripping down my face. With one hand, I dialed 9-1-1, putting the phone on speaker, the screen pocked with raindrops. The call center and ambulance dispatch weren't far from our location, but the hospital was at least ten miles away.

"*9-1-1, what's your emergency?*"

"I... Hello! I need an ambulance—" I yelled in a shout, Terri's eyelids fluttering briefly, her eyes swimming behind them as she tried to register where she was. "—the municipal building parking lot—"

"*I have your location,*" the operator said. Her voice went on, but Terri's condition pulled me from the conversation.

"Terri?!" I shouted when she shut her eyelids. I made a fist to grind against her chest bone. She moved and regained consciousness. "Terri, did you fall?"

She tried to say no, moving her head slightly from side to side. She squeezed my hand, handing me the strap, the end of it torn from the bag, the stitching frayed. She closed my fingers around the purse strap and mouthed the word, "Pushed." Her eyes looked past me, looked to the darkening sky.

"Terri?" I asked, her stare becoming distant as emotions caught in my voice. "Who was it that pushed you?!"

"Push—" she answered, the word carried on a breath as the look of death entered her face. My eyes stung with tears, a cry climbing the back of my throat. I began CPR, one hand over the other to drive a fist against her heart. *Find the center of the chest bone*, I heard in my head. *Apply compressions, hard and fast.*

"Stay with me, Terri!" I shouted, a distant siren wailing. I worked the muscles in my arms, recalling the instructions. I only needed to keep her heart pumping, keep the blood flowing to her brain. The cut on her chin was small, insignificant for her condition, leaving me to think about the mini strokes she'd suffered. What if this was like them? But a bigger one? *A breath!* I opened her mouth and gave her a breath, her chest rising, the tears on my cheeks wetting hers. I was crying, but kept the pace, and begged the woman I'd come to think of as family, "Please, Terri. Stay with me!"

My arms ached and my lungs burned as I panted and kept the count. A moan slipped from my lips as Terri's life seemed to be slipping through my fingers. My heart lifted then as red lights shined against the cars around us, the windows and doors wet and reflecting the flashes. The ambulance drove past us, dousing my hopes like a gushing hose onto a flame. They didn't see us. We were too far in between the parked cars.

"Over here!" I yelled, jumping up briefly and waving my arms. "We're over here!"

The ambulance came to a stop, tires screeching on the wet

blacktop. Doors flung open and a man and a woman emptied from inside and went to the rear, swinging open the bay doors, jerking a gurney from inside, the wheels touching the pavement with a thud. They swung medical bags around their shoulders and ran toward me. Compressions. I resumed them, hard and fast, finding renewed strength as sweat mixed with the rainwater.

A paramedic knelt next to me, his taking over the CPR and matching my tempo. I fell backward to sit on the heels of my feet. The second paramedic produced a mask with a resuscitation bag and planted it onto Terri's face, squeezing air into her lungs. But Terri's eyes were lost, their focus gone. And as the paramedics continued to breathe for Terri, I watched her small frame jostle and shake out of control. There were moments when the pair checked for a pulse and traded dismal looks that told me more than I wanted to know. But like me, they continued, they persevered. They kept squeezing the bag and pressing against her chest.

"Please?" I muttered to myself at one point, wishing they would stop, the sight of Terri like this breaking my heart. I took Terri's hand and looked into her face. If she was still there, I wanted her to see me, to see someone that she knew in life while she moved on to wherever it was she was going. Through the painful heartache and tears, I brought her hand to my lips and kissed it.

TWENTY-FOUR

With her hand in mine and the paramedics trying to revive her, Dr. Terri Swales died at 5:43 p.m. on a rainy late Thursday afternoon. The late night was filled with phone calls that were like waking glimpses of a nightmare. With each, as I shared the terrible news, there were images of Dr. Swales's face flashing in full morbidness. I held it together for most of the calls, but it was when I was face to face with Jericho that I lost it completely. I had to tell him in person and had waited for him at the marine patrol station where he arrived soon after sunset. With his body pressing against mine, his breathing deep, there was a stricken look of tragedy and sorrow. It was a moment frozen in my mind and would haunt me forever.

Terri's cause of death would require an autopsy, but the immediate indications were that she'd suffered from a massive stroke, which had caused her to fall and strike her chin on the pavement. She'd had a series of mini strokes in the last year and had recovered from them, symptoms of what was to come. As a detective, I couldn't help but think about her last words to me. When I shut my eyelids, it was her voice I heard. Her saying that she was *pushed*. Was she disoriented from the stroke, making her believe someone pushed her? But what if she was lucid? What if she had been pushed and it was the fall that caused the stroke? I didn't share any of these thoughts, but it was something I was compelled to investigate. To do that, I'd enlist those closest to me, asking Tracy and Nichelle and Emanuel to help.

When I felt the bed move, I opened my eyes to find Jericho had returned from the shower, a towel around his middle. I went to the edge of the bed where he was sitting, drops of water on his shoulder and back, his hair wet and his eyes red-rimmed and puffy. He'd been crying, the noise of the shower hiding it. I knew he had a special bond with Swales, and that the two knew one another most all of Jericho's life. Swales had also been close to Jericho's wife and helped him through the nightmare of her murder. I couldn't find any words but took a small towel and began to dry his skin, gently removing the drops as I kissed his shoulder and held him in my arms.

"She lived a good life," he said, voice breaking, his chest shuddering.

"Yes, she did," I said, his emotion making me tear. "I can't imagine anyone taking her place."

"No one ever could," Jericho replied. "Although I know she wanted Samantha to eventually take over her job," he continued with a nod, turning to face me. "That's what Terri had told me when Samantha first arrived. It's what Terri wanted to see happen after she retired. That wasn't supposed to happen this soon."

I put on a frown, thinking back to my first introduction to Samantha, how she'd been squeamish. "Is Samantha qualified?"

"She's qualified, but doesn't have the experience yet," Jericho answered, forehead wrinkling as he told me the additional news. "This last year was her fellowship."

"But there is medical school?" I asked, cocking my head, not quite seeing Samantha as our medical examiner. "Isn't there?"

"She might not look thirty, but she's already finished medical school and her residency." He stood up to towel himself dry, stopping a moment to add, "It's almost like Swales knew her time was short."

"That's why she pushed so much to have Samantha working here," I added, knowing it was purely speculation, my mind working through the sadness as though her death had been a small part of some grander plan. Perhaps it was? We'd never know. "The best we can do is support Samantha. If she's right for the job, she'll get it. But she'll also have some mighty big shoes to fill."

Jericho raised his brow with a grin, saying, "Yeah, Swales had the biggest size fives I'd ever seen on a person."

I let out a soft giggle and thought of Laura Jackson's case and where I'd last left things with Swales. Samantha would be grieving, as would we all, but there were DNA tests I was waiting on, and we needed the results. Jericho must have sensed the worry, asking, "What is it?"

"How soon is too soon to talk work?" I asked, not wanting to sound cold or callous. "Swales had this big discovery in the Jackson case that involved skin beneath the victim's fingernails. She sent it to the lab to see if there was recoverable DNA."

Jericho reached out to me, inviting me to stand with him. I took his hand and got up, the first of the daylight peering through the window. "Send a text to Samantha. I have a feeling she's a lot like her aunt Terri."

"I hope you're right," I answered. As Jericho continued to get dressed, I texted Samantha as he'd suggested, asking how she was doing. There'd been nothing official about her being our new medical examiner, but she'd been close to the latest case— Laura Jackson's which included the carnival murders. All this time, I'd thought Samantha was an assistant. She looked young for her age, but so did Swales.

Beneath my words, I saw Samantha texting, the words appearing

Not bad. Just sad, she replied. *And you?*

That was kind of her to ask, my replying with the same line. I added, *Not to press, but would you be able to help with the Laura Jackson case?*

She was typing again, but then the three bouncing dots dropped. I waited for them to resume, my concern for the case's sake climbing. The dots resumed, her text following: *I'll do everything I can to help.*

Thank you, I texted to her, and added, *If there's anything I can do, let me know.*

Can you meet me at the morgue? she replied without hesitation.

Sure, I texted her with a flick of nerves. *I'll have Tracy join us?*

Yes. I've asked Derek to be there as well.

I'll leave in a few minutes.

I sent Tracy a text and then put my phone down, my earlier hopes dashed. When Jericho saw my face, I told him, "I'm going to meet with Samantha this morning at the morgue."

Jericho gave me a hug, saying, "I think Terri is there. Want me to go with you?"

I don't know why I didn't think of Dr. Swales being there already, my thoughts concentrating on the work. "I think Samantha wants to discuss the case."

"That's encouraging?" Jericho said, questioning. He shook his head. "No?"

"It is," I said as a rush of nerves came, unsure about the private viewing we were about to have with Dr. Swales.

. . .

My heart ached as I entered the room outside of the morgue. Tracy said nothing as we followed the regimen Dr. Swales had showed us. We slipped paper booties over our shoes and sleeved our arms through a lab coat, hanging it over our jackets, knowing the cold in the room had a sinister bite. Derek opened the pair of thick resin doors to see who'd arrived. He said nothing but gave us a nod, the look on his face saying plenty.

"Dr. Swales? She's here?" I asked, having thought we'd meet with Samantha first.

He nudged his chin, focus shifting to the morgue. "Just arrived."

He held one of the doors for us as we entered. Emotion stung my eyes when I saw Emanuel, Nichelle and Samantha standing next to the gurney with Dr. Swales. Their faces were like stone, the sadness etched deep. It was our own private viewing, a chance to be alone and to say goodbye. We'd lost one of our own and the setback would be felt for some time.

"May I?" I asked Samantha. She blinked me into focus, her black bangs bouncing. I motioned to the gurney, Samantha nodding an approval. I went to Swales and leaned over the rail to touch her face and to hold her hands, her skin cold and lifeless. I couldn't feel Swales at all, couldn't feel her energy or spirit that I'd loved so dearly. Her body was here, but she had gone somewhere. I thought of everything she'd given me since arriving to the Outer Banks, and kissed her cheek, whispering, "Thank you."

"Casey," Emanuel said as I returned to the group, his large hand on my back. "She's going to be impossible to replace."

Samantha's eyebrows jumped with a slight twitch, hearing Emanuel. She looked at us, eyes filled with tears, saying, "I don't know if I am ready for"—she spread her arms wide—"for all this."

I went to face her and took her hands, lowering her arms. "Samantha, your aunt Terri thought you were ready."

"I barely made it through med school, or my residency." The tears flowed then, leaving me to wonder if this was something she wanted. But I'd seen glimpses of her work that had surprised me. This was hers if she wanted it. "If I'd had a little more time with her."

I gripped her hands firm, forcing her to look at me. In the middle of the Jackson case, we needed someone who knew all the details. Someone with Samantha's knowledge. "You have me, and the team."

Samantha fell into my arms to sob, the cries strong, her chest heaving. When she was ready, she put space between us saying, "Okay."

One by one, each of the team said goodbye. When we were ready, we followed Derek and Samantha's lead, helping to cover Dr. Swales and to transfer her body to the morgue's cold storage. When it was only me, Tracy and Samantha, I asked Samantha, "I'm sorry to ask, but there's some time-sensitivity around the tissue samples, possible DNA recovered—"

"From beneath Laura Jackson's fingernails," Samantha said, interrupting while we walked to the small desk in the corner of the morgue. It was where Swales managed her work, an ancient computer on the desk with a monitor that stole most of the space, the keyboard and mouse buried beneath a muss of paperwork and receipts.

I gave the desktop a hard look and asked, "I'm guessing it's here somewhere?" In my head, I could hear Swales saying, *I keep a clean house.* It was a favorite saying of hers, but from the looks of her workspace, what she practiced in her morgue did not translate to her desk.

"Right! It's hard to believe it, but Aunt Terri said she had a system," Samantha said as she sniffled and wheeled the chair out from beneath the desk. She stopped herself before sitting, a look of reverence on her face.

"It's okay," I told her with a faint strum of concern. We needed the lab results. "It's your seat now."

She eased into the chair as though trying on a new pair of shoes. Around the keyboard and the monitor were stacks of papers, most looking to have been spat out of a dot-matrix printer sitting atop thick medical journals on a neighboring shelf. "I was with her when the sample was submitted."

"Maybe she recorded it on the computer?" I asked, fearing we could lose a vital piece of evidence. It wouldn't be the first time the chain of custody had been broken.

Samantha lifted and dropped paperwork. "I know the paperwork is somewhere around here," she answered and flicked on the computer. The monitor hummed as it warmed, an amber glow at the center of the tube turning bright. Sitting back in the seat, Samantha waved her hands over the desk as though chanting a magic spell. "This is something I'm good at. I'll get it organized and find the lab work."

"Worst-case scenario, the lab will have what was submitted?" I asked, trying to sound confident for her sake and mine.

"Yes!" she exclaimed, pressing the heal of her palm against her head. She shook her head, adding, "Dunno why I didn't think of that."

"Because you've had a lot of other things to think about." I took her hand, giving it a gentle squeeze. "This can wait for now. Be with your family. I'll go to the lab to get the results."

She frowned with the corner of her mouth twisting. "I will, but could I do this?" Before I could answer, she continued, "I think I need to do this."

"Of course," I told her, understanding the escape from mourning that came from busywork. "I'll leave you to it."

As I walked away, my gaze locked on the drawer where we'd put Swales's body, I could feel the weight of her loss. For Laura Jackson's sake, I hoped Samantha could make up for it.

TWENTY-FIVE

I wanted to see Samantha succeed. Hoped to see her jump into Swales's shoes and take off running. But I had concerns. Though not shared, I thought of Nichelle and her new role in the FBI. When she'd worked with me in the past, Nichelle was often tasked to coordinate DNA submissions to the FBI's CODIS and NDIS databases. In her time with Swales, she could have picked up a name. A point of contact Swales used when sending lab work. I found nothing in my notes, including the oldest of them, the ones dating back to my first case in the Outer Banks. The sound of papers shuffling came from Nichelle's desk, or what used to be her desk before she moved on.

I rested my arms on the wall that separated our cubicles, asking, "Any chance you kept your notes from all our old cases?"

Nichelle cocked one eyebrow as she busied herself with a video cable to finish connecting it to a desktop computer I recognized. She'd brought her gear back to the station, the sight of it giving me hope she was staying through the end of the case. "Casey. Absolutely I kept my notes." My gaze fell to the paperwork strewn across her desk. She wagged a finger, "Uh-uh! Not my mess. I have no idea who parked in my old spot, but they were a slob."

"Let me help out," I said, reaching down to scoop a handful, knowing full well that half of the coversheets and printed forms were from my laziness. "Your old notes, can we take a look at some work you've done with Dr. Swales?"

Tracy joined the conversation, leaning against the cubicle opening. "What do you need?" she asked, holding her tablet. "I kept mine too. Every written note, scanned and indexed."

"For you, Tracy, can you get Laura Jackson's tablet?" I told her, wanting to research the teen's emails, to pick through them for anything overlooked. We needed this since Jane Finley wasn't talking. As she'd said, *Shawna was safe*. There was nothing else for her to do. "We'll work that while Nichelle helps with the tissue samples."

Nichelle straightened, a look of surprise showing. "Tell me you collected DNA from one of the victims?" She picked up her phone. "Mind if I make the call to my team?"

I shook my head. "Not yet."

She heard the tone, asking, "What happened?"

I moved closer, sitting in a lean against her desk, my voice low. "This is sensitive, but I need to ask for some help locating the samples. Swales sent them to the lab. I was hoping you had a point of contact and could follow up with them."

She put one leg over the other and crossed her arms, asking, "What about Samantha?" She tilted her head confused.

I decided to bend the truth a little and to keep my concerns to myself. "Poor girl is going to have her hands full," I answered, sounding reasonable. "There's her family and also any help with the funeral."

"Say no more," Nichelle said, flicking on her desktop computer, the red, green and blue lights flashing through the glassy side-panel. "I'll check my phone. If I don't have it there, I'll pull my contacts and notes once this is booted. But—"

"Yes," I answered before she asked. "We're a team, including yours and mine. Any findings are shared."

"Excellent," she said while pulling a wall calendar from her backpack and tacking it to the wall, piercing the material with a straightened paperclip. The picture for this month was a pair of kittens sitting amidst pumpkins and surrounded by autumn foliage. She sat back in her chair with a content look. "I know it's just for this case, but it feels good to be back."

"Consider it your home," I told her. "Whenever you feel the need, the door will always be open, and the desk will be available."

"Thank you," she said, handing me a crumpled coversheet, my name on the face of them. "And, Casey, maybe empty your recycle bucket?"

"Will do," I answered, caught in the act, faint heat rising on my neck. The largest of her monitors flashed to show folders and documents. "The tissue sample is from Laura Jackson. Swales recovered it from beneath the girl's fingernails."

Tracy returned with Laura's tablet. "I'm ready when you are."

"What's on that?" Nichelle asked, standing to see the tablet, her curiosity wandering.

"It's the victim's school tablet I told you about, the one where she'd created a secret profile account," Tracy explained. She showed the school profile, the default apps on the screen. A moment later, it changed to Laura's profile, the apps changing to icons for popular social media platforms.

Nichelle returned to work her computer, saying, "Let me know if you need any help with that one. Your victim might have hidden other surprises."

Tracy put on a smile, answering with an edge of competitiveness, "Well if she did, I'll find them."

"I am sure you will," Nichelle said, and quickly added, "I haven't shown you all my tricks."

"We'll grab you if we run into anything," I said, settling the conversation and getting my chair. I rolled it to Tracy's desk, sitting next to her, Laura's tablet with her email inbox opened. "Did you say you transferred the data, made a backup?"

"Oh yeah, I did," Tracy said, chair wheels squealing as she rolled around me to her laptop. She opened the folder with the data, saying, "It's point in time, so it'll be everything from when I performed the backup."

"What if Laura's accounts were active after her death?" I asked, thinking of how I'd posted a sad note on my ex-husband's Facebook page after he'd died. "Anything new since you did the backup would only be on the tablet?"

"That's the only place it could be," she answered and wheeled back around, bumping the wall on her way. "Let's try Instagram. She posted pictures of her and her sister on there. I can mirror it on my monitor too."

"Please," I said, anxious to see if anyone had tried to contact Laura since her murder. Tracy drove while I watched the monitor, Instagram appearing, the heart showing a few days of activity with comments on Laura's last post. "What do they say?"

Tracy clicked on it to show Laura's post, a picture of her and Shawna, the two wearing thick hoodie jackets with the letters OBX on the front. It was nighttime and behind them I saw the lights I recognized from the fair, the Ferris wheel towering behind them. "She must have taken this picture with her phone."

"We never recovered her phone," I said with an understanding I had overlooked until now. I nudged Tracy's arm, adding, "This account on the school's tablet, it's using the same accounts Laura used on her phone."

"Which means everything she did on the phone is going to be here as well!"

"Let's get all the social media activity taking place after her murder," I said, giving her a task she was well suited to handle. "I'm curious, open up her email. Maybe she got something new?"

Tracy opened the tablet's email reader, the unusual quiet in the station interrupted by a flurry of ringing bells. Laura's inbox began filling with new mail, the subject lines made up of sorrowful comments, her friends sending heartfelt words that Laura would never read. When the swirling animations completed, Tracy ran her finger down the side of the tablet, saying, "There was an email buried in the *Sent* folder that I missed."

I saw the name FINLEY in bold letters, my palms itchy with curiosity. "*Another* email to her birth parents?" I asked, glad to have her picking through the tablet again.

Tracy read the draft email, her lips stopping as she moved closer to me. "Casey, look at this line."

She handed me the tablet, her finger pointing to the words as I read them, "'I know it is too late for me, but please save Shawna from the same fate.'"

Tracy clapped my arm, asking, "That supports abuse, right?"

I wanted to agree with her. Felt almost desperate to agree with her. But the statement only led to more speculation and questions. The Finleys never saw this email, and I'd been certain the carnival killer was our lead suspect. But now? Was it time to reconsider the Jacksons and abuse? "We do have the neighbor's statement about school absences and urgent care visits," I began, speaking of what we'd learned, hearing it aloud to see if it corroborated with what the draft email might be insinuating.

"There are the old fractures found in the autopsy," Tracy

continued, and then added a reminder, "Some healing on their own."

I brushed my neck, wrapping my fingers until I could almost touch the nape of it. "A broken bone in the neck, the bruising that appeared different from the carnival murders."

"And now there is this email." Tracy moved to the edge of her chair with excitement. She tapped the top of the tablet. "She asked them to save her little sister."

I didn't like it when a case left me feeling perplexed. The look on my face must have spoken volumes, Tracy's enthusiasm replaced with annoyance. "There's the carnival murders, that's a solid lead too."

She sat back and crossed her arms, the pile of evidence to support both leads accumulating. She touched her neck like I had, her thoughts returning to the point of the girl's death. "The bruising looked different on Laura's neck. What if the abuse in the Jacksons' house got out of control? Maybe they'd seen the Greenville murder and tried to copy it?"

"With the other girls, their strangulation didn't involve a broken bone in the neck. That could have been enough to change the pattern of bruising." I ran my fingers through my hair wanting one piece of evidence that solidly pitted the Jacksons as Laura's murderer or the person we believed to be hiding amongst the carnival workers. I lifted the tablet, saying, "There is one other thing from this that raises a huge question."

"What's that?" Tracy asked. My gaze shifted to the station's holding cell. A spark shined in her eyes as a question came to her. "The Finleys? You want to talk to Jane Finley again?"

Jane Finley hadn't spoken another word since we brought her to the station. Her silence was exactly how she was helping her husband. And she knew it too. I put on a frown and saw the immediate discouragement in Tracy's face. "Jane Finley isn't going to help us."

"Then what?"

"It's more a question about this email," I told her. "If this email helped the Finleys kidnap Shawna, then why didn't they save Laura?"

It was called agonal breathing. Those last moments with Dr. Swales before the paramedics arrived. I thought she was struggling to catch her breath, gasping for it. But she wasn't really breathing at all. I learned later that what I saw was a natural reflex. It happened when her brain stopped getting the oxygen needed for her to survive. I hope that meant she was without pain. That she was already in a better place, a kind of distant dream state where there was warmth and happiness. I had to hope for that because I hated the idea of her being semi-conscious and aware. What a terribly frightening thing being unable to move or sense what was happening to her.

She'd still had the strength to say a final word. "Pushed." I still didn't know what it meant.

"Casey?" Alice, our station manager, asked with a light rap of her knuckles against my cubical. I kept a stare fixed on my monitor while reading more of Laura's emails. When I looked up, Alice continued, "There's a reporter insisting he see you."

"You know the policy," I answered, annoyed by the disruption. It wasn't a hard policy. In fact, I wasn't at all sure it was a real station policy. But since joining the force in this part of the Outer Banks, reporters stayed in their place, and we stayed in ours. The waist-high gate at the front of the station was the point of demarcation. "When I have information to report, I'll find them."

The skin beneath her chin wagged as she rocked her head. "I know and I am sorry to bug you. But he's insisting. He says it's about Dr. Swales."

"Terri?" I asked, my attention stolen entirely. I stood up and scanned the station's front, quickly finding the reporter I'd known since first arriving to the Outer Banks. He was wearing an expensive gray suit with a pleated jacket, a purple silk tie that shined, and slacks that were tighter than anything I had in my closet. It was a far cry from the adolescent wear I'd seen him dressed in when we were first introduced. When he saw me, he held up his hand, a small baggy pinched between his fingers. I waved him through, saying, "Thank you, Alice."

I knew the reporter to be a blogger where web clicks had replaced print and become the news media currency. He'd since turned the blogging gig into a full-time reporter career and had covered most all my cases. And I'd also known him to always be authentic and unbiased.

"Detective," he said, greeting me thin-lipped and without the bright smile I was used to seeing.

"Casey," I said, our speaking informally.

"Jonathon," he said, my having heard his name before, but never collecting it, registering it with his face.

"Alice said this is about Dr. Swales?"

"I have this," he answered and handed me the clear baggy, a memory card inside it like the kind Jericho had helped me retrieve from a boat's navigation system.

"What's on it?"

"It's from my news van's dashcam," he answered while I opened the baggy and removed the card. I had a reader already plugged into my computer, courtesy of Nichelle, and inserted the card. The video played back, showing the view in front of his van. "That's the municipal building—"

"—it is," I said, finishing for him. Jonathon drove past Dr. Swales as she exited the building, the image of her making me gasp. I recognized the clothing and asked, "This is before she died?"

"I thought you would want it," Jonathon said and took to leaning against my cubical. The video continued, Terri's frame leaving the video. I slapped my keyboard and paused the video when I saw it. "What's the matter?"

"Thank you," I said and clicked the screen to throw the video to the background. "May I keep this? Make a copy and return the card later."

"Absolutely," he answered, and offered his hand. I took hold and stood to walk him toward the gate. "Dr. Swales was always great to me and I thought you all would want to see her in the video."

"Yes," I said, eager to get him out of my cubical. "That was very thoughtful of you."

"Keep it as long as you want," he said, the gate slapping shut behind him.

I didn't reply and ran back to my desk, heart racing as Terri's voice rang in my head like steeple bells. Only, the sound was her saying the word, *pushed*. I kicked my chair to the side and played the video in a loop. On it, I saw Terri walking to her car, her Walkman cord around her chin, the foamy orange headset on her ears. Jonathon drove by, passing Terri's parked car. But then across the parking lot, I saw the car I recognized. And from it, there was Barbara Newman, the Jacksons' neighbor, walking with a limp. Was she there to see Dr. Swales?

Terri was an ardent sewer. From the baseball stitches of an autopsy, to quilts and sweaters and scarves. She would have never left home with her purse strap half torn. There was the cut on Terri's chin too.

Was Barbara Newman the last person to speak to Terri Swales?

TWENTY-SIX

The sky had darkened in the latter half of the afternoon, clouds forming and dumping a relentless rain that I feared would hamper our search of the Delight's Funfair grounds. It was the FBI who'd pushed the necessary paperwork, their attaching my case, along with Emanuel's and Detective Jeremy Watson's. When the clouds broke, we made our way to Corolla, a few miles above the Currituck Beach Lighthouse. Tracy and Nichelle found Delight's next location, the schedule showing they'd be on the east side of Route 12, taking over the parking lot of a shopping mall for the next five days.

We parked in the lot next to the carnival, the rain turning into a light drizzle, the grounds wet enough to form puddles and small creeks along the cracked asphalt, funneling into larger flows that raced along the edge of the street. There were two dozen uniformed officers we placed strategically around the perimeter while my extended team entered from the front. Raindrops trickled down my face, the damp cold making me shiver. It could have been the building adrenaline too. I stood at the entrance, sizing it up, sizing up our efforts and thinking we could have used more patrols in case the suspect decided to run.

There were no suspects yet though, but that could change once the search and questioning began.

"It's a lot bigger than I imagined," Nichelle said, rainwater dripping from the bill of her FBI cap. She eyed the colorful banners spelling out the carnival's name and the spiraling red and white striped pillars. "Where do we start?"

"Right there," I answered and pointed at the attendant sitting in a booth. It was the same woman I'd seen when we first visited the carnival. We began to walk, the team filing behind me, our badges in clear view. The attendant picked up a walkie-talkie, the size of it fitting snugly in her hand. She said a few words I couldn't hear over the music, and then waved me in without question. I passed beneath a speaker, the carnival music playing loud, mixing with the jocular sounds of the games which were open. There were whoops and hollering from a few visitors braving the weather, some of them winning and others losing. What was missing were the yells and screams of delight that came with the mechanical clacking of the rides, the weather dousing everything and shutting them down. A part of me was glad for the thinner crowd. It meant less people, less danger to them and, particularly, to any more victims.

"They're not liking this," Tracy said, following alongside Nichelle. She was plain-clothed like me but wore a jacket with Kill Devil Hills Police logo, an eagle at the center, and memorializing the Wright brothers' first flight. It was Nichelle and her team that got the recognition, the few visitors parting way, the carnival workers talking amongst themselves or into walkie-talkies like the girl in the booth. When I made eye contact with one of them, he spat a ribbon of tobacco juice, the wad splashing the asphalt near us, an affront to our being there. Beyond the worker, appearing between the ring-toss game and a miniature tilt-a-whirl ride, I saw Jimmy Delight. He waved his hands at us, his face beet red and wearing a fierce scowl as he stomped toward us in a rush. "Man, that guy is really mad."

"What! What is this!?" he spat, lips wet like his graying hair. Nichelle handed him the warrant as the FBI agents behind her began to fan out in a coordinated manner. The carnival turned quiet while he opened the warrant and began to read. Shoes crunched the pebbles atop the pavement as carnival workers moved subtly behind their concession stands and gaming counters. The rain had bled through Jimmy Delight's pale shirt enough to show a body filled with tattoos, one of them creeping from his shoulder to his collar. It danced with the thick cords bouncing on his neck, his muscles straining. "This is total bullshit."

"Is that him?" Tracy asked. I followed her gaze through the chains of the swing ride to glimpse a red color that shined bright against the dim gray weather. The green hair and white makeup came next. It was the clown from the fliers. He watched us and held on to one of the swing's chains, pressing the side of his head against the metal. Two children were near him and urged the clown to do a trick. But he paid them no mind, his focus concentrating entirely on us. I shuddered when his gaze met mine and he tilted his head as though a ghost had whispered something into his ear. I wanted to think that perhaps it was one of the girls that had been killed, their telling him we were coming. I shook my head with a double take, hearing Tracy ask, "But it can't be?"

"Sir?" I asked with raised concern. My voice was enough to steal Jimmy Delight's attention while I unfolded one of the fliers Tracy had printed and handed it to him. "This is you?"

Even with the carnival owner standing in front of me, I could see the resemblance to the clown in the picture. Hidden beneath the wild-haired wig, and behind the thick makeup and oversized clothes, it was Jimmy Delight's face. "That isn't me," he replied, the fury that had been on the face dissolving like a look of heartache.

"But you know who it is?" I said, asking with demand.

That's when the revelation hit me and made me suck in a wet breath. "You've always known! It's why you move abruptly—"

A crashing thump knocked against my shoulder with a shove coming from behind that was hard enough to slam me into the carnival owner. We toppled forward, Tracy trying to save me, only to fall when Jimmy Delight grabbed her arm for support. From the corner of my eye, I saw the red hair and tall build of Detective Jeremy Watson, his shoes a blur as he raced to catch the clown. My arms pinwheeled with a threat of falling, but I regained my balance while Tracy and the carnival owner crashed to the ground. "It's my brother, Robert," Jimmy wheezed. "Please don't hurt him."

I didn't respond and ran after the detective from Greenville. He'd heard enough of what Jimmy Delight was saying and convicted the carnival owner's brother without a trial. I held my breath when a cart rolled out from between two tents, narrowly dodging them, but losing ground to the detective. The clown jumped when he saw us coming, his funny face showing fright as he ran over the children, knocking them out of the way. "Stop!" Watson screamed. In the detective's hand, I saw his gun appear, the dangers suddenly rocketing. "Stop or I'll—"

"Holster your weapon!" I shouted, picking up speed, the tread of my shoes feeling loose against the wet pavement. Breathing heavy, my chest pounding, I tried screaming again, "Detective Jeremy Watson, stop!"

Emanuel was next, his gait massive with his tall legs. He didn't speak a word as he passed but turned a hard right to slip through two concession stands when the clown disappeared. I neared the back of Detective Watson, his shirt loose, the back of it coming untucked. I risked the retaliation and snagged it, slowing down, forcing him to stop. "What are you doing!"

I heaved and bent over to catch my breath. "Gun!" I said, waving my hand at it. I looked him square in the eyes with a thought of a reprimand. "Detective, you know better."

He holstered his gun, his face slick from the wet air. He covered his eyes with his heels, saying, "I told them I would get Jeanette's killer!"

"Then follow me," I said, tugging on his shirt when I resumed the chase. Behind the concessions where Emanuel had gone, there were dozens of cables snaked across the pavement that threatened to trip us or twist an ankle. We held a makeshift fence, the metal cold and wet, using it to guide us to the other side of the carnival where Emanuel stood in front of a funhouse. It had a row of ruby-colored flags lining the roof, their lying still without a breeze to lift them. The funhouse was painted and black and white, a giant circle at the entrance with its insides striped like a barber pole. "Where is he?"

Emanuel's hair and face were beaded wet, his breath a cloudy gust as he spoke, "He went inside... there, that house thing!"

The line of us jumped with a start when music suddenly trumpeted and strobe lights flashed like lightning, the funhouse windows turning into giant teeth. The house became electric. It was alive. The round entrance began to spin too, the red and yellow paint spiraling in a motion that made me feel wobbly. I forced myself to look away. "We've got to go inside."

"What did I miss?" Tracy said, joining us. "FBI have the owner in custody—hey, the power is on with this one."

"Robert Delight must have turned it on before he went inside." I looked for movement in the windows, but the strobe lights blinded me. Delight was using the funhouse as a shield, and it was my guess that he probably knew the inside layout better than anyone. It might be that this was his lair where he sat like a spider and waited for his prey. What web of tricks did he have for us?

"Are we going in?" Tracy asked. I saw her look to me and then to my hip and my gun. Her focus went to the other detectives, their weapons. When our eyes met, she answered her own question, "I'll wait out here?"

"It's best you do that, but I got a task for you," I said. She clasped her hands eager to help. "Get the owner and see what you can do about the power."

"You bet," Tracy answered, leaving my side as Nichelle and some of the FBI joined us.

I tugged on Detective Jeremy Watson's shirt where I'd torn a hole. "Sorry about that."

"You can make it up to me by catching this guy," he grunted without turning away from the funhouse. He was ready. Maybe too ready.

"We want him alive," I warned, tugging on his shirt, forcing him to look at me. The hard scowl from earlier remained. There was blood in the air and he was hunting for revenge. I needed him, but suggested, "We can handle this if you think it best to sit out."

"No way!" he scoffed. I dipped my chin with a hard look, making him recognize that I had seniority on the site. "Alive. I'll do everything by the book."

I turned to Emanuel, noticing his face was the color of ash and his lips moved silently. I couldn't make out what he was saying and asked, "Hey? Are you okay?"

"Um. Is it too late to tell you I hate funhouses?" he asked and bit his upper lip. "I almost hate them as much as I hate clowns."

I felt a laugh erupt from deep in my gut, thinking he was joking. But when the look on his face didn't change, I asked, "Do you need out?"

He blew out his lungs and answered, "Let's do this."

"Remember, guys, he's just a man. And if he's who we think he is, then he's a killer too. A predator."

"Are we ready?" Nichelle's manager asked, coming along-side me with another agent. She was petite and looked young enough to have been one of the victims in this case. She was nervous too, her stare fixed on the funhouse, a hand saddling her firearm.

"Yes," I said, taking the lead to enter. There was the scuffle of feet, the rest of the FBI joining us. They hurried to guard the front and circled to the rear, the funhouse bordering the temporary fencing. As we ascended a metal ramp, I told the team, "There's no place for Robert Delight to go."

"Watch your step," someone said, the metal ramp slick from the rain, our shoes squelching as we climbed.

"Cargo trailers," I commented, looking over the railing at the ground. That's what the funhouse was built from—two, maybe three of the trailers buttoned together to form one structure. Which made sense since they traveled from town to town. I spoke over my shoulder at the agent behind me, "I think the exit is ground level."

"We've got that covered," he said in a breathy voice. "We'll capture anyone going in or out."

We reached the entrance. There was pitch-black darkness on the far side, giving me pause. Nobody moved. "I'll go," I said, daring to take a step, the red and yellow tube spiraling. On the second step, my feet were swept out from beneath me, my middle and arms tightening as I fell on my side. "Crawl," I yelled, getting back to my hands and knees, cold wet seeping through my pants as I scurried to the other side.

"What's there?" Emanuel asked while he knelt and gauged the spinning tube.

I unclipped my holster, not knowing if the suspect might be armed. Emanuel landed on his shoulder with a thud, his yelling and cursing. "Move fast," I told him, stretching my arm for him to take hold. "You have to move fast."

His face was wet and he wiped it while we took a step into a room, "Can't see a thing."

"Funhouse or not, we're here on police business," I said and turned on a flashlight. Its beam fell on a shadowy figure as it jumped out of the light.

"Shit!" Emanuel yelled into my ear, his voice a raspy whisper. "This fucking guy!"

"Easy," I said, breathing furiously, a lump growing in my throat with the taste of metal rising on the back of my tongue. When my foot landed on a lump, I shined the light at the floor.

"Shit! Are those rats?!" Emanuel shouted and squeezed my arm hard enough to make me pull away.

"They're not real!" I told him, showing him the hard rubber mounds and the loose twine used to mimic rat tails. "I'm guessing you hate them too—"

A gun's hammer clicked into place, the unmistakable sound shutting me up. In the terrible silence that followed, I realized my mistake and killed the light. By shining the flashlight into the dark, I'd made us a target. The tiny room exploded in a brilliant white flash, a fire scorching the air and an immense burn teasing my leg. I dropped at once, landing hard and drawing my gun. There was a rapid run of thumping against the floor as I pressed my body painfully flat against the rubber mounds, the fake rat tails winding around my fingers. The footsteps were growing distant, it was Robert Delight running from us, leaving the room. "Emanuel!"

"Casey," he grunted, his voice wet. "That damn guy!"

A flash of lights blinded me, three of them with a voice beckoning from behind them, "We heard gunshots!"

"Your lights!" I shouted. Before the flashlights were doused, I saw the blood. I saw the dark pool, saw the direness of what it meant. "Emanuel!?"

"I can't go with you," he answered with a slur. "That guy shot me in my thigh."

"We'll take care of him," the young agent with the FBI said, her fingers on my hand, tapping gently to let me know where she was.

I looked at her skeptically, the size of Emanuel compared to the agent daunting.

"Casey, go!" Emanuel demanded. More footsteps came, along with the fall of a body, agents entering the spinning mouth only to be tripped up by it. "Fucking guy ruined my pants."

There was a hand on my arm, urging me to stand. "Come on," I heard Detective Watson say.

The detective's fingers glided down my arm, the touch aggressive to make sure we didn't lose contact. When I felt his fingers in my palm, I gripped his hand tight, weaving my fingers with his while we moved forward into the inky black. Pain knifed my thigh as I took a step, "Hold up," I said, trading hands, clutching my leg. It was wet and sticky, warm with blood.

"What's the matter?" he asked, voice short.

"I think I was hit," I told him, uncertain what was my blood and what was Emanuel's. "But I can go on." We squeezed hands, moving into the next room. In my head, I imagined another cargo trailer and where the walls would be.

"What is this place?" Detective Watson asked, the room opening to what was the length of a concert hall. I squinted until my eyes could adjust and reached out in front of me. Where there should have been air, I found glass, the tip of my gun bumping it.

"We're in a maze," I said, letting go of his hand. "It's a hall of mirrors."

A gunshot pierced my ears, shattering a wall of glass, the bullet ricocheting from striking metal, whizzing by us with a distorted sound. We dropped behind the entrance, the safety of the dark concealing us, the mirrored room a mirage of reflections with flashes of green hair and white makeup. Detective Watson's face remained firm with a scowl. His gaze fell to my leg and softened. "You did get hit," he mouthed.

I dared to look down, afraid to see it, knowing the adrenaline was pumping fully to keep me moving. There was a cut the width of a bullet. It had torn my thigh open and must have struck Emanuel in the leg. I looked in the detective's eyes and pointed behind him. There was a path around Robert Delight's location. It was our chance. "Cover me!"

With the detective's nod, I lurched forward. He jumped up and returned fire in a fury so rapid, it kept Robert Delight down. I hurried on my hands and knees, shards of glass cutting, the small space exploding with the acrid smell of burnt sulfur. Glass rained down around my head and shoulders, Robert Delight having enough and returning fire, shooting wildly in any direction. When I saw the back of him, I got up and screamed, "Freeze!" and stared down the barrel at a tuft of his green hair. Robert's clown face turned around, eyes weepy with tears staining his cheeks. "Drop your weapon!"

"Okay! I will," he said nervously, his arm sleeved in blood, the wound superficial. On the floor, he placed his gun and faced me. His face was painted with the red smears of a smile.

TWENTY-SEVEN

The smell of the autumn season was thick outside the station, yesterday's downpour caking the sidewalk with wet leaves. The sun was still low, the sky a warm pink that hinted of good weather today. The sky's shade reminded me of the cotton candy I'd seen at Delight's Traveling Funfair. The carnival was closed and would be for the foreseeable future. We had both Delight brothers in custody, though only one was considered a suspect in the murders.

I didn't believe Jimmy Delight had anything to do with the murders his brother carried out. But in my gut, having seen the look on his face, I was certain he knew something. It was the only explanation to their moving when they did—the suddenness on the tails of a newly discovered body. The FBI might try to make a case, and for now, we had his cooperation, his telling us his brother had always been troubled.

And he had been troubled. His rap sheet was as long as my arm, filled with offenses that included cruelty to animals and a collection of assaults. There was even a court order psychiatric hold when he was younger, his custody turned over to his older brother. I wanted to know what happened before he'd reached legal age, but those records were sealed. Had he killed before, or had he been testing the waters as serial killers sometimes do?

I entered the station with a slight limp that must have been noticeable enough to fend off the reporters, their giving me distance and staying out of my way. But the questions came anyway. Not that it mattered. Even if I could say no comment or offer something, they'd interpret as they wanted, making sure there was a story. With my last case, I'd grown weary of reporters and their questions and motives. It was almost to a point of distrust. After all, as cold and heartless as it was, for them another murder was another story. Since my last case, I purposely kept the answers short, if I gave any at all. When I reached the gate, the top of it smoothed from years of use, I lifted my head enough to see the usual faces, the usual suspects seeking a comment that they might present or misrepresent, depending on how it fit their needs. Sometimes it was for the better, and sometimes not.

"Can you tell us how Detective Wilson is doing?" Jonathon asked and held the gate for me. He was the reporter who'd given us the dashcam footage, the contents of which I know he reviewed. I appreciated that he hadn't asked about the video, knowing to do so in a public forum could jeopardize an investigation into Terri's death.

I grinned at the politeness, answering, "Detective Emanuel Wilson required short surgery. His status is stable, and he is expected to make a full recovery."

Another reporter approached, shoes scraping the floor, a reminder of the funhouse and the dark hallway. I grew tense and braced the gate, a cold sweat forming on the back of my neck. "Casey?" the reporter holding the gate asked.

"I'm okay," I said, assuring him as I turned to face another question.

"And the carnival murders?" the reporter asked, her hair tied back in a bun. She wore a blue pantsuit and cream blouse, a camera recording us. I glanced at the station monitors to see if we were being broadcast live. We weren't, which was good since the FBI would hold a press conference this morning.

"No more questions at this time," I said, hurrying past the gate to get to my desk, where there was a clutter of FBI agents working, the logos on their hats and jackets big and bright. At the center I saw Nichelle and her manager. They'd had the first hours with Robert Delight, their investigation preceding mine by eighteen months. A raw feeling stirred in my gut. When they broadened their search, I was certain they'd find more murders.

"How are you feeling?" Nichelle asked, looking to my leg with a concerning smile. Her shoulders drooped then, asking, "And Emanuel? How's he doing?"

"I'm fine," I told her. I shut my eyelids when an image of the blood pool blinked in my mind. Forcing a smile and opening my eyes. "He's—"

"That bad?" she asked before I could finish, fright showing.

"He'll have a limp for a while, but the doctors are sure he should make a full recovery."

"Oh good." She took my hand in hers and gave it a squeeze. "I was worried about you guys."

"And how is our suspect?" I asked. From my bag I took a folder I'd prepared for this morning.

As we made our way to the interview room, she answered, "He complains a lot, but he only needed a couple of stitches."

"Other than the complaints, did he spill anything?" I asked, a part of me hoping he was being stubborn, so I'd have a chance to question him. "Am I too late?"

"Not a word." She motioned a closing zipper across her lips, answering, "I don't know that he's going to admit to anything."

"The tissue samples. If there's a match to his DNA then we

can convict on the evidence for Laura Jackson." Her brow rose as she fidgeted with her hands. Noticing she was uncomfortable, I asked, "Have you had any luck tracking down the samples?"

Her mouth puckered like it sometimes does when she doesn't want to disappoint. And disappointment was what I felt. I narrowed my eyes. A DNA match was a certain lock. When she saw my reaction, she answered, "But we're still working on it."

"Well keep at it!" I said, unintentionally sounding short. She regarded the tone. "Sorry, that's not directed at you. If we end up going to trial, I don't want to see us without a critical piece of evidence."

"Understood," Nichelle said, her brown eyes shining gold as the morning sunlight entered the narrow hallway. "Good luck in the interview."

I tapped the folder I'd prepared, my fingers tingling with anticipation. Our suspect hadn't budged and that meant it was my turn.

Nichelle twisted her mouth again, looking unsettled, and asked, "Want me to join you?"

I took note of the time on the clock, the minute hand swinging by the top of the hour. "Give me fifteen minutes with him first, and then come in with your laptop." She nodded and exited the narrow hallway, leaving me alone with two patrol officers standing guard. The bigger of the two couldn't have been more than a few years older than our victim. He opened the door for me, tipping his cap as I passed by him.

The interview room was thick with the smell of perspiration, the walls bare and empty of color. There was one window with black glass, my reflection in it muted. Sitting on the other side, watching and listening, there was the FBI and possibly our local sheriff. In the center of the room, a single metal table, which was bolted to the floor, welded guard bars along the side were empty, Robert Delight sitting free of any handcuffs or chains.

He regarded me as I entered. His clown clothes had been replaced with an inmate-issued jumper. The outfit he'd worn was evidence now. His clown wig was gone too, leaving behind stringy hair which he'd dyed the same lime-green color. Loose strands hung limp over his face, pink skin bleeding through the creases and cracks of the remaining white makeup which had worn thin in spots. What was left of the red makeup around his mouth had smeared across his cheeks, giving the impression of a smile that wasn't there. His bulbous clown nose was also taken into custody, leaving the tip of it bare like the walls around us.

There was black eyeliner around his brow and dabbed in blotches on the puffy skin beneath his eyes which gave him a sinister look, and nothing like the jocular clown we'd first seen on the flier. At the table was Nichelle's commanding officer. The FBI agent sat stone-faced, his focus buried in a myriad of paperwork as he shuffled it from one side to the other. He glanced up at me, a look of frustration and exhaustion, and then glanced at the contents on the table. It was the string of colorful handkerchiefs used in the magic trick where Robert made them appear out of thin air. Next to it, the ruffled collar, the material bright red, the small evidence bag with a single thread found on Cynthia Harriet's body, the colors the same.

"You like magic?" I asked Robert, his eyelids droopy as though he were bored of the questions.

He cupped his right arm, showing me a gauzy bandage with dried blood on the material. "You have a trick to make the pain go away?"

"Afraid not," I said. I put my hand on the back of a chair, the metal cold. I used it to lean, deciding I'd stand for this interview. I poked at the chain of handkerchiefs, eyeing the knots that bound them together. "Want to tell me about this magic trick?"

My heart jumped when I saw a flicker of motion on his left cheek. It was faint and subtle enough to have been overlooked, but I saw it. His face went stone cold again, his stare as dead as the bodies lying in the morgue. "Could I get some aspirin?"

"We can do that," I said, opening the interview room door. The burly officer who'd held the door turned to face the room. "Some aspirin?" I asked. I looked at Robert, asking, "Water? Coffee?"

"Pop, diet," he answered. "Anything as long as it's diet."

"Thank you, officer," I said, leaving the door open, a gush of air circulating to clear the room of its staleness. When Robert's focus went to the folder in my hands, I opened it and placed a picture of Jeanette Klause on the table. It was the Greenville victim, the niece of Detective Jeremy Watson, who'd decided not to partake in the interview, which I thought was best for him and the suspect. Robert Delight brought his arms together, weaving his fingers and placed them on the table as he leaned forward. The tremble appeared again like a rattly pipe stirring behind a wall. It was faint, but I saw enough to know to look for it. "Recognize her?"

"Can't say I do," he answered coolly, sweeping scraggly green hair behind an ear. It was a lie. I knew it, and so did the FBI agent.

"Mr. Delight, let me be blunt." His brow rose to form new creases, the caked makeup cracking. I motioned to the table, saying, "There is enough evidence in front of me to seek a guilty verdict from a jury. Cooperate with us and we'll cooperate with you." I wanted to include the death penalty as a possibility but would wait for the district attorney.

He shrugged and spoke slow and without interest. "But there's no evidence."

"Are you sure?" I asked. From my folder, I presented a

picture of Cynthia Harriet's body, bumping the edge of it, the print gliding across the metal. It stopped in front of him, the girl's throat showing the worst of the ligature marks. His pupils expanded immediately, an irrepressible response, the twitch in his left cheek following. It was barely noticeable, the trembling just a shimmer over his makeup, but I saw it. Like an amateur poker player, our suspect had a tell. What was even better, I don't think he had any idea about it.

He shoved the picture back to me. "Doesn't prove anything."

I'd made sure the picture was printed at a one-to-one scale with the victim's size, her neck a match to what it was in life. On it, the colors were a purplish swarm with a well-defined pattern that resembled a butterfly. Only it wasn't a butterfly. I slipped on a pair of gloves, taking my time, the elastic nylon snapping around my wrist. I picked up one of the evidence bags, samples already taken for analysis, its next stop being an empty space on the shelf of our evidence locker. The plastic crinkling made our suspect stir. It was a tell, and it urged me to open the bag, my fingers covered tight with nylon.

Robert Delight squirmed when I touched them, his disposition changing to uncomfortable, another tell perhaps. "What are you doing with my stuff?"

"I thought I'd perform a magic trick of my own," I answered with sarcasm, Nichelle's manager taking notice and sitting up. Robert Delight grew more restless and began to scratch his chin as I handled the handkerchiefs. I moved to the center of the table where the photograph was, his gaze serious, brow furrowed. "That's okay with you?"

He splayed his fingers away from his chin, fanning them in a sleight-of-hand manner the way a magician performs a card trick. "Why shouldn't it be?"

I was touching what we believed to be the murder weapon.

What I had in hand wasn't just a string of handkerchiefs knotted together though. There was a wire strung through the middle which explained why they didn't appear quite as flaccid as was expected. Between my fingers, I pinched the wire, guessing it thin enough to provide flexibility, but stiff enough to use as a weapon. It explained why the handkerchiefs didn't come loose or tear. He'd hidden a garrote inside the string of handkerchiefs. It was the knots that had me curious, the picture on the table was like Cinderella's foot, the handkerchief knot in my hand her slipper. Nichelle's manager saw what I wanted to do and stood up for a better look. "If the shoe fits," I said, laying the knot atop the picture, the size and shape a near-perfect match. "I think we can confirm this as the murder weapon."

There was dissatisfaction on Robert Delight's face as he lowered his head. "What kind of magic trick is that?" he asked, surprising me. I'd thought he'd ask for a lawyer, but it was the trick I'd mentioned that he wanted to see.

"I suppose it isn't much of a trick after all." He scoffed and sat back, his focus locked on me as I handled the murder weapon. How many innocent lives had he stolen with it? The thought of what it was, and how it was used sickened me, my stomach flipping. My mouth went dry as I tilted my head, and told him, "The real trick is what the district attorney will do." I dropped the string of handkerchiefs onto the table, leaning over the edge, adding, "Or what the other inmates will do to you. I doubt they'll take kindly to your clowning around."

"Funny," he chided. But I could see he wasn't laughing. He wiped his mouth, red smearing from the sweat on his upper lip. "We'll see."

"How about these?" It was time to show more pictures. One by one, I placed the life-sized photographs showing ligature marks, a picture of the victim next to it. Robert Delight mussed his hair as the shape of the handkerchief knots aligned with each picture. The twitch continued as well, his recalling their faces and what he'd done. "Remember her?" I asked, placing Laura Jackson's school picture on the table. Next to it, an enlarged photograph I'd taken in the morgue.

Robert Delight sat up, muttering, "Uh-uh." He quickly corrected himself, waving his hands over the photographs and collected evidence. "Got nothing to do with any of these." My chest tightened when I placed the knot onto Laura's picture, the bruising around her neck not the same shape. We'd already seen that it was different, but until I put the murder weapon there, I didn't know how much. I said nothing and produced a picture of the fulgurite we'd recovered from her throat. "What? You think I killed a rock?"

I ignored the comment, asking, "Do you know what it is?"

He leaned in to give the picture a second look, his interest waning, his gaze drifting to the victims he knew. "Like I said, a rock." I gathered the pictures as Nichelle's manager gathered the murder weapon and the evidence for placement into custody. "We done?"

"We are," I answered. "Officer," I asked, voice breathy as I tried to fight the heaviness of doubt. "Could you escort the prisoner back to his cell."

"What? That's it?" Robert Delight yelled, jumping up. His fist banged the table suddenly, the metal clamoring sharp and loud.

"No, sir! That's not it!" I yelled as the officer subdued our suspect. We didn't have the DNA yet, there were still tests to be done. "The district attorney will decide what's next."

Robert Delight was led out of the room, the FBI following with the evidence, leaving me alone with my folder. I opened it, the smell of the photographs still fresh. I stared long and hard at the fulgurite and at Laura Jackson's neck. Somewhere in the Outer Banks her killer was walking free. A wrenching despair hit me hard. He could be anyone. He could be tall or short. Or black or white. I didn't know who he was, but imagined he was reading a newspaper or maybe monitoring the case online. If he was, then I'm sure he knew that we were missing something, that he'd gotten away with murder, that he could get away with it again.

TWENTY-EIGHT

The walls in the interview room began to close around me, the flat white paint inscribed with Laura Jackson's name. I saw her pictures too, her face as it was when she was alive, when she was vibrant, beautiful. There were the autopsy photographs too, along with the ones we'd taken on the beach where her body had been discovered. I shut my eyelids with a stormy pressure building in my head. In the darkness, I saw her sister, Shawna, walking alongside their birth parents. I was willing the truths to come to me as if some spiritual force of nature could cast a spell. My eyelids sprang open with the understanding I'd need science and technology and the deductive powers of being a detective. Those were my tools. To find Shawna and find Laura's killer, I had to keep working.

I'd entered the narrow hallway of our interview rooms when I heard the voices of Carla and Frank Jackson. Had they come to the station? Like an echo that has you spinning left instead of right, I saw they were nowhere to be seen. It was the station monitors hanging from the ceiling that had everyone's attention. On it, a news conference with the familiar faces of reporters that cover our station, along with Carla and Frank

Jackson. The words *Carnival Killer in Custody* scrolled along the bottom of the monitor, the letters in bright yellow with a red background, the colors clashing purposely to pop the contrast. I felt my mouth go slack when I saw Detective Jeremy Watson standing behind the Jacksons, along with a woman who shared his chin and eyes and hair color. His sister, I thought, the mother of Jeanette Klause. I'd be lying if the sight of them together didn't bother me. We still had work to do, still had a case of kidnapping and murder to solve. But Detective Jeremy Watson didn't work for me, leaving me little choice but to watch and listen. I joined Tracy and Nichelle and the staff of FBI agents, our standing silently, chins up as the broadcast continued.

Mrs. Jackson stood at the microphones, her pink skin glistening in the daylight, her eyes big enough to see they were bloodshot and welling, a look of relief in them as she spoke. She half-turned, her hand patting Detective Jeremy Watson's chest as she spoke, *"I'm so grateful to the detective."* She held up a picture of Laura and Shawna, continuing, *"So grateful Laura's killer is in custody."*

She covered her mouth with a cry, the sight of it painful to watch. Mr. Jackson put a consoling arm around her, taking the picture. His eyes were different than his wife's. They were tear-filled and desperate as he pleaded and looked into the camera, *"Please!"* he began and shoved the picture of the girls forward, its filling the screen with blurred colors. The cameras refocused as Mr. Jackson spoke, *"If anyone has seen our other daughter, Shawna, please contact the police!"*

"Tell me we have a case?" a voice spoke loudly from the front of the station. Heels clapped the floor and the front gate slapped shut, the district attorney making her way toward me. For a Saturday, she was dressed in her usual all-business attire with her golden hair pinned tight behind her head, a pair of heavy, thick horn-rimmed glasses in tortoiseshell. She was tall and lean, with long fingernails that seemed to me to be too burdensome. She glimpsed the station monitor as she reached us, her thumb in the air pointing at it. The look on her face showed every bit of annoyance about the press conference that I was feeling. "I've been on the phone with Greenville and Elizabeth City all morning. They feel there is a case. What do we have?"

"Ma'am," I said, keeping my voice calm, but hearing it edge concern. "With the FBI's help, there is a case. A strong case that can persuade any jury to favor a verdict of guilt."

She regarded my words, giving me a hard look. She balled her hand in a fist and set it against her hip. "You know, Detective, I swear it's like talking to a statue with you. You got this stone face that I can't read."

I felt a smirk warm my cheek, but held it in. "I guess I can take that as a compliment?"

"Yeah," she said, shaking her head. "A compliment. But don't get me wrong. Stone face or not, I think I heard a *but* in that explanation. Talk to me."

"A second?" I asked, seeing the press conference continue with Detective Jeremy Watson and the parents of Jeanette Klause taking to the front and answering the reporters' questions. In the corner of the screen, they showed the picture of Robert Delight as he appeared on the Delight's Traveling Funfair flier. "I want to see this."

"Jesus!" the DA grumbled when the picture of the flier was replaced by a video of Robert Delight performing as the clown, his hooped pants swaying as he did cartwheels. She groaned when the video cut to another segment showing him performing a magic trick for kids, yanking the string of handkerchiefs from his hand. "And there goes a local jury selection. Defense lawyers are going to argue unfair bias. They might even try for a change of location."

"Let them," I said, trying to defuse her emotions. "The

evidence will speak for the victims regardless of where the trial takes place."

"What don't I know yet?" she asked.

"The Jackson girls," I answered, picking up Laura's tablet. "Robert Delight had nothing to do with Laura's murder, and nothing to do with Shawna's kidnapping."

The DA typed on her phone, fingernail scraping the glass. "And you still believe it was their birth father you saw with the younger sister?" She continued her text message, speaking to us while looking at her phone. "Even though there's been no corroborating sightings to confirm it?"

"I know what I saw," I said, nerves jangled by the questioning. Wheels from Tracy's chair screeched as she stood up. "We both saw Shawna Jackson with a man who resembled her birth father. And from later interactions with Jane Finley, we can assume he has her."

The DA peered over her phone at Tracy, saying nothing as she assessed the two of us. From behind me, I heard Tracy fidget, her left shoe moving as she pegged her toe behind her right foot. The DA let out a sigh, showing her phone screen briefly. "Well, there's been no talk of a defense attorney yet, so we've got a little time to clean up any loose ends."

"Speaking of loose ends," I began to say, her stopping me with a raised hand.

She briefly closed her eyes as though preparing. "What is it?"

"There was a tissue sample recovered from beneath Laura Jackson's fingernails, only we're having an issue reconciling Dr. Swales's notes and her... her system."

There was an apologetic look that softened the hardness on her face. "Listen, I am sorry for you and your team. Swales was an amazing medical examiner." She returned to her phone when it buzzed. Without looking up, she continued, "I've got to take this." She turned to leave, but stopped and asked, "The tissue sample. You said Delight had nothing to do with the Jackson girls?"

"That's right," I answered.

"Then his case is solid," she commented. A knot formed in my belly, knowing what she was about to say. "But to find who killed Laura Jackson, you're going to need that tissue sample."

The DA was right. What she didn't mention was that our list of suspects had plummeted to zero. It was the only tissue sample, and even if we had the DNA sample, we had no one to compare it to. My palms were sweaty with nerves, Laura's tablet between my fingers being the only thing we had that might offer up another clue. "Thank you, ma'am," I said and returned to my desk.

The Jacksons appeared on the monitor again, reporters asking more questions as another video snippet of Robert Delight in full clown makeup played in the upper corner. It was a long shot to disprove any abuse in their home. Even if we could show the slightest history, their alibi for the night of their daughter's death was firm. I opened the statement from old man Peterson, a crab fisherman. He'd been to the station while we chased down Robert Delight. In the report, he'd followed up on the charter the Jacksons had told us about and confirmed the fishing party was at Oregon Inlet's fishing center on the night Laura Jackson was murdered. He also supplied still images from their parking management, a towing service that monitors vehicles parked on the property, removing those that stay beyond a twenty-four-hour limit.

"Want to keep looking?" Tracy asked, her hand on my shoulder. I didn't want to show her how I was feeling, not when the case was this low. She sensed it though, saying, "Yeah, I know. I feel it too."

"All the good leads, or what we thought were good leads, they're gone," I said, gripping her hand in mine, appreciating the sentiment. For the sake of trying to fight defeat, I flipped open the cover of Laura's tablet once again. "Did we search everything?" I asked, rolling my chair to the side to give Tracy room next to me.

She plunked her spiral notebook onto my desk and sat down, air whistling from the chair seat. "Well, let me check. First there was the school's account, and all those applications." She tore a sheet of paper, crumpling it into a ball and throwing it at my trash can. It bounced off the lip and scuttled out of my cubicle. "Next there was Laura's account, and all her social media accounts." Again, she tore the paper from her notebook, made a ball and tossed it into the trash can. This one bounced twice, once on the wall as a backboard, before landing.

An idea came to my mind like a blink, on and off as I thought through it. With my focus on the paper ball on the floor, I asked, "What about her trash?"

Tracy scratched at her cheek, unsure of what I meant. She looked over my shoulder at the trash can she'd been aiming at, and asked, "Like her trash at her home?"

I tapped the tablet and clarified. "I mean her digital trash can. You know how when you throw something away, it isn't permanent, how there's always a trace of it. Maybe Laura put something in her trash?"

Tracy jerked her head back with a gasp. "We never looked!" She flipped through the pages of icons, finding the social media app that had the most use and clicked on it. "Let's hope the retention policy is relaxed."

"Anything?" I asked while writing down every possible digital trashcan I could think of. Tracy shook her head. "Okay, try the Photos App next."

The listing of photographs was in the thousands, there having been collected from across multiple devices, but with one single account which was Laura's personal cloud. "We've seen the school stuff, and the ones of her sister," Tracy mumbled while flipping through the options. "Casey! There's a folder called Recently Deleted!" Wide-eyed, she added, "We never looked in there."

"Open it!" I said, sitting at the edge of my seat and holding my breath. Inside we saw more of the same, photographs that were duplicates or blurry. "Sort on the most recently taken."

"That makes sense. We want to see the last photographs—" Tracy stopped talking when we saw a picture of Laura, a selfie, her arm extended to hold her phone, the camera set on a wide angle. The teenager was sitting on the same couch we'd sat on when speaking with Barbara Newman. Next to Laura was Geoffrey Newman, Barbara's husband. The two were alone and sitting close together, considerably close, enough to question given that the photograph was deleted. "Do you think something was going on between them?"

"I don't know," I answered, feeling sick to my stomach with the thought of sexual abuse, an older man taking advantage of a young girl. But the photograph of them could be completely innocent too. In it they were smiling and fully clothed, the time-stamp showing it was taken the night of the carnival, after it had closed. While it was very easy to speculate and to suggest the worst, it was also impossible to conclude anything from what we had.

The time of the picture did not line up with the story Barbara Newman told us, of driving the girls home earlier that evening. I tapped Tracy's arm, nearly punching it when I saw the background of the photograph. I pinched the screen, expanding my fingers to zoom into the room. "Tracy, take a look at that."

In the corner of the room there stood a handsome chestnut curio, the glass shelves illuminated and rimmed a bright emerald green, the tops lined with stony figurines that could be anything at first glance. When I zoomed in a little more, we both saw the fulgurite. Not just one piece, but a collection the way some people would collect and showcase Hummels or antique clocks and cameras. Mr. Newman's treasure of choice, his beachcombing appetite, was the same precious fulgurite stones like the one we'd discovered buried deep in Laura's throat. "I think we might have the source of that glass that cut into Barbara Newman's foot too."

TWENTY-NINE

Wind swept through my hair as I exited my car, the black-and-white stripes of Bodie Island Lighthouse ahead of me. Sea salt filled my nostrils with sunshine behind my head, throwing a long shadow of my body onto the grass. There was a small farmhouse, picturesque with windows dotting the second level, two red-brick chimneys on each side of the roof, a white picket fence along the front deck with a shallow ramp. It was the keeper's quarters, a man and woman standing in front of it. They wore hunter-green slacks and a jacket of the same color with a name tag and gold badge I recognized as the National Park Service. One of them had called the station to tell us they'd seen Robert Finley.

Tracy exited the car as tourists parked alongside of her, the lighthouse crowded for a Sunday. The weather had an autumn touch but had stayed just warm enough to spend the day outside to see the sight. I'd checked the hours of operations to confirm the call placed, discovering all the national sites hosted in the Outer Banks were open year-round except for Christmas Day. A woman in a minivan parked next to me, tires crunching loose stone on the asphalt. Every seat was filled, a look of excitement on her face as she eyed the sky and the lantern room sitting atop the lighthouse spire.

There were three buildings that I could see from the parking area, including a small one-room building at the foot of the lighthouse, a red-brick walkway stretching from it to the main house. There was a great lawn surrounding the property, the grass manicured, and bright green given the time of year, the previous day's rains helping. Another building edged the property to the north, a graying boardwalk running along the property and disappeared into the marshes where visitors ventured for a look at natural wildlife.

"Casey, there's a lot of people here," Tracy said, the sunlight shining gold highlights in her hair. She was scanning the parking lot just as I had when I first arrived. There was no truck that matched the one we'd seen Robert Finley driving. His had been impounded. I wouldn't expect to see the dusky blue pickup parked in front of the lighthouse. But that didn't mean he wasn't hiding from us, but doing so in plain sight. "Walk the grounds?"

"Yeah, let's move around, check in with them first," I said, eyeing the east, Route 12 where we'd driven from, the lighthouse on the west side of the highway and close to where we'd discovered Laura Jackson's body. "We're a mile from the Newman residence."

"Figured that'd be our next stop," Tracy answered, zipping a cotton jacket with the letters OBX embroidered on the front. I made my badge clear and ensured my gun was holstered, the safety strap buttoned. We came to the lighthouse without the FBI, but I had two patrols on the property to help cover the many acres in case Robert Finley was hiding here. If he was here, and the National Park Service personnel was on site, where would he have hidden?

"Ma'am," a woman in her fifties said, greeting me with a handshake, her fleece jacket swishing as she moved her arms.

She tipped the bill of her service hat to shield the sunlight that reached her eyes.

"You made the call?" I asked, guessing.

"Yes, ma'am. I work part-time up at the Currituck Lighthouse," she said, holding her hip and rocking as she spoke. "The lighthouse site manager told us about Robert, that we should call the police if we see him."

Yells and yips carried on a breeze, children running across the lawn, a purple and bright pink kite chasing after them. I kept my gaze on them as I asked, "How long ago did you see him here?"

"Thirty minutes, give or take," she answered, following my gaze to watch the kids play as kids do, one of them stumbling, the soft grass a cushion. "Does this have to do with his kid?"

Alarm rang in my head, making me turn back with that question and ask, "You spoke to him about his kids?" The woman looked down at the ground as she shoved her hands into her jacket pockets. The tops of her shoes were polished and shiny as she stewed over what to say and what not to say. "We just want to make sure Shawna Jackson is safe."

The woman looked up with reluctance on her face. She shook her head, saying, "I don't know where she is, but I can tell you Robert was here."

"You can tell us if he was alone or not?" I asked, trying to sound hopeful.

She frowned with the struggle, answering, "Listen, he's a good guy. He'd never hurt anyone."

I dared a step closer, turning my back to the wind, my hair blowing around my head and face. "We know he's been in contact with his older daughter—"

"—the one that got killed, what a horrible thing!" she said, her face losing all expression. The whites of her eyes were like saucers as she shook her head, adding, "But Robert would never—"

"I understand that, ma'am. It sounds like you worked with him closely?" I said, asking as she gave me a nod. "When was the last time you were in contact with him or his wife?"

"Not since the last shift we worked together," she answered, her gaze returning to the children running, the kite bouncing against the ground. She commented, "He was only trying to help them."

Tracy shot me a hard look. "Mr. Finley shared his plans with you?" The woman dipped her head, the bill of her hat covering her eyes. But I could see her lips tighten and turn white. "Ma'am, we only want to help Shawna Jackson."

Her eyes returned, soft and with an eagerness that said she wanted to help. "He's inside."

"Inside the lighthouse?" I asked, the crook of my arm bending to bring my fingers close to my gun. I began to walk, waving to a patrol officer to join us. "Is there anyone else inside?"

"No, ma'am, the next tour doesn't start for another hour," she answered as I moved past her, shoulder brushing her shoulder.

Reaching the entrance I held my hand behind me, keeping everyone back, the patrol officer taking to the opposite of the entrance. "Robert Finley," I yelled inside, my voice bouncing. When I dared a look, I saw the entrance was empty. To the officer, I mouthed, "On three... one, two, and—"

"Three," she responded as we held our guns toward the ground and climbed the concrete steps.

"Clear," I said, entering deeper, the concrete steps splitting to the right and left, the round room lined by an iron staircase that spiraled upward, the floor a black-and-white checkerboard. Sweat itched my palms, the nerves bringing heat from beneath my collar. "Robert Finley?" I yelled to the top of the lighthouse. A moment later, my own voice replied in an echo.

"Guess we've got to climb," the patrol officer said, her gaze following the spired staircase as it disappeared above our view.

"Then we climb," I said impatiently, hoping to have heard a response by now. I climbed six steps, looking behind me to see her following. She was breathing heavy, her face already blotchy. "Easy does it." I motioned for her to slow her breathing.

"I will," she said as another patrol officer entered to join the climb behind us, his boots ringing out on the metal treads. We turned to face the steps and began the ascent, taking our time as we wound our way up and around the lighthouse.

"First window," I muttered, thinking it a third of the steps behind us now as a burn inched up my calves. The gunshot wound on my thigh, just a graze, woke with the labor too and forced me to slow down.

"Just a third?" I heard the officer in the back ask.

A commotion bounced against the walls, raining like a distant patter. We stopped to listen, hearing the shuffle of shoes against metal. "We just want to talk to you," I shouted, and resumed the climb. Nothing else was said as we moved beyond the second window, my lungs tight, concern growing that we'd have no strength when we reached the top. But as I wound around the stairs, my feet heavier than I could ever imagine them being, I saw a flash of gray, and a pair of the National Park Service pants. It was Robert Finley standing alone at the landing of the third window.

He was fully dressed and appearing like he was ready to work. There was a look of dismay on his long face. I could see the resemblance to Laura Jackson, their having the same color hair, a strawberry-blond, though his was specked with grays. His complexion was the same, and there were freckles peppered across his nose and cheeks. But it was the golden-brown eyes that instantly told me he was their father. "Mr. Finley?"

"I just wanted to protect our girls," he said, wrinkles etched deep across his brow. Panic set in and my face turned cold when I saw him reach behind his back. I swung my gun around to the front of me, lowering my body until the steps ahead became my shield.

"Robert Finley!" I yelled. "Keep your hands where I can see them."

"She was safer with us," he said and began to weep. In his hands was a keyring the size of a baseball. And on it, there hung a hundred keys or more, some long and others short.

"Stay still!" I commanded and eased forward, the sight of my gun trained on his chest, a single shot in place. But I saw both of his hands and lifted my index finger as I blew a hot breath from my mouth.

When we were on the platform, his eyes were deep and sad, but seemed relieved, a ray of hope for a dire situation. For Robert Finley, it *had* become dire. "You'll help protect her?"

"Where is Shawna Jackson?" I asked, slowly taking the keyring from him. With his hands free of any instruments, the patrol officer took over, searching Robert Finley, patting him down before placing a pair of handcuffs on his wrists. "Sir, where is Shawna?"

He looked stunned and muttered broken sentences and fragments. "We got the letters. Knew it was best. But Caroline was killed. We had to save Janet." This was a form of shock or mental lapse and I was afraid he'd become despondent.

"Caroline and Janet?" I asked, desperate to reach him. Hearing me speak the old names of his daughters helped. Through his bloodshot and weepy eyes, he saw me and nodded to the names he and his wife had given their children. "Robert, can you tell us where Janet is?"

"Up," he answered and took to staring at the spiral staircase above us, the remaining steps leading to the top. "She's safe now."

She's safe now. With his words, my mind froze. Would Robert Finley harm his child?

I didn't ask another question and leaped onto the steps ahead, taking two and sometimes three at a time. My pulse rang in my head like my shoes striking the metal, another pair echoing as the officer followed the same pursuit. When we reached the top, we found nothing.

"Where is she?" I asked, my voice a heavy rasp, barely able to catch my breath. The top of the lighthouse was a round room, empty with a door that exited to a balcony outside. I stopped moving, the officer joining my side next to a shallower staircase, the steepness more like a ladder. She pointed up as I nodded. Above us was the lantern room and it was closed to visitors. But for someone working the National Park Service, responsible for the lighthouses, Robert Finley had the key and he'd given it to us. Like the woman we'd met outside had said, he wouldn't harm his child. He only wanted her protected. I jangled the keyring, the soft touch of metal echoing, and said, "It's one of these."

"Which one?" the officer asked while I climbed the remaining steps and knocked on the door above me. No answer. I tried five keys, maybe eight before seeing the one with masking tape around the head. It went in and the door opened.

"Shawna?" I asked. A gush of cool air came, filled with the scent of French fries and cheeseburgers. It was strong and gave me hope. Finley had been here to bring his girl food. I climbed inside, the room surrounded by windows. In the center was a giant lens the shape of a circle. The pieces of glass were oriented like louvers, each of them carrying the reflection of rainbows. It was beautiful like artwork, and in the slats, I saw the frightened eyes of a child staring back at us. I knelt next to the lenses, their towering above us with Shawna on the inside next to the lantern. Her cheeks were mussed with mustard and ketchup, hair tangled, clothes dirtied. Next to her was an open bag with a few toys, abandoned as Shawna ate her food. "My name is Casey."

"I'm Shawna," she said, gazing behind me as footsteps rifled up the narrow pass.

"Hello there," I said with a soft voice. "Aren't you a pretty lighthouse girl."

She put on a toothy smile, though it lasted only a moment. "Is my sister here too?"

I couldn't be the one to tell her the terrible news about her sister, and instead asked her, "Would you like to go home? I know your mom and dad really miss you."

"Home?" she asked, blinking fast as though the idea were impossible to consider. "I can go home now?"

"Come on, baby," I said, holding out my hands and standing. There was a commotion below us as officers finished the climb, the raucous noise making Shawna flinch. She held up her hands for me to take, her eyes wide with fright, her fingers small in my palm. I crouched down and put my arms around her body, lifting her and calmly saying, "I'll take you home."

THIRTY

Less than a few miles from the Bodie Lighthouse, the Newmans' home sat across from the Jacksons' residence. The timestamp on the photograph found in Laura's digital trash can proved she was inside their home the night she was killed. This was not what Barbara Newman had told us. Where was Geoffrey Newman after the photograph was taken? What happened to the fulgurite collection on display? The Newmans were hiding the truth, but not for long.

Shawna Jackson clung to me, her skin sweaty, her arms and legs wrapped around my neck and hip, the sight of additional police frightening her. There was a benefit to being a detective and wearing plain clothes. Minus the badge and gun, I could easily fit in with everyone else. Shawna saw that, her tiny face filling with panic. From a patrol officer's radio, I heard the raspy call that Child Protective Services had arrived on site. There was also mention of the child's parents, Carla and Frank Jackson, Mrs. Jackson's voice rising in the background. It was brief, but enough for Shawna to hear.

"That's my momma?" she asked as we descended the spire,

easing around and around the metal staircase with one hand clutching the railing. "My other mom."

Shawna's birth parents must have told her who they were. I eased my head back until I could see the child's face. "You want to see her?"

"Yes!" she said, nodding vigorously before tucking her face into my neck and hiding her eyes as we continued down the stairs. "I don't want to be here. I want to go home."

"Yeah, this is a little scary," I said, speaking softly, feeling her chest against mine, her heart pounding in her chest. "But it's only a building."

"It's tall," she said, continuing to talk, which was a terrific sign that told me she hadn't suffered a trauma. "My other dad showed me all of them."

"Is that right? Your other dad showed them to you?" I asked, beginning to enjoy the conversation, the descent much easier than the climb. Thinking of the lighthouse names in the Outer Banks, I asked, "Did you see Ocracoke and Currituck?"

"Uh-huh," she answered, leaning back so I could see her face. She was small for her age and thankfully light. I tightened my hold when she let go of my neck to count the lighthouses on one hand. "And we went to Hatteras and Cape Lookout, which was closed, but we still went to the top."

"Is that right?" An eager nod. "And did you stay inside them long?"

"Sleepovers," she answered. She held up a hand, wiggling her fingers. "He had the keys, and we could see the big light at nighttime."

"That must have been something," I said, reaching the bottom step, the arches in my feet sore. The sun had slipped across the cloudless sky to stand high in the west, rays of buttery light pouring through the lighthouse doorway. A crowd had formed. Bodies were in silhouette, reporters jockeying for position. There were rapid camera clicks and shoes striking the red-brick walkway. Shawna collapsed the space between us, tightening her firm grip. Through the rush of bodies, I found the Jacksons, saw their desperate eyes, saw the pouches beneath and the endless worry all parents feared. "It's okay, baby."

"Shawna!" Carla Jackson yelled amidst a rain of mechanical clicks and clacks as I stepped onto the walkway. A white fence bordered the path which had been kept clear, the reporters standing on the sides of it. "My baby girl!"

"Ma'am," I said, greeting her as Frank Jackson joined us. I'd seen reunions before, always the look of utter despair squashed as relief sprang to life on their faces. Fingers clawed the air with an eagerness to hold their girl while camera flashes turned their faces ghostly white. When I felt Shawna's grip loosen, I whispered to her, "Would you like to see your mom and dad?"

She never answered, but released her tight hold, the back of my neck turning cold when her hands were gone. There were no other words when the Jacksons took their child in hand, only tears and cries, the world around the family of three disappearing. Days before, it had been a family of four. Through the crowd I found Tracy, our job continuing at the Newmans' place.

When I pulled up to the house, Barbara and Geoffrey Newman were packing their minivan, the side door open, a bag of groceries on the floor, their daughter rifling through it while holding a juice box in one hand. There was a hot pink duffle bag and luggage on one seat, a cargo carrier atop the car that Geoffrey Newman worked to secure to the roof. When I opened my car door and exited onto the street, Barbara Newman stopped what she was doing. She said something to her husband, her voice too quiet for me to hear. He shot a hard look in our direction, a question forming on his face.

"Mr. and Mrs. Newman?" I asked with insistence for their

attention. I walked around the front of my car, Tracy joining me with Laura Jackson's tablet in her hand.

"Officer," Mr. Newman said, tossing a bright orange tie-down strap over the top of the car roof. "What can I help you with?"

"I'd like to go inside to ask some questions," I said, my tone questioning, purposely inquiring and staying forceful.

The couple exchanged a look, Barbara Newman answering, "We... we're kind of in a hurry to beat the traffic."

"Headed out of town?" Tracy asked as we walked across their lawn and onto the pavement.

"What is this?" Mr. Newman asked, his eyeing a patrol car pulling up and parking in their drive to box the minivan in place. Another patrol drove from the opposite direction, parking perpendicular to the first. "What's going on?"

"Inside, please," I insisted.

"What questions?" Barbara Newman asked, leading her daughter out of the minivan. "Do we have to? Geoff—"

"It doesn't look like we've got much of a choice," Geoffrey Newman said and dropped the orange tie-down straps, the buckles striking the ground with metal clanking against stone.

We filed into the house, Barbara Newman sending her daughter up the stairs. The girl shuffled in a run as I watched her disappear at the landing. Shadows shifted in the hallway as a door shut closed, telling me she was in her room. When we entered the family room, the den with the fireplace and where the curio display cabinet with fulgurite had been, I went to the spot. With my phone's flashlight shining onto the carpet, I saw the faint impression of the cabinet, the shape matching what was in the photograph. "Mind telling us what was here?"

"There was a cabinet there," Geoffrey said, joining my side, his arms folded across his chest. He nudged his chin toward his wife who'd stayed in the kitchen where she watched us. Tracy stayed next to her, Laura Jackson's tablet in hand.

"Can you tell us what happened to the cabinet?" I asked, moving to the kitchen as Tracy opened the tablet. "What about what was inside? On display?"

"They were rocks... or a kind of rock," Geoffrey Newman answered with a shrug while following. He looked to his wife, adding, "It was Barbara's collection."

"Mrs. Newman?" I asked, wanting to hear an explanation before we showed them the picture.

She shook her head, the corner of her mouth in a curl. "I guess I got tired of it is all."

"How is your foot?" I asked, thinking of the glass shard she'd stepped on, the thick carpet in the den possibly hiding more evidence. She didn't answer, her eyes glazing with dullness as color drained from her face.

"Barbara?" her husband asked with concern as he touched her arm. "What's going on?"

I tapped Laura's tablet, the picture of him on the couch with her and spun it around for the two of them to see. "The time," I said, pointing to the watermark in the lower corner, the timestamp clearly showing. "Mrs. Newman, this shows that Laura Jackson was in your home the night she was killed."

"Laura took that picture of us after the carnival," Geoffrey Newman said. He picked up his phone, clicking through the apps and then turned it around to show another picture, similar, but from a different angle. "I took one too, so we could both have a picture."

"Jesus!" Barbara Newman said in a breathy voice that shuddered. "Geoffrey!"

"May I?" I asked, his handing me his phone.

"What's this about?" he asked, slapping his hand onto the granite, oblivious to his wife's previous lie.

Barbara Newman covered her face, lowering her head, her hair falling forward. On the side of her neck there were faint scabs. Barely visible, having mostly healed. "Mrs. Newman, can you tell us how you got those scratches?" I asked.

Geoffrey Newman's jaw fell slack, his cheeks flushed, his neck turning red as he gazed at his wife. "Barbara, what happened?"

She lowered her hands to stare at the pictures, brow rising slowly as she mumbled, "I told her to delete it, but she wouldn't."

"It was just a picture," he pleaded, his eyes turning wild. "What happened?"

"It wasn't just a picture!" she said, a frown forming, mouth twitching. "I've seen the way she looked at you and sat close to you. You can't tell me you didn't look at her differently!"

"Oh my God!" Geoffrey Newman cried, his strength draining as he dropped his arms onto the counter and rested his head. A sob. Guttural, heartbreaking. "She was a child!"

"Mrs. Newman?" I asked, thinking back to the search of Laura's room, and our finding the origami paper fortune teller with the initials Laura must have written. They were LJ and a GN. There could have been a young crush that resulted in a deadly misinterpretation by Barbara Newman. "The picture?"

"She wouldn't delete it," Barbara Newman said, her face turning soft again, brow raised as she stared blankly ahead. "When you left the house, I begged her to delete the picture. But she wouldn't do it."

"You fought with Laura that night?" I asked, hearing the confession begin, the woman's state of mind clearing with the emotions gone. "The fight got out of control?"

A chuckle, but not the kind that came with a laugh. It was one of disbelief, her answering, "She got so mad! I didn't know she could get so angry!"

Geoffrey Newman looked up with a look of hope showing. "Did Laura attack you?"

"She showed me she deleted it," Barbara Newman

explained. "But then she started screaming about it, calling me crazy... and I, I pushed her."

"Into the curio cabinet?" Tracy asked, Barbara Newman nodding.

I took out a picture of the fulgurite recovered from Laura's body and placed it onto the countertop. "Could you explain how this was found with Laura?"

Barbara Newman choked with shock, clutching her chest, the picture appearing to her like a ghost. "I searched everywhere for it. The cabinet was smashed, my collection was all over the floor."

Geoffrey Newman's shoulder shook as he cried silently while I asked, "Is it possible Laura picked it up?"

She continued to nod, but the effort was lacking, her looking at the wall distantly. She held up her arms, her fingers shaped like she was choking someone. "When her back was turned, I grabbed her"—she stopped and sucked in a breath, her chest rising—"around the neck as hard as I could. She must have picked up the fulgurite." She began to shake her head. "Must have taken it."

"She died when you grabbed her?" I asked.

Her eyelids snapped open wide enough to see the whites of her eyes. Her husband froze as he waited for her to answer.

"I felt it," she said, mumbling the words, her focus moving to her fingers which shook. "I felt the bones break." The shaking traveled into her arms and her body. "Laura... she just collapsed. I didn't know I was squeezing that hard."

"Ma'am," I said, hearing enough. We'd finish at the station with the district attorney present.

I pulled up a photo of the note found in the Jacksons' home, asking, "What about the note found in Laura's home? Did you write it and place it there?"

"Oh my God!" Geoffrey Newman said, opening a kitchen drawer, the sound of the casters urging me to place my hand on my gun. From the drawer he revealed a large plastic bag, the kind used for leftovers. Inside was a mess of scrap paper, torn pieces with the same calligraphy writing as the note found in the Jacksons' home. "That's one of Laura's notes."

"You save her notes?" Tracy asked. Barbara Newman's shoulders shook with a cry, an understanding of what was going to happen to her clearing the storm in her mind.

"When she babysits, she writes notes. Practicing her calligraphy," he answered as he opened the bag, showing a few. "We were going to make a scrapbook and give it to her to show off her writing."

"She wasn't heavy, and it was so dark," Barbara Newman began to say, her confession continuing. "Nobody even noticed. They didn't even see me."

"You carried her body to the ocean?" I asked, thinking of where we'd parked on Route 12 when we were first called to the sight of Laura's body.

"Light as a feather," she answered with a blank look on her face. "Lighter than Abigail."

"Barbara?" Geoffrey Newman asked, his hand on her arm. He looked to me for permission, his fingers on his phone. I gave a nod, his picking it up and scrolling through a contact list. "Babe, please. Don't say anything else."

"I put her in the minivan," Barbara Newman continued, ignoring her husband's request. I imagined she had to keep talking, had to purge the confession, release the sickness plaguing her soul. "We drove to the beach—the girls love the beach, you know," she said to me as if a part of a conversation between friends. "There was nobody anywhere, and I put her into the water gently. She looked so peaceful—"

"Barbara!" Geoffrey Newman yelled. "Hello, Frank!?" he asked, speaking into his phone. He put a finger in one ear and turned away. "We need a lawyer."

With the mention of the minivan, I showed my phone

again, the reporter's dashcam video playing back on the screen in a loop. Tracy recognized the minivan, her mouth dropping when she saw Barbara Newman. "Can you tell us why you were at the municipal building?"

"Because Laura was there," she answered dryly as though hypnotized, waiting for her next cue.

"Did you speak with Dr. Swales?" I asked, her husband's attention torn between his phone call and what his wife was confessing.

"Thought she would listen to me," Barbara Newman mumbled.

"Listen to you about what?"

"I just wanted to explain to the medical examiner about Laura's sicknesses and the absences from school. Like I told you too when I went to the station."

By now, her husband had put their lawyer on hold and was watching and listening. "Barbara? You spoke to the medical examiner?"

"She wouldn't listen to me. No matter how much I tried to explain things," she gasped and began panting. "I got so mad. I only wanted her to listen!"

"Dr. Swales?" Tracy said tearfully, her face pinched with sad understanding.

"Did you strike Dr. Swales?" I began to ask as Barbara Newman nodded with a cry. Terri's stroke may have been induced. It may have been a reaction to a confrontation. Was this another chargeable offense? Would the district attorney seek charges of second-degree murder?

"Oh my God!" Barbara's husband covered his face, his shoulders bouncing as he sobbed quietly.

"Mrs. Newman," I began, knowing it was past time to move, to stand behind her while Tracy collected the evidence, "you have the right to remain silent. Anything you say can and will be used against you in a court of law." I jerked her wrists together, holding them tightly with one hand and clapped an open handcuff on one, and then the other. "You have the right to an attorney. If you cannot afford an attorney, one will be provided for you. Do you understand the rights I have just read to you? With these rights in mind, do you wish to speak to me?"

"Uh-huh," she answered. Metal struck metal, handcuffs clicking until each was tight enough to turn her fingers cold. "I'm sorry. I didn't mean for this to happen."

"Ma'am?" I asked, standing to her side, having to know more. "When you were fighting with Laura, what happened to Shawna?"

"She ran." I heard a noise from the hallway. We swung around to face the entrance of the kitchen. There, standing in her stocking feet and wearing a jeweled white shirt with unicorns and rainbows, was their daughter, Abigail. Mrs. Newman looked at her with a heartbroken smile. "When Mommy was fighting with Laura, I told Shawna to run."

"Jesus!" Barbara Newman cried, understanding her daughter was witness to the horrific crime she'd committed. "Geoffrey!"

Her husband ran around the counter and stood between us, his arms opening wide as he lifted his daughter into the air. She was crying and talking, her words choked between the sobbing. But as they returned to the hallway and the staircase, I heard Abigail asking, "Why did Mommy do that?"

THIRTY-ONE

Old twisting oak trees edged the cemetery property, the bark pale in the gray daylight as the last of its yellowed and browned leaves flittered in a breeze and clung to neatly pruned limbs. Like the leaves, I held on tight to Jericho's arm, the ground still soft in parts as we slowly walked by headstones with popular Outer Banks names that read Gray and Scarborough, the lettering etched deep into the stone and having turned black with age. The grave site was already growing crowded and amongst those gathering I saw the mayor, her entourage fifty yards behind her. There was the fire chief and his wife. And standing tall, his face carrying the sadness of the day, a lone reporter from the wolf pack that followed us with every case. He was free of pen and paper, a hand over the other, his eyelids closed and his lips moving silently to reflect the moment.

"I don't like funerals," Jericho confided, leaning toward me to keep his words hidden. I peered up to see his face was wet, and the whites in his eyes red. Jericho was as rough and tumble as they come, but this was the funeral for Dr. Swales, and I could feel him struggling. I squeezed his arm, muscles beneath his jacket quivering as he held back the emotions.

"I'm here, babe," I said, placing my head against his shoulder. The two of us held one another as friends and family gathered around the burial plot. Songbirds flew across the treetops, bouncing between the bare branches as if to move closer and attend Terri's funeral. And maybe they were. Dr. Terri Swales was an avid birdwatcher, her backyard filled with houses and feeders of all shapes and sizes. From what I was told, it didn't matter the season or weather, she kept the feeders filled, and as she'd often said to us, she kept a clean house, including the ones built for her backyard birds. Had they come to see their friend? To say goodbye? I liked to think they did. "I'm going to really miss her."

Three men wearing dark green and gray dungarees stood against a sycamore tree, their gravedigger shovels perched alongside of them, a puff of smoke rising from a cigarette while they waited for the service to end. Behind the grave, a breeze lifted the green tarp covering the mound of dirt, causing it to flap and stir the dry earth beneath it. Derek and Samantha came forward to hold the tarp as another man covered it with a stone, his sharing a resemblance with Samantha and Dr. Swales, leading me to think Samantha had a brother. When Samantha stood and returned to her place, she gave me a nod.

"Thank you," I mouthed, appreciating her hard work in recovering the Laura Jackson tissue samples. Nichelle found the name, the point of contact Dr. Swales used at the lab, the Outer Banks using a commercial lab on the mainland. It wasn't long after that Samantha had made sense of her aunt's system and recovered the same, including the DNA results.

We already had a solid confession from Barbara Newman, including how the scratches on the back of her neck had occurred while she fought with Laura. The DNA from the skin recovered beneath Laura Jackson's fingernails locked the case, making any defense moot. We also had my witness account of Dr. Terri Swales having said she'd been pushed and Barbara

Newman telling us she'd had an altercation with Terri. The DA was considering second-degree murder as additional charges for Barbara Newman.

Charges against Robert and Jane Finley remained pending. They were cleared of any connection to Laura's murder, their oldest daughter. However, they had kidnapped their youngest daughter, Robert Finley explaining it was a chance happening when he saw her late at night, alone and walking on the street after she'd been sent running from the Newmans'. While they broke the law, I hoped the charges decided by the district attorney would be minimal.

"You're welcome," she mouthed in return as Tracy and Nichelle joined us alongside of the grave, sunlight peering briefly between the clouds to warm the red woodgrain in Terri's casket. The color suited her. It was bold and confident and powerful and matched the colorful life it'd carry into the grave.

"Hey, guys," I whispered as they stood arm in arm, supporting one another, their heels playing a dangerous game like mine. Their eyes were puffy, Tracy's mascara wet, the grief contagious with tears returning to my eyes.

"Sorry," Tracy whispered, looping her arm in mine. "Can't stop crying."

"I know it's hard," I said, my breath short. "Funny thing is, she'd want us laughing and dancing."

"Then that's what we should do," Nichelle said, her stare fixed on the casket as long-stem roses were handed to us.

"He made it," Jericho said, voice breaking. Next to him, Emanuel and his wife had arrived. His limp was bad, his left leg in a medical brace that stretched from below his knee to his thigh. He gripped a cane as he made his way to take a place next to us. His face looked thinner since the shooting, but he was alive and with us today. Jericho patted his shoulder, saying, "It's good to see you."

"It's good to be seen," Emanuel replied. "Would rather it be over a couple beers and a football game."

"Yeah," Jericho said somberly as he put his arm around Emanuel. "Me too."

Emotions tugged on my insides like high tide ripping a shoreline, the pang of heartache growing as anguish and grief overtook the crowd. I dabbed my cheeks dry, the breeze turning my face cold as a pastor took to stand in front of Dr. Swales's casket and speak the words we'd all gathered to hear. Her voice carried well over the crowd, the songbirds chirping, leaves drifting over us like snowflakes. I tugged on Tracy's arm, pulling her closer to me, Nichelle joining us as we huddled together.

I stood with my family, the core of my life, saying goodbye to Dr. Swales. We'd lost a giant, her partnership with each of us going beyond solving crimes. There was a lasting essence from her life that would stay with us as we moved on with new cases. When the pastor gave her cue, we carried our roses to place on the casket. A hundred roses, maybe more, covered the red wood. And when it was my turn, I recalled how Dr. Swales looked in the morgue, her body a shell, her spirit already gone. I couldn't feel her anymore, not like I had when she was alive. But today, surrounded by the love she'd brought into this world, she was with us. I held her memory close to my heart. It was there I'd keep Dr. Terri Swales the rest of my life.

It had been a week since the funeral, our days and nights running together as they returned to the normalcy of working the river of paperwork that floods in after a case is closed. There was a new case coming. I could feel it in my bones. However, there was one detail remaining that I'd put off.

We needed something to blow off steam and to shed the weight of the pressures, even if it was just for the one night. A night out with drinks and food was one of the best ways to team build, and everyone was on board. Considering Terri's death, I'd thought to postpone indefinitely, but Jericho made a point to tell me that now was the best time for a get-together. Who was I to argue with that?

It was well past six in the evening, the sun at rest below the horizon, when we filled up a corner of a local Korean restaurant. Emanuel and his wife arrived, along with Derek and Samantha, her hair up in a ball that reminded me of her aunt Terri. She'd ditched her usual footwear, the purple Crocs, replacing them with a pair of high-heeled open-toed red shoes that added a few inches to her height.

She took my hand, leaning in to plant a kiss on my cheek, and asked, "You heard?"

"I did," I answered and put on my best smile to shade the disappointment I felt for her. She would not be taking Terri's place in the morgue. It was decided that she might eventually step into that role, but for now, she would continue working under an interim medical examiner. I squeezed her hands, assuring her, "Give it time. You're a natural."

"Thank you," she said warmly and grabbed Derek's hand to lead them toward the small bar the restaurant set up for us.

"She knows?" Jericho asked, handing me a tropical drink, the fruit juices thin, the smell of alcohol strong. I nodded as I took a taste and cringed, batting my eyelids. He let out a laugh and bumped his glass of diet cola against mine. "I'll be your designated driver."

"After having a sip of this, I'll need it," I joked. We surveyed who had arrived from the team, seeing Tracy with Nichelle and her team. The FBI had ditched their hats with the bright yellow logos and changed their jackets to look like civilians, dressing informally, the invitation having gone out to everyone who'd been involved. Even Detective Jeremy Watson had made the trip, bringing his wife. The two gave me a wave as they paired up with Emanuel and his wife and found seats.

Like the food, the time flew into the evening as the courses were served, the team stuffing their faces and catching up on one another's lives. Soon after, the first round of shots were delivered, the smell of them mixing with the Korean barbecue, a camaraderie forming with a toast to catching the carnival killer and bringing resolution to Laura Jackson's murder. Glasses clanked, a round of speeches was made, and laughter hit the ceiling.

"I needed this," I yelled into Jericho's ear, my arm around his middle as I held on to him and danced to the music.

He put his mouth near my ear, a rub of stubble touching my cheek. "I'd say you all needed this." He nodded his head toward the table where the team from the FBI sat with Jeremy and Emanuel, three pitchers of beer at the center of the table. "It's good to see Nichelle."

Emotions stirred, some of it fueled by the shot of liquor they'd ordered, the words gliding easily, "She's doing amazing—"

I couldn't finish, Jericho asking, "But?"

She was doing terrific, but deep down I held a reservation. Call it selfish, or my just being a mother hen looking out for her own. "I wonder if she could have used more time working with us?"

As I spoke, Tracy and Samantha danced, and were soon joined by Nichelle and Derek, the bartender turning up the music, the beat reverberating through me. "Another round," Nichelle ordered. She pointed toward her co-workers, and requested, "Another pitcher for my friends."

Jericho smirked, answering, "She's doing fine."

"Yeah," I said, a part of me hating that I had to agree.

"By the way," Jericho said, eyeing the shot glasses on the bar. "Tomorrow is a workday."

"Yes, it is," I said with a wave to the bartender, mouthing the word coffee and went to the center of the dancing. Their faces were colored by the warm lights, their eyes half-lidded as they swayed to the music. It was time to wrap this up and thank everyone for their hard work. Nichelle took my hand, urging me to dance with them, her skin bathed in gold light. Tracy grabbed my other hand as Samantha joined us, putting Derek in the middle while we danced around him. The sight of his offbeat movements made me laugh giddily, his feet trying to keep up, but stuttering with an extra step between the music's beat.

"I love you," Nichelle said, her voice rising and directed to Tracy. A look of shock came to Tracy's face, the boldness of Nichelle's statement being a surprise. Nichelle turned to face the team, adding, "I love all of you guys."

"We love you too," I said, finding myself suddenly alone, my dance partners leaving me. I let out an insecure laugh, my head buzzing and thinking the team was forming a dance circle. It wasn't though as I tried to make sense of what was happening. I looked into the faces of Nichelle and Tracy and Emanuel, and then to the rest of the team, questioning what they were doing. "Guys? What's going on?"

Tracy pointed toward the bar. My heart stopped when I spun around to find Jericho. He'd changed his clothes and was wearing a pair of black sweatpants and an oversized T-shirt with a tuxedo printed on the front. It was perfect. He knelt on one knee, balance wobbly, and offered me a diamond ring, the lights striking the facets, its brilliance sparkling. My insides warmed like they never have, and I lowered myself so that our eyes were level.

"Will you marry me?" he asked, wearing the biggest smile I'd ever seen.

"Woo-hoo!" Tracy yelled and pumped the air with her fist.

"Jericho—" I said, trying to speak, emotions stealing my strength, my answer a difficult one.

"Well?" Jericho asked, the shine in his smile dimming. We'd met on a fateful day years earlier when I'd ventured onto the barrier islands in search of my daughter. It was a chance meeting, two broken souls crossing paths. Little did I know, meeting him would change my life.

I glanced at the ring, mountainous thunder in my chest that made it hard to breathe, the boisterous fanfare continuing to raise the roof. The ring was lovely, and when the time was right, I would cherish it the rest of my days. But for now, I needed to know who I was first. I needed to know who I was with a daughter who'd just come back into my life. "It isn't a yes," I answered him in a weepy voice. "But it isn't a no either."

"But not a yes?" he asked. Disappointment struck, the look of it putting a pain in my heart. I gripped his arms, the team becoming quiet. If there was anyone in this world who'd understand, it was Jericho.

"Not yet," I told him with a plea in my eyes. His gaze drifted to the shuffle of shoes, the team dispersing behind me.

"It's Tracy?" he asked and tucked the ring back into his pocket. He saw the answer and with a somber smile, he added, "I think I can live with a 'not yet'."

I wrapped my arms around the love of my life. "I love you, Jericho."

He whispered into my ear, "I love you too, Casey."

A LETTER FROM B.R. SPANGLER

Thank you so much for reading *The Lighthouse Girls*. With each in the series, I continue to be fascinated by the Outer Banks as a setting, the sciences and the crime research, as well as the growth of the characters in the stories. I hope you have enjoyed reading them as much as I have enjoyed writing them. If you did enjoy it, and want to keep up to date with all my latest releases, just sign up at the following link. Your email address will never be shared and you can unsubscribe at any time.

www.bookouture.com/br-spangler

For some of the help with this book, I want to say thank you to Meghan Agresto. Meghan has been the resident site manager of the Currituck Beach Light Station for more than sixteen years. During my research, Meghan was very helpful in answering everything I needed to know about the Currituck Beach Lighthouse.

Want to help with the Detective Casey White series and book 6, I would be very grateful if you could write a review, and it also makes such a difference helping new readers to discover one of my books for the first time.

Happy Reading,

B.R. Spangler

KEEP IN TOUCH WITH B.R. SPANGLER

www.brspangler.com

 facebook.com/authorbrianspangler
twitter.com/BR_Spangler

Made in the USA
Monee, IL
02 May 2022

95774404R00152